Joachim B. Schmidt, born in 1981, emigrated from Switzerland to Iceland in 2007. He is the author of several novels and short stories and is also a journalist and columnist. Joachim, who is Swiss and Icelandic, lives in Reykjavík with his wife and their two children.

Kalmann and the Sleeping Mountain is the sequel to the best-selling *Kalmann*, published by Bitter Lemon Press in 2022.

KALMANN AND THE SLEEPING MOUNTAIN

Joachim B. Schmidt

Translated by
Jamie Lee Searle

BITTER LEMON PRESS
LONDON

BITTER LEMON PRESS

First published in the United Kingdom in 2024 by
Bitter Lemon Press, 47 Wilmington Square, London WC1X OET.

www.bitterlemonpress.com

First published in German as *Kalmann und der schlafende Berg*
by Diogenes Verlag AG Zurich, 2023.

The translation of this work was supported by the Swiss Arts Council Pro Helvetia.

Copyright © 2023 Diogenes Verlag AG Zurich
English translation © 2024 Jamie Lee Searle

A CIP record for this book is available from the British Library.

PB ISBN 978–1–916725–003
eB USC ISBN 978–1–916725–010
eB ROW ISBN 978-1-916725-027

Typeset by Tetragon, London
Printed and bound by CPI Group (UK) Ltd, Croydon CRO 4YY

swiss arts council
prohelvetia

For my greatest treasures
Heiðdís Elisabeth and Rögnvald Anton

Land, steeped in black shadows
Dark nights, your fate held there
The path
the path
lies ahead, but to where?

Landið sokkið í svartan skugga
Sorta nætur þú vígður ert
Leiðin
leiðin
liggur áfram en hvert?

JÓNAS FRIÐRIK GUÐNASON,
poet, 1945–2023

1

COFFIN

If only my father had never written me that letter. If only he'd left my mother and me in peace, so we could have spent our time watching movies and eating pizza, just she and I. We were doing fine up here in the Northland, through the rainy summer days and stormy autumn nights, and our grief, it belonged only to us. If my father had never written that letter, the FBI officials wouldn't have twisted my arm behind my back and slammed my face against the bonnet of the black Cherokee Jeep. And I wouldn't have missed the New Year's fireworks in Raufarhöfn either. Because I've never missed them before, it's tradition, and traditions are important, even if sometimes you can't remember how they started.

Just like this story. Maybe it starts with my father's letter, just an email which my mother printed out at work and brought home with her, and which eventually led to me being arrested by the FBI.

Did I scream? Or did I stay silent? I hate it when my mind takes a dive, like a ship behind a rogue wave. It never bodes well. If only my mother had been there. She could have explained everything to the FBI agents, without a doubt. But now I was here, utterly alone, 4,700 kilometres away from Iceland, in a tiny room which contained nothing but three uncomfortable chairs and a little table, no window, no TV, no pictures – a coffin, and I was locked inside it, lid shut. Bang. Buried deep and soon to be forgotten.

Like Grandfather.

It wasn't really a coffin, of course, but an interrogation room in a giant FBI building, a proper hulk of a thing. My jaw had dropped when we sped up to it in the Cherokee Jeep. Sure, I'd seen buildings before that are even bigger, the church in Reykjavík, for example, or the hotel in *Home Alone 2* – I know that movie off by heart. But with this hulk I had the feeling it might sink into the ground. It was brown and heavy like the basalt rock of the Melrakkaslétta, and so big it could have housed all the inhabitants of Raufarhöfn in individual rooms. Just imagine that: all the inhabitants in one single building, with a school and store and community room and gas station and everything! But here nobody was from Raufarhöfn, and that's why I felt lonelier than ever before.

I used to think a classroom was the loneliest place in the world, when you're sitting completely alone at the desk in the back row and don't understand what the teacher at the front is explaining to the class. Everyone's listening attentively or writing something down, and they sometimes glance back at you, happy there's somebody who's dumber than them. No one wants to be the dumbest. But somebody *has* to be the dumbest, and if you're somebody like me, the smartest thing is not to deny it.

A teacher once said that you couldn't knock knowledge into my skull even with a sledgehammer. That was Sigfús, who was the principal at our school. But our teacher was sick that day, and Sigfús had to cover.

He's pretty old now, but seems to go on and on; he walks through the village slowly and with small footsteps. He leans on ski poles, even in high summer, because he can use them to shoo away Arctic terns and tourists. He's not so mean to me nowadays, actually he's really nice, as though he's completely forgotten I used to push him to the brink of despair with my stupidity. He once threw a massive Danish dictionary at me over my classmates' heads. But because I ducked at the last moment, the book crashed into the map of the world on the wall behind me. It made a hole in the Atlantic Ocean. Because I was the only one who found that funny, Sigfús sent me out of the room, and I probably broke something out there, smashed in the glass cabinet with the stuffed birds and made them fly, the short-eared owl, the golden plover, the snipe, I can't remember exactly any more. But I didn't touch the raven, definitely not. These predators scare me, because they're sneaky and cunning, maybe smarter than Sigfús, even though they can't speak Danish. Ravens like death, they feed on carcasses. Like Greenland shark or Arctic foxes or wolf fish. The wolf fish isn't really a wolf, it's not even half a wolf, it's a fish. They're striped or flecked and are actually eels that got too fat. The wolf fish is probably the ugliest creature in the entire Norwegian Sea. Its jaw is so horrific that even the best dental surgeon would get a fright. But everything has a purpose, especially in nature, and that's why dental surgeons aren't needed in the ocean, they only exist among us, because the human being is the only mammal that uses its teeth to give a friendly smile.

Luckily, after the incident with the stuffed birds I didn't have to go to school for a while. Grandfather took me out to sea, so I could help him catch shark, spike bait on the hooks and stand at the wheel while he was having a nap down in the narrow cabin or stretched out on the deck. Though I should have been at school, like every other kid. That's the law, after all. But back then I didn't realize that. Grandfather said I'd learn much more out at sea than in the classroom, because you can't eat the alphabet.

When I eventually went back to my school desk, I had to stay late on my very first day, until it got dark. Until Grandfather appeared in the doorway, stooped, shaking. I remember it well, because I'd never seen him in a classroom before. He asked Sigfús to tell him whether he had a screw loose or something, and Sigfús, who had jumped up from his chair, explained that he'd just wanted to help, a private lesson of sorts, so I wouldn't have to repeat the year yet again. But Grandfather retorted that it wasn't possible to repeat a year, no one could do that, a year could only be lived once, and after that it was over. Period. And with that, my career as a schoolboy came to an end.

At this point, I wouldn't have minded staying late in the Raufarhöfn classroom, because anywhere was better than in this FBI coffin. At school, at least I'd have been able to look out of the window and watch Halldór shovelling snow in the parking lot or leaning on the shovel while he was talking to somebody about the snow. And after staying late I could have gone sledding with the other kids in the Pallabrekka or had a snowball fight. Me against everyone, until someone started crying, because someone always did. Then someone would have sent me home, but I would have wandered through the village instead, until I'd tracked Grandfather down somewhere, at the harbour perhaps or in the curing shed. Grandfather usually didn't care when people complained about me. And besides all that, he would still have been alive.

2

DAKOTA LEEN

The tall FBI agent who had arrested me, driven me to the station and left me sitting here, poked his head in the door and asked whether I was thirsty or hungry. I ordered a cola. That's something I know. When you're being interrogated by the police, you're allowed to order a drink. That's the law.

Half an eternity later, the door opened again, but this time it was a young female FBI agent I'd never seen before, neither during the arrest nor when we'd walked through the giant building. I certainly wouldn't have overlooked her, even though she was quite small. But she was very pretty and younger than me, and her skin was black, though not as black as her hair, which was plaited into a thousand little braids and tightly knotted at the back of her head. She also wasn't wearing a bulletproof vest like her colleagues in the Cherokee Jeep, and in fact she wasn't even armed, her gun holster was empty. A laptop was clamped under her left arm, a notebook beneath her right, and in her hands she was holding a paper cup filled to the brim with coffee and a can of cola. She paused in the doorway and stared at me, gripping the laptop firmly against herself. "Hello, Kalmann," she said, giving me a brief nod. "Can I call you Kalmann?" she asked in English. She gave the door a shove with her foot, without spilling even a drop from her paper cup. Then she stood there hesitantly. "Do you need an interpreter, someone to translate the conversation?"

I shook my head and, to make it clear I understood, said: "No need to worry."

"No need to worry," she echoed, smiling with relief. "Did your father teach you English? He's American, isn't he?"

"No," I said. "*Dr. Phil.*"

"*Dr. Phil*, the talk show?"

"And *The Bachelor, Top Gear, Gilmore Girls —*" I stopped abruptly, because I hadn't intended to mention *Gilmore Girls.* I hadn't watched that girlie crap in ages.

"I love *Gilmore Girls!*" said the FBI agent, leaning over the table to set down all her things, which didn't look easy. "I'm agent Dakota Leen, but you can call me Dakota or Cody."

I decided to call her Dakota Leen; after all, she was a proper FBI agent. "And the guy?" I asked.

She glanced over at the door. "Mr García? What about him?"

"He said he would take care of me."

"Would you prefer *him* to interrogate you?"

"I'd rather not."

"Good." She opened her laptop and laid the notebook and a pen next to it, all very neatly. Her shirt was buttoned right to the top.

The light from the laptop cast a blue shimmer on her face, which had a constantly curious expression. Dakota Leen typed something on the keyboard.

"Just a minute," she said, before standing up abruptly and going to fetch Mr García, who then leaned over the laptop too and explained where to find the programme, where to enter the code, that she needed to turn on the camera and microphone, here and here, but first she had to select the room – we were in number four – and that he wouldn't show her again. "Got it." Dakota Leen cleared her throat, and I now know that even people with black skin can blush, but you have to look really closely to see it.

"You can do it!" Mr García laid his hand on her shoulder, looking at me while he did so, properly staring, like he'd only just noticed me, and as though by some kind of magic I felt his hand on my shoulder now too. "There's a first time for everything, isn't there?" He winked at me and left the room, slamming the door behind him, and Dakota Leen brushed her hand over her shoulder and exhaled tensely. I took a few sips from the cola can.

"January the sixth, 2020, no, nonsense, it's already 2021! I'm agent Dakota Sage Leen, twelve, zero, two, eleven. I'm speaking with —" And then she looked right at me, and because I stared back as though all my lights were off, holding the cola can in mid-air, she prompted: "Please state your name!"

"Kalmann," I said hurriedly, suppressing a burp. "Óðinsson." She typed on the keyboard again and I summoned my courage. "Can I ask you something?"

She nodded. "Of course."

"Am I under arrest?"

She leaned back in her chair and rocked the backrest a little, making her shirt strain over her chest. I did my best not to stare. "Do you think you're under arrest?"

People only answer a question with a question when they don't know the answer themselves. So I shrugged and turned my attention back to the cola can. It was bigger than the ones in Iceland, but otherwise identical. I raised it to my lips and drank it down to the last drop.

"Kalmann." Dakota Leen bent forwards. "You just have to answer a few questions for me, okay?" I nodded. "Let's make a start. What were you doing out there?"

I thought of my father and got a lump in my throat, as though I were breathing through a straw. My hands stiffened, making a dent in the cola can. "I was looking for them."

"Who were you looking for?"

I squeezed the can even harder. "They were all gone suddenly. My father, Uncle Bucky, even Sharon, there were so many people, and I got shoved around, and I lost my cowboy hat too."

"Where are they now, your father, Uncle Bucky and Sharon?"

I flattened the can so much with both hands that it looked like a truck had driven over it. Dakota Leen shifted a little way back from the table in her chair, keeping her eyes on me the whole time. "Am I under arrest?" I repeated the question quietly, and the FBI agent sighed.

"No, Kalmann, you're *not* under arrest. You're free to go at any time. The door's there. It's not locked. But I'm the only one who can help you now. For me to do that, you have to answer a few questions, do you understand? Because there are a lot of things I don't know. That only you know. And after that I'll help you find your people. Deal?"

I agreed, and with that the interrogation began. It was only the beginning of an hour-long conversation, though, so I had made a terrible deal. But I didn't yet know that. I told the FBI agent we had wanted to visit the president in order to go for a walk with him. But the president hadn't come with us, even though he had promised to. "You're not allowed to break promises," I explained to her, thinking about the angry mob of people, who perhaps were disappointed for that very reason, because so many promises hadn't been kept.

There's barely anything worse than disappointment, because it destroys so much: trust and anticipation, fun and hope. And when disappointment spreads like a drought, it ignites rage. I tried to explain that to the FBI agent, but she stared at me thoughtfully and didn't say a word.

3

GRANDFATHER

"Are you taping the conversation?"

"The room's equipped with everything. Microphone and camera." Dakota Leen made a sweeping gesture with her arm. "Back to my question. What were you all planning to do? Were you really intending to go in?"

"I wasn't, but the others were. Just to be on the safe side, you could record the conversation with an iPhone. We always do it like that in Iceland." I thought of Birna, who is probably the best police detective in the world, and glanced discreetly around me. Up to the left beneath the ceiling was a circular lens, as large as an eider duck's egg, but completely black.

"Yes, that's one of our cameras. Kalmann, what happened then?"

"And the microphone?"

"They're all over the room. Don't worry about it. Kalmann, please tell me what happened. Did you lose your people in the park, before the steps?"

"Correctamundo."

"Were they armed?"

"Uncle Bucky..." I hesitated.

"Was Uncle Bucky armed?"

"I'm not totally sure if he's even my uncle," I said.

"That's irrelevant right now. Please answer my question. Was the man armed?"

"Always."

"With what?" Dakota Leen wanted to know, but because I hesitated, she explained to me that it was important they find out whether he posed a danger to others. That it was entirely possible I was saving lives today! "Perhaps your uncle is angry."

"He's probably not my uncle."

"You've already said that."

"Is it actually against the law to carry weapons?"

"Sometimes, yes."

I felt awful, guilty, even though I hadn't done anything wrong. "He always carries a Glock on his ankle, sometimes a Walther too, and an HK under his arm. But you can't see that one."

"HK? Heckler & Koch?" She typed it into the laptop.

"And a knife."

"A pocket knife?"

"No, a hunting knife. Quite a big one." I demonstrated the size.

"But what's he hunting?"

"Normally deer, but today lizards and pigs."

Dakota Leen's face became paler. She stared at the laptop in concentration, and that's why she didn't notice that I was looking around for more cameras. I found another black egg behind me. And in the walls there were these little round spots with holes, which probably contained the microphones.

"Why didn't you go in with the others?"

I shrugged. Why had my father left me there in the crowd of people and not looked for me? "I was suddenly completely alone. That's why. And when you get lost, you have to stop right where you are and not move an inch. Everyone knows that."

Dakota Leen looked at me and bit her lower lip. She was perhaps the most beautiful woman I'd met in the United States. "Kalmann," she said, "do you have a legal guardian? Do you know what I mean by that?"

I nodded and stared at the surface of the table. "My mother."

"And where is your mother?"

"She's 4,700 kilometres away. In Akureyri. That's the largest city in northern Iceland, but it's fairly small."

Dakota Leen stood up and was about to leave the room, but when she opened the door, Mr García was standing right outside. "Leen!" I heard him say in surprise. "Are you done already?" She pulled the door slightly to behind her, which meant I could only hear snippets of their conversation. They were talking about a protocol, the correct way of doing things, rules, and that someone needed to be informed, at least the embassy.

But Mr García sounded annoyed. I distinctly heard him say that Dakota Leen wasn't at the Academy any more, nor at a beauty contest. She was in the field now, and it was war out there. "Welcome to the real world, honey."

When Dakota Leen sat back down with me, she stared angrily at her laptop for a long while. Her chest rose and fell quickly, and her hands trembled almost unnoticeably, but she closed her eyes and exhaled slowly. "Kalmann, let's rewind again. Why were you out there today? Why are you here?"

Well. Why was I where I was? Why is anyone anywhere? It was a question as big as the ocean, and Dakota Leen was sending me out on it in a little boat. But she seemed to want to know at any price. So I thought hard about it. After all, we were in the boat together, she and I. I understood that now.

Grandfather. I pictured him before me in his holey woollen jumper and foreign military trousers, the tobacco pipe clamped between his teeth. He sat with us in this boat and stared out to sea, puffing. The Slétta, as the Melrakkaslétta was known up here, in the far distance. I remembered the many hikes we had done across it. Sometimes I would flop down on the moss because I was so exhausted, and Grandfather said that when you're walking a long distance, you don't do the whole stretch at once but just one step. And then another, and then another. Always just one step at a time, no more.

"Step by step," I murmured, and now I knew where I had to begin, so that the whole story would make sense. At the beginning, in other words. "My father wrote me a letter because my grandfather Óðinn was murdered. That's why I'm here," I explained.

"I'm sorry," said Dakota Leen, though she seemed somehow relieved. "Tell me more."

I told her everything. And right from the beginning. I told her that until a few weeks ago, I hadn't even properly known my American father, that he had been stationed on the military base in Keflavík in the 1980s and had donated my mother the seed for my conception, even though he really shouldn't have, because he already had a wife and two children, and that's why he was pulled out of Iceland when I came into the world nine months later. That my mother moved with me into Grandfather's house and I grew up with him there, the man who had taught me everything, for example how to process Greenland shark or to stand with your back to the wind when you're peeing on the Melrakkaslétta.

Dakota Leen smiled and looked at me again with her curious gaze, and because this made me lose my thread, she said I should go on, that I was doing a good job.

So I told her I'd encountered a polar bear, and if I hadn't had my American grandfather's Mauser with me, I wouldn't be sitting here today. So perhaps the story actually started with the polar bear or with my American grandfather, who had fought in the Korean War and taken this Nazi pistol from a Korean. And a sheriff like me was of course responsible for —

"Sheriff?" Dakota Leen looked back at her laptop in confusion.

I pondered for a few seconds, wondering how to explain to her that a sheriff in Raufarhöfn presumably isn't the same thing as a sheriff in Washington DC. But she waved her hand and said it didn't matter. She would much rather know whether my grandfather had taught me how to handle firearms.

"Correctamundo!" I said proudly, and then I felt sad, because it made me think about him.

I wished Grandfather hadn't been murdered. As I told Dakota Leen everything, word for word, it felt as though he were sitting next to me on the frozen moss and staring out at the straight-as-a-die horizon, and somewhere beyond it was the sea, which never looks the same, it changes its colours almost every day, and there are so many there probably aren't any names for them. Like feelings. Grief has a colour too, a dark one, like the sea during a storm, deep and bottomless. Grief recedes and surges like the ebb and flow of the tide. And it whooshes, not in your ears, but in your chest.

"Tell me about your grandfather," Dakota Leen instructed me, leaning back in her chair and drinking from her paper cup. "And please take your time."

Time.

I sniffed and nodded, thinking about Grandfather.

When you see somebody for the last time, it's better if you don't know. You presume you still have time, that you'll see each other again soon, you simply say "bless", and these goodbyes are the best, because they don't hurt.

Grandfather hadn't been able to walk for a long while, no longer wanted to eat, and couldn't go to the bathroom by himself any more, he even needed diapers. And he couldn't remember how to hold a spoon or a fork, even though I'd shown him a few more times. That's why I presume he couldn't see any more, or just very blurrily, because his eyes looked like dead jellyfish on the shore. And beneath the jellyfish lie the grey stones which were once part of a cliff. Grandfather didn't recognize me any more either. Someone once explained to me that very old people are almost like newborn babies, but Grandfather hadn't been sweet or curious in a long time, and sometimes he smelled like rotten dulse seaweed, so you had to hold your nose.

The fact that babies are curious and also smell much better than my grandfather is something I can confirm. Because this one time I was allowed to hold one in my arms, a real one, not a doll. It's really true! Perla, my ex-girlfriend, had a sister called Lilja who doesn't have a disability. Lilja had a baby when I was still with Perla. And when we visited her once, they put the baby in my arms, there was nothing I could do, no way, because you can't give back a little thing like that, it would be much too dangerous. You have to wait until the baby is taken from you again. So I made my body stiff, like a statue, and practically forgot to breathe. The baby smelled like vanilla cream. It opened its eyes and blinked at me, probably because it wanted to see who I was. And I blinked back, as though we were communicating in Morse code, which everyone found charming, even though I unfortunately didn't understand a single word.

Sometimes I knelt right in front of Grandfather on the floor and looked at him or did Morse code with my eyes.

The tips of our noses almost touched, and sometimes a jolt went through him and he would sit up straight, nod at me, say "hmm" or clear his throat and squeeze out a few words that sounded a little like baby language but rougher. His voice was spent, so I didn't understand a word. Sometimes I laughed, even though that wasn't at all what I wanted to do.

My mother had explained that Grandfather could still understand me, even though he didn't react. That his heart was listening, guaranteed.

That's why I told him everything that came into my mind. Sometimes he laughed, and sometimes he cried, regardless of what I'd just said, and I longed to know what was funny, or how I could have comforted him, but my mother said only he knew what was going on in his head. He had slipped too far inside himself, she said, and wouldn't come out again, and the only thing we could do for him was to be with him, because then he wouldn't be so alone, and everything's better when you're not alone, like watching TV, for example, or eating, or driving a car, or reading, or dancing, or cooking, or sleeping —

My mother didn't want to stop listing things that are more fun together. So I interrupted her, because there are some things that are much better when you're alone. Like sitting on the loo or talking to an Arctic fox or being grumpy. And sometimes it's also wonderful when you're alone at sea, because then you can think about who you'd like to have with you, and that could be anyone at all, for example Lady Gaga or Rihanna.

That's pretty much how I explained it to her, and then my mother looked at me oddly and leaned over to give me a hug, but she didn't really succeed. We were sitting close to Grandfather, after all, and he was studying us surreptitiously, without a clue what was going on.

"Kalli minn, you're a wise one," said my mother, her eyes suddenly damp. To this day I don't know why. Being a wise one isn't anything to be sad about, but perhaps my mother was sad because I wasn't supposed to be the wise one in our little family; my grandfather was, that's how it had always been, even though my mother had often complained about his wisdom. "It's a shame you don't have any hákarl with you," she sighed, and sniffed. "Perhaps we could take him home with us just once, to say a proper goodbye. Before it's too late. That would be lovely."

And then I felt annoyed, because on that particular day I didn't have any on me; hákarl, that is, the fermented shark meat he loved so much. It was the second to last time I saw Grandfather alive.

Once I knelt before him on the floor and laid my head in his lap, and he stroked my hair as though I were a cat.

4

KALIBER

Ever since the thing with the polar bear I'd been tormented by nightmares, and I was no longer the Kalmann I once had been. The world around me wasn't the same either. Cocoa Puffs were forbidden, because someone had found out they were unhealthy, spoiling everyone's appetite for them in the process. I had to switch to Honey Nut Cheerios, and had almost got used to them – when suddenly there were Cocoa Puffs again! It was so confusing. My best friend Nói still hadn't been in touch, and Iceland had become one glacier worse off.

In Raufarhöfn, too, quite a lot had changed. After Dagbjört's father had disappeared and been declared dead, she had sold the Hotel Arctica and moved, with a heavy heart, to Akranes, 575 kilometres from Raufarhöfn. The school authorities searched desperately for a replacement, even sharing the ad on Facebook, until a Polish woman called Valeska declared herself willing to teach the few children. But there was no reason to worry: Valeska can speak Icelandic so well you'd think she's an Icelander with a funny name.

Around the same time, a man called Hörður bought the hotel. We only saw him in the village occasionally, because he spent most of his time in his villa on the outskirts of Reykjavík, or in Tenerife. Óttar took care of the hotel, with the support of his wife Lin, who made sure he didn't help himself to the contents of the hotel bar or beat anyone up.

Hörður hadn't just bought the hotel, he also brought back part of the fishing quota he and his siblings had taken from Raufarhöfn many years ago. He must have heard the call of his old home, or at least that's what harbour master Sæmundur said, and that's why, for the time being, there was no reason to worry. Siggi and Jújú continued to catch fish by the barrel load, and the freezing facility resumed activity after a brief pause; Raufarhöfn had survived the death of its king.

Sometimes people called me *Kalli Kaliber*. I didn't like this nickname, because I was no longer allowed to own a weapon. The authorities had taken away my gun licence, which, if you want to be a stickler for details, I'd never had in the first place. Because I had patrolled through the village armed even as a kid, no one had thought of asking me for a licence, because the Mauser was as inseparable from my hip as a bad mood is from Halldór.

But after the thing with the polar bear, that changed. Questions were asked. Lots of questions. To save having to answer them, my mother sold the rifle and flint with which I'd hunted foxes and ptarmigan and flicked off sharks' lights, pow. I'd thrown the Mauser into the ocean by then, following Birna's request. That's why I could no longer catch shark, because for that you need a shotgun, to anaesthetize them, that's the law. So "Kalli Kaliber" sounded like a joke, as though the people were calling someone who no longer existed just to annoy him.

Perhaps I didn't like who I had become. Perhaps I had been dead for a while under the polar bear, that can't be ruled out, so it was like I'd been reborn. For a long time, I didn't want to acknowledge it, because Grandfather had always said: Kalmann Óðinsson is how he is! But if I had still been the same Kalmann, I would've had a piece of hákarl with me on that second-to-last visit. The newborn Kalmann was a forget-ful grouch, like Grandfather had been, often getting angry for no apparent reason. Something in me had probably been squashed while I was under the polar bear. After the visit to Perla's sister, I even flew into a rage because then Perla wanted a baby too, and of course I was supposed to be the father, but that's not okay, we're not allowed, at least that's what I heard on a *Dr. Phil* episode once. And also, you can't make babies just by kissing. Possibly Perla didn't know that. And that's why I got more and more angry and eventually broke one of her favourite dolls, twisted off its head, wrenched out its arms and legs, and Perla spent the night at her parents' place. Once, when I had a nightmare, I ripped my Hulk nightshirt and accidentally gave Perla a bruise, because she was trying to calm me down and got too close to me. That's why I wasn't allowed to see her for a while, and if I'm completely honest, I wasn't bothered. It was better for everyone if they left me alone with my nightmares.

After the drama with Perla, I moved to live with my mother in Akureyri. That was totally okay, even if it meant my chances were minimal of ever finding a woman like Perla again. My mother and I had found lodgings in a little, old corrugated iron house in the middle of the harbour neighbourhood of this small town. The bedrooms were slightly bigger than in Raufarhöfn, and I liked the fact that every step on the floorboards and every turn in bed made a squeaking and creaking sound, or that in bad weather you could hear the splashing of the rain because the gutter on the roof was rusted through and had crumbled away in some places. The cellar was constantly flooded, so we couldn't use it.

I found work in the Glerártorg shopping mall, a short walk from home. I was responsible for the shopping carts, which people left scattered all across the parking lot. I had to collect them up and bring them into the dry, and sometimes clean them or oil the wheels. The work was enjoyable, and the people were usually nice, even though I gave them dirty looks when they didn't bring back the carts. But maybe they were allowed to, because my boss, Nanouk, who was actually from Greenland, summoned me to his office and said I wasn't supposed to follow the people to their cars but instead had to wait until they had driven away, then collect the trolleys. Icelanders are lazy, he said, that's just how it is, there's nothing you can do about it. He probably didn't know it's against the law to leave something in the middle of a public parking lot. Probably they don't have this law in Greenland, because they have almost no cars there and so no big parking lots.

So I had a job and even got paid for it, earning more money than I had for my hákarl or the Arctic fox tails. And that's why there was no reason for me to go to Raufarhöfn, apart from to eat an Arctic Cheeseburger with Óttar at the Hotel Arctica, and to say hello to our little house so it didn't get lonely.

In summer I once stayed a whole month. There was a lot to do, things were busy down at the harbour because of the summertime regional quota, and I helped to clean the bulk cargo container with the water hose and shoo away the gulls. One weekend, the pavements in the village were being repaired. The inhabitants of Raufarhöfn gathered and knocked away the broken bits, concreted some smaller areas and reinforced the edges with cement. The local authority in Húsavík, which has been in charge of Raufarhöfn for several years, didn't want to spend any money on pavements, even though they had promised to. That's what Halldór says, anyway. But anyone who's now thinking that the inhabitants of Raufarhöfn got annoyed or even angry because they had to look after the pavements themselves would be wrong. The mood was great, even cheerful, despite the fact that the summer had been damp and cold so far and people were still wearing woolly hats in July. There were coffee and sweet pastries, and the sheep farmer Magnús Magnússon had his accordion with him and serenaded us during a coffee break. Everyone was really quiet and peaceful, sipping coffee and staring out to sea, lost in thought.

But the nightmares – they stayed. They came again and again. Stubbornly. Luckily my mother knew what you had to do with them: breathe them out. Blow them away like a bad smell. Open the window a crack, take a deep breath, then blow everything out into the dark night until you've no air left in your body from your noggin to your tootsies, and then breathe in the fresh night air so there's no space for new nightmares to collect in the body.

I had expected the bad dreams to become less frequent, but they kept coming, almost regularly: the polar bear that lurked behind every hill, sometimes appearing right in front of me, even if I wasn't out in nature in the dream but somewhere in a house, or in the shopping mall. Róbert, staring at me and holding the Mauser to his head.

Pulling the trigger.

Keeling over.

The sawed-up body parts. The blood.

In Akureyri, there's this store for tourists. Next to the entrance is a life-size fake polar bear, standing on its hind legs and moving its head and front paws. When I walked past this polar bear for the first time, I started to shake and even had to throw up. It was totally embarrassing. The tourists thought I was drunk.

The problem was that I couldn't talk to anyone about it. Because the McKenzie thing was a secret, and what's more I didn't know anyone who had been under a polar bear like me and who could even come close to understanding my nightmares.

Then this damn virus came along. My mother, who worked in the hospital and got marks on her face from all the mask-wearing, said I wasn't allowed to work in the shopping mall any more if I wanted to keep visiting my grandfather. It was an either/or situation. So I chose Grandfather; I didn't even have to think about it. Because Grandfather and I, we belonged together like a hamburger and fries.

The very last time I visited Grandfather, he was sitting in his wheelchair like always and staring at the floor with clouded eyes. The nurse who had led me into the room stroked the back of his hand and said loudly: "Óðinn minn, Kalmann's here. He's come to visit you!"

Grandfather jumped and made a noise that almost sounded like a proper word, so it was one of the good days, which had become increasingly rare. "Who?"

"Kalmann, your grandson!"

"Ah." He sank back into the chair in disappointment.

The nurse gave me an encouraging smile and left me alone with Grandfather. I stood there for a while, then knelt on the floor in front of him like I usually did. "Hello, Grandfather," I murmured, but he just gave me a fleeting glance and then went back to staring through me. I don't think he recognized me. But this time I had hákarl with me! A few particularly slimy little cubes from my final stash, probably long beyond being edible, but that didn't matter, because Grandfather wasn't allowed to eat hákarl now anyway. He could have choked on it. But everyone knows you don't just eat with your mouth, but with your eyes and nose too, so I held the little plastic tub open beneath his hooter so he could at least enjoy the scent of the delicacy.

It took a second or two, then it coursed through him like an earthquake. He widened his eyes in surprise, braced himself on his shaky arms, straightened up a little and began to rock to and fro, as though he was dancing to music playing only in his head, because I couldn't hear anything at all. He raised one hand and moved the fingers in the air, as though he were counting stars, froze, and then the words gushed out of his mouth like a kind of alphabet soup. They were completely incomprehensible, strange sounds which somehow seemed familiar. So I tried to listen to the sound of his voice, and that's how I was able to make out one word clearly: "Kalmann," he said again and again – or that's what I thought he was saying, because it sounded more like "Kallakallakalla!" And then he leaned forwards, grabbed me by the shoulders and looked at me in shock. I was stunned. Grandfather was still strong, the little tub almost fell out of my hand, but I gripped it tightly, and Grandfather cried out: "*Gora vzletit! Opasno. Gora letit!*"

"What?"

"*V nutri gory*! The mountain. *Vzletit v vozdukh. Gora! Gora letit!*"

I felt breathless. "Mountain?"

"*Suka amerikanets, suka, suka amerikanets! Opasno. Vnutri gory!*"

Now the little can fell to the ground after all and the cubes rolled across the carpet. I got up and collected them together, which wasn't so easy, because my hands were shaking. At the same time, I tried to make a note of the words Grandfather was repeating over and over.

"*Suka amerikanets. Opasno! Gora letit!*"

Then something happened that I thought was completely awful, even though with hindsight I'm glad it happened: Grandfather stretched out his arms, desperately cried "Kallakallakalla!" and fell forwards. The wheelchair leaped backwards and Grandfather landed on me, pulling me to the floor, a crash landing, boom! Now I was on my back, buried beneath about sixty kilograms of Grandfather. The hákarl cubes lay scattered alongside me, and Grandfather buried his face in my chest, stroked my face with his rigid hand and cried and sobbed like a little child, still repeating these funny sounds over and over: "*Gora letit.*" And that's why I wrapped my arms around him and held him tightly, because when someone's sad, that's what you have to do, even if you're the one who wants to cry.

That same evening I told my mother that Grandfather had flipped out and probably spoken Lithuanian, because that's what it had sounded like. I didn't tell her about the hákarl and the nurse who had found us. You don't always have to tell everything. The nurse got rid of the hákarl for me, holding the tub as far away from herself as possible between her thumb and index finger and hurrying out of the room, blinking; she even went outside the care home to throw the hákarl in one of the big rubbish containers. I watched her through the window while two other nurses heaved Grandfather onto his bed, where he soon fell asleep.

My mother sighed, stared at me silently for a while, then made herself a cup of tea. Whenever my mother makes a cup of tea, there's something to discuss. Usually it's something important, but rarely something that makes me happy.

So we sat down at the kitchen table, my mother even opened a packet of cookies, and before she had time to explain what I'd done to deserve the cookies, I'd already devoured two of them.

"Kalli minn," she began, like she always does when she wants to talk to me. She told me that Grandfather had done this a few times already, the care home had called her today too, and that his attacks were getting increasingly strong and frequent. Sometimes he even shouted at the staff. In Russian, by the way, so my guess had been almost correct.

"But why?" I asked, swiping another cookie before my mother could put away the packet.

She didn't know, but presumed it had something to do with the fact that Grandfather used to be an ardent communist. He'd always had a keen interest in the Soviet Union, she said. But the fact he could speak Russian was a surprise to her. The care home people had also said that Grandfather was declining rapidly, that it wouldn't be much longer before... Then the words got stuck in her throat, but I knew how the sentence would have ended. After all, you didn't have to be a doctor to realize Grandfather didn't have much longer to live.

Strange. The idea that he would die soon didn't even make me sad. My mother had tears in her eyes, and I munched on the cookies. To cheer her up I said: "*Suka amerikanets! Gora letit!*"

In the middle of the night, I awoke with a start from a nightmare. I must have yelled so loudly that my mother woke up too. She knelt next to my bed and stroked my hair, but she was so tired that she laid her head next to me on the mattress. Suddenly her hand went limp on my face. So I tapped her on the shoulder and told her she could go.

The dream flickered in my head for a while longer, so I went over to the window and blew my breath out of the gap into the silent harbour district.

In the dream, I had been with Grandfather on the Melrakkaslétta. We were hiking aimlessly over the plain, and actually I know my way around up there really well, but in the dream I didn't know where we were. So I got scared. And Grandfather, who was always a little way ahead of me, came to a sudden halt and turned around. He had my Mauser in his hand, and he held it beneath his chin. Now I was standing directly in front of him.

Anyone would have woken up shouting in that moment.

The next afternoon, Grandfather died. Luckily my mother was already back from her early shift when the telephone call came. It was 14.40. I remember that precisely, because the doctors on TV always immediately say the time when someone dies. So I looked at the clock and said: "14.40."

We had been planning to visit Grandfather at four that afternoon. Goddammit! Our visiting time was null and void. My mother wanted to go anyway, immediately, but I thought that was unnecessary, he was dead after all, and you can't talk to a dead person. You can't hold hákarl under their nose either, because that doesn't actually wake the dead, even though lots of people say it does.

I didn't move from the spot.

I wanted to watch TV.

At this time of day, the dating show *Temptation Island* was on Station 2, where couples go on a free holiday to a tropical island, with palm trees and swimming pools and champagne and bikinis and everything. But separately. Super-hot single women spend the night with the men, and super-hot single men with the women. Then all hell breaks loose, because you're not supposed to cheat on people, but the singles don't care. They just want to have fun, snog and screw. And when the couples meet up again after a fortnight to tell each other about their holidays, there are usually tears, and then they're all single.

My mother was running around the apartment like a headless chicken, she grabbed the remote control out of my hand, put her shoes on and took them off again, cried and pleaded, because apparently leaving me at home alone was out of the question. But I had no intention of leaving the sofa, because it was too late now. Grandfather was dead. He had died. A corpse! Hadn't she understood that? I yelled at her. My mother promised me until she was blue in the face that we would order pizza tonight and watch a movie together, but they were empty promises. After all, she'd also promised we would visit Grandfather today, but now he was dead, gone, no longer there. My mother had brought a packet of cookies through from the kitchen cupboard, and I shoved them off the coffee table. The cookies wouldn't bring Grandfather back to life, but my mother didn't seem to get that.

Then the telephone interrupted us. It was my Aunt Guðrún from Reykir. And she was crying too, I could hear her all the way from the sofa. Women get so hysterical! My mother was fussing into the phone that she couldn't possibly leave me alone, that I was refusing to come with her.

Things like that make me mad. I don't like it when people say bad things about me behind my back.

Suddenly I was standing. I was holding in my hand one of these owl figurines made of glass that my mum collects and had arranged all over the house. I had no idea why I was holding the damn thing in my hand, so I smashed it next to my mother on the wall, as hard as I could, which, together with my mother's screams, made such a hellish noise I had to beat it out of my ears, the noise, like you would bang out little flies that have sneaked into your ears. I beat myself until it eventually went quiet. It felt pleasant. I didn't know why I had blood on my hands, but I didn't care. It didn't hurt either, not in the slightest. And when two police officers overpowered me, pushing my face against the floor, I relaxed, weirdly, because under two police officers it's almost as dark as beneath a polar bear. In the dark you're somehow completely by yourself, even when others are still there. I no longer had to think about Grandfather and the pointless visiting hour. I simply waited and observed the air draining out of my body, and along with it the rage, from my chest, my arms, my legs and my tootsies.

The voices were so muffled that I couldn't understand a word. My mother was there; I heard her arguing with the police officers. So I could calmly think about something else. Like the shopping carts in the parking lot in front of the mall or the pretty Kacy, who'd had an affair with Mike on *Temptation Island* and pleaded with her fiancé James not to leave her, even promising that she would finally give herself to him.

What had she meant by that?

But then suddenly it was bright again, like when you surface after being underwater. Every sound gets louder. And now I was afraid after all, because my mother was making a horrible face, like a mask. And I couldn't move my arms properly any more, because I had handcuffs on, and that's why I was now flopped on the carpet like a seal and couldn't find any words either, which was really dumb, because I wanted to tell my mother how very sorry I was.

5
RAGE

The next few days were like living in thick fog. I can only vaguely remember them, and I don't really want to think back on it. Mental blackout.

I was hospitalized.

In the nuthouse.

Correctamundo. The Sheriff of Raufarhöfn was locked up. But it wasn't that bad, apart from the rather large pills I had to swallow that made me sluggish and kind of muted but cotton-cosy. I was given a peaceful room, which was the brightest room in the world. There were other people in the nuthouse too – that's not actually what it's called, but if you've ever been there, you can call it what you like. That's what this guy there told me, he's called Pétur and has a season ticket to the psychiatric ward, he said. Sometimes he was having a good day, and you'd wonder why he was even there. And sometimes he was so sad he couldn't get a single word out. It was as though his lips were sewn shut. My favourite nurse was Gummi, who I got to know a few days later, when I wasn't so foggy.

Usually the TV was on, but my brain was off. Admittedly I still stared at it, but the connection to my head was shaky – bad reception. Something was broken. I didn't even notice when James in *Temptation Island* forgave Kacy for her affair with Mike and proposed to her, which bizarrely she rejected, as though she'd fallen in love with Mike after all. Pétur had to explain the thing with Kacy and James and Mike to me a few times, but eventually I found my way back to the living, received a signal again and no longer felt so numb.

Gummi the nurse gave me a good tip: the next time I flipped out, I should count backwards, from ten or twelve to zero, whichever I preferred, it didn't matter. And we practised it together.

My mother picked me up on a Tuesday and drove me home via the direct route. She talked the whole time, but I didn't listen, because I was mad she hadn't picked me up sooner, she was my mother and guardian after all. I sat there with my arms crossed and didn't say a word, not even at the kitchen table, even though my mother dished up pizza and cola while I stared at the kitchen wall and tried to ignore the smell of the pizza.

"Oh, Kalmann," said my mother, sitting down with a sigh and looking at me in that way only mothers do. Then she laid her hand on the table, facing upwards, so I could put mine in hers. And when I did exactly that, she said she could imagine why I was angry with her. But I just shrugged. "No, I'm sure you are," she assured me. She said she understood, but that anger was a silly emotion that hangs around your neck like a weight, making life heavy. "I'm sure you're still angry, aren't you, Kalli minn?" I nodded sullenly. "And where is it, your rage? Can you show it to me?"

I looked at her. Did she know that every feeling is located at a specific point in the body? "Here," I said, pulling my hand away from hers and pointing towards my shoulders, my upper arms and my ribcage. "Here and here."

"Okay," said my mother, looking at me with satisfaction. Her eyes sparkled. "Listen up, now I'm going to take your rage away, just like that!" She stretched her hand out towards me, gripped my left shoulder as though she were grabbing a tiny, invisible spider that had been crawling around there, then she did the same thing on my right shoulder, touching me lightly, and a third time at my chest. Then, full of pride, she showed me her fist. "Now I've got it, your rage."

"Nonsense!" I said, laughing in surprise.

"Look, you're laughing! You're already feeling better!"

It was true! I was amazed. Where had my mother learned this trick? I was about to ask, but then she got up and went over to the bin, opened the lid, threw all the rage in and brushed her hands as though she were trying to get rid of the final crumbs of anger. Lid shut, bang! But she still wasn't done, she sat back down with me and asked whether I was sad about Grandfather's death. I nodded, because it was only logical.

"And where is it, your grief?" Her voice was soft now, as though she didn't want to startle the grief.

I pointed to my throat. And my heart. I couldn't get a word out.

My mother nodded, stretched her hand out then tenderly reached for my grief, touching my neck and chest – it tickled – and holding my grief in her hands for a while, but this time as though she were holding a butterfly captive. "Grief isn't a bad thing. It's actually good, did you realize? It reminds you that you loved someone, and loving someone isn't bad." She pressed her hand gently against her chest. "I'll keep your grief safe for you for a while, if that's okay with you." Suddenly she had tears in her eyes, probably because she was now carrying my grief in her heart too. "And when you're ready, Kalli minn, I'll give it back to you."

6

SAUÐANES

Grandfather was buried in the Sauðaneskirkja cemetery, about an hour's drive from Raufarhöfn, just a few kilometres beyond Þórshöfn. That was only logical, because Grandmother, who unfortunately I'd never met because she had been dead for thirty-six years, was already buried there in the small cemetery. She was probably hopping mad at Grandfather for having kept her waiting so long. My grandmother was originally from Þórshöfn, born and raised, that's why she was buried here and why Grandfather was joining her.

As we drove south over the Melrakkaslétta, in a long convoy of about twenty cars, I wondered why Grandfather and I had never visited my grandmother's grave. He didn't seem to have missed her at all.

"I can still remember when the entire fjord filled with pack ice once," said my mother as we passed through Þórshöfn and had to stop in the middle of the road for a throng of children. "I was as little as those kids, just imagine!" She smiled, pointing at them.

I couldn't imagine it, so I counted them. There were fourteen children. There weren't that many in the whole of Raufarhöfn.

"We wanted to pick up my father, who was supposed to be returning from a tour, but couldn't because of the ice. The trawler had to divert to another port. So we were allowed to climb around out there." She gestured towards the wide bay.

"I'm sure that's forbidden," I commented.

"You're right, Kalmann! It wouldn't be allowed today. Far too dangerous! We kids were probably accompanied by an entire flock of guardian angels."

"So when did Grandfather come home?"

"The trawler sailed to Akureyri, but the roads were closed because of all the snow and we couldn't pick him up there either, so he went straight on the next tour without a break. When he did finally come home, he brought lots of presents with him."

"Presents!"

"Weird stuff."

We soon left the last houses of Þórshöfn behind us, and I saw the beach at Sauðanes. I couldn't help but think of the wolf fish, and I heard Grandfather telling me about them. Wolf fish are proper gourmets even though they're as ugly as sin. But they're industrious, and process the seabed like construction machines, chewing up clams, shrimp and lobster, the kind of delicacies you usually only get in an expensive restaurant in Reykjavík. The wolf fish chew stoically on the shellfish, crunching them to a powder, he told me, and that's why he would advise anyone against holding their finger between their teeth, because when they bite, even stones turn to dust, bones to crumbs, shells to sand, which is then carried away by the tide and washed up on the beaches.

The beautiful beach is an overpowering sight. The wolf fish have done a good job here over many thousands of years, chewing on the shells until the beach has turned as white as my behind. Astonishing, really, that these ugly beasts can create something so beautiful.

As everyone gathered in the parking lot in front of the church, I wondered whether Grandfather had been pulling my leg. Are wolf fish actually capable of creating a kilometre-long sandy beach? I wanted to ask my mother, but she had flung her arms around her sister Guðrún. They didn't want to let each other go, they hadn't seen each other in a long, long time because of the dumb pandemic. Guðrún's grown-up children formed a queue behind her: my cousins Nonni and Íris Ósk. They nodded at me shyly, and I thought about the shell-munching wolf fish. They're probably not very talkative creatures, these creatures of the deep sea.

"Kalmann, come on, it's time."

The church in Sauðanes is, like many old churches in Iceland, small and, well, old. It's made of driftwood, on a foundation of natural rock, with a small tower, whitewashed boarded walls and a red corrugated iron roof. The inside would be comfortable if only the church pews weren't so hard. You can only sit on them with a really straight back, otherwise your bottom slips forwards. But if you tilt back your head, you can gaze up at the blue domed ceiling. Lots of church ceilings are painted blue, and sometimes even decorated with gold stars, so people feel like they're in heaven. Or they would, if their bottoms didn't hurt so much.

The front pew was reserved for us relatives – luckily, because the church was already half-full! The people from Þórshöfn didn't have as far to come as us, after all, and were waiting impatiently, craning their necks as we stepped on board ship. They were mostly sat on one side of the church, starboard, that's the sunny side. I had to sit between my mother and Aunt Guðrún, an arm's length from Grandfather's white, plush, shiny coffin, which was adorned with golden handles. A black-and-white photo stood on top of it, of Grandfather about twenty years ago, and he was looking at me, so I turned around.

Behind me, the people from Raufarhöfn were making themselves comfortable port side. I tried to count them, but didn't manage, because they kept waving to me. The only sure thing was that more people had come than was allowed, because during the pandemic only so many people could be in one room, that was the law.

Beads of sweat were forming on the priest's forehead; she was called Séra Agnes. For sure she was too hot under her thick robes, because somebody had turned the heating up to the max. The sun was also shining fiercely through the three windows; little dust particles danced in the rays of light above people's heads, flashing like thoughts. Once everyone had found a seat, Séra Agnes made a signal with her hand, upon which an old, scrawny man reached for the keys of a small organ. He played a sad song, rocking back and forth, and by the time he was finished the church was completely silent. Séra Agnes, who reminded me of an Angry Bird on account of her thick, black, painted-on eyebrows, black habit and white collar, greeted us warmly and explained that too many people were in the church. If anyone felt uncomfortable, she said, they could leave and she would understand. But anyone willing to take the risk should stay seated, she would allow it, because not a single case had been registered so far, neither in Þórshöfn nor Raufarhöfn. The virus hadn't found us up here yet, or perhaps it had forgotten us, she said with a strained smile. So she would also overlook the fact that not everyone was wearing masks – but we weren't to tell anyone, otherwise the authorities would ban public funerals up here too.

Five rows behind me sat my neighbour Elínborg, nodding emphatically because she wasn't wearing a mask. Siggi wasn't either, and actually I had never seen him with a mask on, but Óttar and his wife Lin were masked, as was Sæmundur, who was waving to me from the back, but his mask had slipped below his nose. Sigfús had his on the wrong way round, which as far as I knew wasn't forbidden.

"Sit back down, Kalli!" whispered my mother, pulling me down onto the pew by my suit.

The priest looked at me expectantly and gave me a friendly smile. Then she turned back to everyone and explained who this Óðinn Arnarson, to whom we were saying goodbye today, had been.

It was astonishing. It turned out I hadn't known my grandfather that well after all. I'd presumed he had always worked in Raufarhöfn as a fisherman and hunter, and that he'd always been old. But he'd been born in Reykjavík as the youngest of six children, a latecomer, and that's why his siblings were already long dead. When the Royal Navy warships anchored in Reykjavík harbour one beautiful morning, he stood there wide-eyed. The Second World War had come to Iceland. So my grandfather had lived aeons ago! Later he moved with his mother to Hafnarfjörður, and I didn't properly catch what had happened to his father. In any case, my grandfather went to school for a while longer. I would have loved to see that: Grandfather sitting on a school bench, forget it! I almost laughed. The fact that he had begun to work in construction at fourteen, that fit him much better. As a young man in the 1950s, he came up here to Þórshöfn and helped the Americans build the road from the small airfield near here to the Heiðarfjall mountain. The priest even said that the road had long been considered the best in all of Iceland. She actually said that! I glowed with pride, it was so exciting. He continued to go out to sea from time to time, she told us, and two or three rows behind me a man muttered that Óðinn had been an excellent marksman back then, really excellent. He had gone out to sea with him during the herring boom, he said, and Óðinn had shot dozens of orcas from the rocky boat, because they were eating too many of the herrings.

The priest continued undeterred, but her voice became a little louder. Grandfather had spent a summer on Grímsey and after that lived in Neskaupstaður —

"Little Moscow, there you have it!" said another man, loud enough so everyone could hear.

The priest paused and raised her painted-on eyebrows.

"That was a long time ago," called Sigfús from further back. I knew his voice well. "There aren't any commies or pinkos there any more. They rotted themselves out." He raised his hand apologetically and added: "Sorry, Séra Agnes. Please continue."

But Séra Agnes didn't get the chance to continue, because someone else needed to get something off their chest, even though they didn't speak as loudly as Sigfús.

"Well, they still vote Red." It was someone from the Þórshöfn half.

"There are Reds everywhere," commented Sigfús, whose mask had completely slipped off his face.

"Didn't he try to form a communist party, up there in Raufarhöfn?"

"Yes, together with Lúlli Lenin," confirmed Siggi.

"My dear mourners!" The priest waved both hands as though she were trying to stop a car driving towards her. "I'll get to his years in Raufarhöfn in a moment. Can I please continue?"

"Please!" called Sigfús generously.

My mother, who was sitting right next to me, was staring at her hands, which were folded in her lap, and shaking her head almost imperceptibly. Aunt Guðrún was doing the same. You could tell they were sisters.

Séra Agnes then spoke of how Grandfather had worked on a cargo ship for a while and travelled the entire world. He returned to Þórshöfn in 1962, back to where he had met his wife in the 1950s. A short while later they were married, and the young couple settled in Raufarhöfn. My Aunt Guðrún was born in 1963, my mother in 1965. The priest also listed my aunt's children, Íris Ósk and Jón, who everyone called Nonni, and then *I* was mentioned, Kalmann Óðinsson, honorary citizen of Raufarhöfn! A few people craned their necks. The pews creaked.

Everything the priest said after that, I already knew. Finally I was back in familiar waters. But now I felt miserable, because even I realized I would never experience any of it again: the boat trips, the shark processing, the hikes across the Melrakkaslétta, the visits to the care home in Húsavík. I looked around at my mother, whose eyes were as hard as stone. She stared ahead into nothing and paid no attention to me.

"What about the Communist Party though?" called the person from Þórshöfn. "We're almost at Óðinn's death."

The priest bundled her notes together and cast a questioning glance at my mother, but it wasn't returned. "There's, er, actually not anything in here about the Party. I think —"

"That's because nothing came of it!" muttered Bragi beneath his mask.

"You can't milk an ox," confirmed someone else.

And then the guy from the front again: "Poet, you were in it too, weren't you?"

Bragi shrugged and looked up at the blue heaven ceiling, as though it had nothing to do with him.

Elínborg turned to the person next to her and said: "All poets are pinkos."

My mother let out a sound like a grunt, then Aunt Guðrún pressed her hand to her mouth and her face went red.

The priest finally intervened: "My dear people, we've gathered here to say goodbye to Óðinn!"

"But you haven't said anything about the dances either!" cried someone else from Þórshöfn. "We remember that hooligan well. He was always up for a fight."

Lots of people nodded now, some muttered, others shook their heads, probably because they disapproved of fighting.

"There was only one time he didn't fight, do you remember? He'd come straight from a tour, and said you don't beat people when you're in work clothes."

Laughter. Séra Agnes gave us an apologetic look and my mother lifted her hand understandingly.

"Was that in Sólbakki, the old community house?"

"No, that had burned down by then. A goddamn disgrace. Sorry, Séra Agnes."

"Did anything come of the fight?"

"Of course! Óðinn came to the next event in a suit and tie and really dished it out —"

That was all we found out, because Séra Agnes gave a sign to the scrawny guy at the organ. And as we all listened to the organ music and lost ourselves in our thoughts, I wondered whether Grandfather had been listening. Perhaps he would have liked to join in the conversation or thrash the men from Þórshöfn. I was very proud to be the grandson of a man that people talk about. And I still am. All I have to do is think of Grandfather, because pride is like a little tub of hákarl that you carry with you in your trouser pocket. Nourishment for the soul.

7

GULLS

I helped carry the coffin outside to the small cemetery. Final stop. We stood close together, because the autumn breeze coming off the sea was really packing a punch, even though the sun was putting up a good fight. It was one of those October days when the colours are particularly strong, overripe and intense. The sea tries to be bluer than the sky, the crests of the waves whiter than the clouds, and the grass shines golden as though it were our most valuable commodity. The air was so clear that the horizon slipped even further away.

Those of us remaining gathered around the grave, which was filled to the brim with coal-black shadows, and the scrawny man who had been sitting at the organ, pounding the keys in such a way that all conversation about Grandfather had fallen silent, used a winch to crank the coffin down into this uncomfortable-looking hole. I looked around for my mother, who had tucked her arm through Aunt Guðrún's and closed her eyes. I felt that the scrawny guy was rushing things unnecessarily; he cranked and cranked until a boom signalled that Grandfather had arrived at the bottom. Séra Agnes said a prayer and threw down a shovelful of dirt, which made a clattering sound. Nobody complained. They probably couldn't wait to finally be rid of Grandfather! I leaned forward a little and peered into the hole, because

I could have sworn I heard a knock on the coffin lid. I stepped so close to the edge of the grave that dirt and pebbles loosened beneath the soles of my shoes and tumbled down into the depths. Someone grabbed my forearm and pulled me back.

It was Bragi. The village poet. He pulled the mask off his face and gave me a serious look. His lips were painted dark red, so he'd clearly made an effort to look extra nice for the funeral, though of course you wouldn't have seen it under the mask. He was actually one of the people who'd always worn a mask since the pandemic began, even when they didn't need to, for example when walking outside or when they were alone in the car. "Kalli minn," he said, pulling me away from the grave as though it were something urgent. "Look, look out there, at all the seagulls. Just look!"

My mother let out a sob and held her hand over her mouth, and I looked out to sea, in the direction he was pointing, to where seagulls were circling over a particular spot and working the surface of the water with their beaks. There must have been a shoal of fish, maybe humpback whales had herded the fish together, but you couldn't see properly because of all the little waves. One thing was certain: there was something to feed on out there, because seagulls hit every buffet, even when they're not invited.

"What could be out there?" Bragi asked me. "Herrings? Waste?"

"You can't tell from here," I told him. "But it must be fish. Maybe caplin on their way south."

"I think so too," said Bragi in relief, as though we had solved a riddle together. "I think so too."

"Grandfather always liked seagulls," I said.

"Because they showed him where the fish were?"

I shook my head. "He just liked talking to them."

"Seagulls." Bragi clicked his tongue. "Most people don't care much for seagulls, they call them the rats of the sky." He pointed towards the small excavator that stood off to the side of the cemetery. "Look, Gulli is ready, do you see him?" I nodded, although I hadn't known the skinny organ player was called Gulli. "He'll shovel the earth into the grave. That's his job." Bragi waved at him and Gulli, a little startled, waved back. "He used to be a farmer way out on Langanes, but the farm doesn't exist any more."

Bragi was talkative today, and not wanting to be rude, I listened to him.

My grandfather was in the earth now, he explained – Séra Agnes had spoken of this too – and he would become dirt, like we all will, like thousands, even millions, before him. And dirt is life, he said. Everything grows and thrives on it, including me and him and everyone else. Then he stamped his foot on the grass. "That's just how it is, do you understand, Kalmann? It's the cycle of life."

I looked at my feet and nodded.

We walked back to the grave, and I cast one last glance into the dark hole, burying my hands in my trouser pockets, which unfortunately didn't contain any hákarl. So there was room for my fists. My mother rested her head on my shoulder, and we stood there and watched Gulli slowly drive up, the little excavator juddering and rumbling. We left because we didn't want to watch Grandfather get shovelled over.

On the journey back we didn't talk much, we just looked out of the window and dwelled on our thoughts. At the Hotel Arctica, coffee and cake stood at the ready. I'm sure Grandfather wouldn't have wanted us to be in this hotel, which had once belonged to the capitalist Róbert McKenzie, filling our bellies. Was he annoyed?

But then I stopped worrying, because I was allowed to eat as much cake as I wanted, nobody prevented me from doing so, and I even started to feel sick. People were really nice to me and told me to tuck in, like they had when I was made an honorary citizen. Even Dagbjört, who I hadn't seen in ages, had come all the way from Akranes just to tell me how sorry she was. But she swiftly said goodbye again, gave me a quick wave from across the room and hurried out of the hotel with a stony expression, as though the place were on fire. I felt annoyed I hadn't told her how happy I was to see her.

"Would you like another piece of cake, dear Kalmann?"

I turned around. An old woman was standing behind me, holding a plate with a slice of cheesecake under my nose. I had noticed the old woman before, in the church and by the grave, because she was wearing a crazy red felt hat decorated with bird feathers.

I shook my head. "I'm about to throw up," I told her.

The old woman smiled and set down the plate on one of the tables. Then she held out her hand to me, almost as if she were expecting me to kiss it. "My name is Telma."

I looked down at the ground. Then I looked around for my mother. She was standing by the coffee pots with Aunt Guðrún and gave me an encouraging nod.

"My name is Kalmann Óðinsson," I said eventually, wondering if anyone would eat the piece of cheesecake left on the table. "Óðinn was my grandfather and my father is American."

"I know," said the old woman, pulling her hand back but still smiling. "I'm very sorry your grandfather died."

"No reason to worry," I mumbled, then regretted having said it.

"I was very fond of him."

"Me too."

"I'm sorry we're only meeting properly now." She paused, and so I quickly glanced at her face. She looked like a nice old woman, even though she was wearing too much make-up and a lot of jewellery, around her neck, wrists, and on her ears. For sure she was stinking rich. Even though I'd never seen her before, she seemed somehow familiar.

"Did you make the hat yourself?" I asked her.

"Yes. Do you like it?"

I shrugged. "And those are seagull feathers, right?"

"Exactly. Gathered from the beach on Langanes."

"You can find tons of feathers over on the Höfði," I informed her. "Gulls are the rats of the sky."

She smiled again. "I think seagulls are very beautiful and clever creatures, much more beautiful than rats, don't you think?"

I shrugged again. I would have to think about my answer.

"I'm your grandmother's sister. You and I are related. Isn't that lovely?"

Now my eyes widened, because I'd had no idea my grand-mother had ever had a family.

Telma hurried to say: "When my sister died, shortly before you were born, I... well, lost contact with you all."

"Okay," I said, acting relaxed.

"But it's lovely to finally meet you." I nodded and looked around for my mother again. She was chatting with Óttar's wife Lin. "Better late than never, don't you agree?"

"Correctamundo."

"Will you come and visit me sometime?"

"Where do you live?"

"On Langanes. So just outside Þórshöfn."

"Where we were just now?"

"Another few kilometres along. My house is completely alone there, by the sea. That's why I'm always glad to receive visitors."

"Did you grow up there with my grandmother?"

"No." The old woman smiled and stared past me, as though she were gazing back into the past. "We grew up in Þórshöfn. I didn't move out to the peninsula until later." She suddenly looked a little sad, but kept smiling regardless and touched me on my upper arm, as though she were checking I was real. Her hand was manicured; the skin shimmered almost translucently. It was like you could almost stare inside her but still see nothing. She asked me whether I had a phone to call her if I was going to visit. I pulled out my Nokia, which wasn't a smartphone but still smart enough to make calls and send texts, and we exchanged numbers. I said "bless", and because the old woman gave me a slightly confused look, as if perhaps she had wanted to chat with me for longer, I went outside. Besides, I was feeling really sick from all the cake, even though I'd turned down the last piece.

The fresh air did me good. I walked through the village, went down to the harbour and hid myself away in my hall.

I hadn't been inside here for ages, seeing as how there hadn't been any reason to. The neon lights took even longer now to shine evenly and stop flickering like a disco. My bait barrel was empty, but still smelled like it used to. My fridge, also empty, was humming. I'd once heard somewhere that fridges start to stink when you turn them off, so that's why I left it on. The processing table was black, and so were my knives.

"Everything okay, Kalli?"

I turned around in shock, not having heard anyone come in. It was Bragi. He was standing in the doorway, a black silhouette in the dim daylight. "No need to worry," I murmured, putting the knife back on the table.

"You disappeared, and I promised your mother I'd find you and bring you back."

"Okay," I said. "I'm here."

Bragi came to stand next to me and looked at the processing table, touching it carefully. "Are you sad?"

"I just felt sick from all the cake. But I didn't have to throw up."

"That's good. Do you want to start shark hunting again?"

I shook my head. "I'm not allowed to go out to sea alone. And they took all my weapons away."

"I see. I'm sorry." Bragi looked around and pointed at the blue bait barrel. "Is there still something in there?"

"It's empty," I said. "Has been for ages."

"The sharks can have a siesta now," said Bragi contentedly.

"Sharks don't sleep," I explained. "They have to move constantly, otherwise they die. They drown. Four hundred and twelve years, constantly on the move."

"At least they don't need to be afraid of you any more. That's kinda nice, isn't it?"

I thought about it. For sure sharks could feel fear. Only stupid things didn't feel fear. And sharks aren't stupid. Because they've been around much longer than us humans, and anything that survives that long can't possibly be stupid.

"Kalli, don't worry. Take everything one step at a time, okay? Your grandfather has been buried, we've had cake, and now we want to hold onto the memories."

"Of the cake?" I asked.

"No, of your grandfather," answered Bragi.

"Okay," I said.

"Come on," said Bragi. "I'll go with you back to the hotel."

*

The evening meal was in the Arctica too. Óttar the Pressure Cooker made the food, Lin served, and my mother helped her. After that we went home to the cottage, my mother, my Aunt Guðrún, Nonni, Íris Ósk and I, and that's when the party really started. We played Poppkviss and watched an Adam Sandler movie where he buys a magic remote control that he can use to fast-forward time or mute people, like women who nag him. I would've liked a remote control like that. My mother and Aunt Guðrún found an old wooden crate containing all kinds of junk and photo albums, which they flipped through while drinking vodka and cola. I only drank cola. We had a great time, even though no one but me and Nonni took any interest in Adam Sandler's remote control. Strange. Even though Grandfather had died, and even though it felt cramped and noisy in the cottage, I felt happiness in my belly. I didn't even mind going outside to pee behind the cottage because Íris Ósk had been throwing up in the toilet for ages and was sitting by the bowl with her head resting on the rim.

My mother and my aunt started acting like teenagers, giggling and almost falling off the sofa with laughter. "No way!" they shrieked, leaning over the photos. My cousin Nonni and I exchanged glances and shook our heads. Women! But anyone thinking this was the high point of the evening would be wrong. The two women tossed the photo albums aside and put on music, pushed back the furniture and danced in a carefree way, even using as a dance partner the column that held the entire cottage upright, embracing it, spinning around it, balancing their half-full glasses, which looked kind of dangerous. And it was! They spattered the column and the floorboards and the coffee table with vodka and cola, so I turned the music down, because Grandfather wouldn't have taken kindly to this nonsense.

But it was pointless. My mother and Aunt Guðrún laughed themselves silly and turned up the music again, hugging me and pulling Nonni and me onto the dance floor. He even let them, which I was miffed about, because I'd thought we were on the same team. I had no choice but to pull away and flee upstairs to the attic room. I pressed two cushions against my ears, because the music was unbearable even up there; the entire cottage was groaning and shaking.

Soon I felt bored, and that's why I went back downstairs again, but not to dance, because Kalmann Óðinsson doesn't dance. I sat down on the sofa with my arms crossed, next to my cousin Íris Ósk, who had fallen asleep with her mouth open and eyes half shut. The women left me in peace now, but my mother gave me these really loving looks from time to time, and I don't think I've ever seen her so happy. And that's why I felt happy again too, but I stayed sitting down.

The next day we said goodbye to Aunt Guðrún, Íris Ósk and Nonni. They were pale and barely said a word, hungover, and that's why the goodbye wasn't as warm-hearted as you would expect after such a fun evening. But I was familiar with that. When people are drunk, they're your best friends. By the next day, they've forgotten all about it.

Outside, heavy swathes of fog were creeping through Raufarhöfn, a drizzle that gets caught in your eyelashes and eyebrows and forms beads on your face. Shivering, we waved after the car until it had disappeared behind the discarded fish oil tanks, and my mother even waved for a bit longer than that, which is why I told her that Aunt Guðrún, Íris Ósk and Nonni could no longer see us. "Spoilsport," said my mother, giving me a teasing jab in the side.

Inside the cottage, it was oppressively quiet without our relatives. We stood around for a while, my mother sighed, then we cleaned up the mess. Once we were finished, she wanted to go right away, to be anywhere but here, as though she were in a hurry.

"I'm staying," I said, feeling offended, because I had assumed we would spend the entire day in Raufarhöfn. My mother probably couldn't wait to cut and run. I don't think she has ever felt comfortable in Raufarhöfn.

She didn't object, and so I carried the old crate containing Grandfather's stuff out to the car for her.

"Will you be okay, Kalli minn?"

"No reason to worry."

I waved after my mother until she had disappeared behind the fish oil tanks, and even for a little longer. Then I turned around to the cottage. It just stood there, silent and old. I had the feeling all the life had ebbed out of it, that it was a husk. Bled out. A corpse of the past. Grandfather was dead, and with him the cottage had died a little, because houses have souls too, you notice it immediately when you go inside them.

I was afraid of its inside, where the empty silence echoed loudly. Like in a dark cave. So I went down to the harbour, because the harbour is the heart of a village, and with every step I felt better.

8
FRIENDS

"Come on in!" Sæmundur waved at me from his container. He was sitting at the computer, the fingers of his left hand tucked into his trouser pocket, his right hand clasping the mouse, his legs up on the table so that his office chair tilted and creaked at the slightest movement. He was wearing knitted socks and slippers; the container was his living room. "Today would be a wonderful day to lay some lines out there, don't you think?" He looked at me and his bushy eyebrows shot up. "Dead calm."

"No chance," I said, annoyed that my shotgun had been taken from me. I wasn't allowed to go out to sea alone with Petra any more either. Sæmundur already knew that; after all, he was the harbour master. "I don't feel like it," I added, sitting down on the small leather sofa which was half-covered in papers and folders.

Sæmundur clicked around on the mouse, occasionally typing something into the computer, then the phone rang and he talked for a while. Once he had hung up, he turned to me. "Are you all right, Kalli? It feels like it's about to start raining in here!"

I shrugged and looked up at the ceiling. "No reason to worry."

"Well, when the sheriff leaves his cowboy hat and sheriff star at home, there definitely *is* reason to worry."

"I'm not on duty."

"I'm sure you're sad about your grandfather, aren't you? I'm really sorry. Óðinn was very old and had a full life. Others spend day after day sitting in a container!" Sæmundur clicked his tongue and turned back to his computer, saying that if he were to die like my grandfather, suddenly, without suffering, he would throw a party.

"Will I be invited?" I asked.

"Of course!" Sæmundur laughed so loudly the entire container shook. "You'll be my guest of honour! VIP!"

Siggi poked his head in the door. Outside, the brown-speckled young gulls were circling over the harbour, making a racket. "There's going to be a party?" he asked.

"You're not invited!" said Sæmundur, but he didn't mean it seriously, because he was still grinning and he isn't mean to anyone. He would invite the entire village to his funeral for sure. "You'd only drink all the Brennivín."

Siggi turned to me: "Kalli Kaliber, where's the party?"

"As soon as Sæmundur dies," I explained.

Now Siggi's face brightened. "Oh yes, then we'll really pop the corks!"

The men laughed, and so did I, even though I'll surely be sad when Sæmundur dies.

"Can you sign for my load before you kick the bucket?" asked Siggi, who never laughed for long, but briefly and loudly and rarely.

"I sure can!" cried Sæmundur, wiping a tear from his eye. "What lovely stuff do you have for me today?"

"One thousand, one hundred and seventy-eight kilos of cod. I mean, it's right there, you can see it."

"On the line?"

"It's certainly not in my car."

"Well I never! The sleepyheads at the fishing ministry will be pleased!"

"They get a shock when they actually hear from us."

"When you remember how things used to be... We had dozens of boats here, and today? Kalli Kaliber, now you're not allowed to hunt sharks any more, there's not much going on up here."

"There's still a fair bit going on in Þórshöfn, and that's not so far away," I informed him, because I didn't feel like talking about sharks.

Siggi didn't move from the spot, still standing in the doorway. "Yes, but their quota belongs to the Westman Islands. If they withdraw it, Þórshöfn will shut up shop." And, addressing Sæmundur: "Has that scoundrel supervisor made an appearance yet?"

Sæmundur rolled his eyes. "Well. Unfortunately, you never know when he's coming. He turned up in Kópasker last week, apparently."

Siggi let out a contemptuous snort. "The fishing ministry has enough money for that, it seems! Kalmann, what do those guys in Reykjavík have against us?"

"I don't know," I said, and I meant it.

"Kiddi on Grímsey told me they're using drones now, that there's no other way he can explain it. He threw a fish back, one single one, he said. And a short while later the bill for it came fluttering into his house. Shame on them!"

"Amen," said Sæmundur.

Siggi pulled his head back and disappeared for a moment, but we heard him cursing outside. Then he poked his head back in the door. "And the big guys with their dragnets?" he asked, without expecting an answer, because he continued, saying that the fishing ministry closed their eyes when it came to the big companies, one eye for each net they drag behind their trawlers, each one as big as a football field. And that we in Þórshöfn got the bill if we threw just one single fish back in the sea. Just one! Grotesque!

While Siggi was outside transporting vats of cod into the freezing facility on the forklift, I asked Sæmundur if he knew my grandfather had spoken Russian. He let go of the mouse, swung his feet off the table and crossed his hairy arms, which almost made it look as if he were holding a cat. "Russian, hmm. Yes, there was talk of that."

"I heard it with my own ears."

"Are you absolutely sure it was Russian?"

"*Suka amerikanets!*" I cried. "*Gora letit!*"

"Aha. *Amerikanets.* That sounds a lot like your grandfather, and Russian too. He must have been annoyed with the Americans, and it's probably easiest to do that in Russian." Sæmundur rubbed his face with his heavy hands. "You think you know someone, and it's only when you carry them to the grave you realize you're burying a stranger."

I stayed a good while longer in the container with Sæmundur while he reported Siggi's catch to Reykjavík, so they wouldn't forget we were still up here. At noon I got hungry and went back to the cottage, where I scoffed the leftovers from the day before, including cake. I sat down on the sofa to digest it all.

The TV stared at me, black and expectant. The remote control wasn't on the coffee table like usual, but by the TV. My mother must have put it there. So I picked up my old laptop from the table and opened it. I wanted to watch that Adam Sandler movie again, the one with the magic remote control, but I didn't get round to it because the laptop started beeping.

"Bear Killer!"

"Nói?"

I almost fell off the sofa! I had assumed my BFF was no longer alive, or that he was in jail, or – as I had sometimes thought since being in the psychiatric unit – that he had never existed in the first place. I mean, it's possible. Maybe he'd been a figment of my imagination the whole time. So I pinched my arm to make sure I hadn't gone completely mad, because there was clearly a Gandalf sweater and a thin neck on my screen. No head; it didn't fit in the picture. I had never seen Nói's face, neither on my screen nor in real life.

"Nói, are you… is it actually you?" I stuttered.

"Behold!" boomed Nói, then he burst out laughing. "You should see your face! Properly handicapped!"

"Where've you been?" I cried indignantly. "I could have really used your help!" I felt a little startled at myself. Seeing Nói in such a good mood made me angry.

"I'm damn sorry, Sheriff," he said, then he paused to think, picking up a Rubik's cube, whose colours can only be organized by super-intelligent people. "I had surgery again, you know? Operation Black Heart. This time it was life and death. It was a pretty tough time. Bro, I'm telling you, I was already on the other side, but I came back!"

"On what side?"

"In the afterlife, dude, in nirvana, capeesh?"

"In Valhalla?"

"Correctamundo. But even there they threw me out again."

I wondered if I had run into Nói back when I was lying under the polar bear.

He put the Rubik's cube aside and pulled his sweater up to the neck until his bare, weedy chest appeared on my screen. There was a bright red scar on it, stretching from the navel to just beneath his neck. "The master butcher almost cut me in half. My medical team said my chance of survival was thirty per cent, that's why I didn't want to tell you. No drama. So long, my friend, you see? I wanted to slip out the back door. Goodbyes are for losers."

I was stunned. "How long were you dead?"

Nói pulled the sweater back down over his ribs. "All I know is that I was gone quite a while. Four operations in total. And then rehab! I was in there longer than Charlie Sheen and Amy Winehouse put together."

"Who?"

"But now I'm a new person."

"Great!" I didn't feel angry at Nói any longer, and gave him the thumbs up.

"But enough about me. It's nuts what you went through!"

"Oh." I waved away his comment.

Nói pointed an invisible gun into the camera. "You talking to me? Bam, bam, bam! Die, polar bear bitch!"

"Well, actually I felt pretty bad. It was a beautiful animal. In fact, I think it was probably the most beautiful animal I've ever seen."

"You or me, baby! You did absolutely the right thing. Nature knows no mercy."

"That's true. The animal almost flattened me. I had to go to hospital too. In Akureyri."

"That's serious shit."

"Sometimes I have these dreams. Nightmares. Where I can't catch my breath. I wake up drenched in sweat in the middle of the night, or I hit someone or scream or smash things."

"Bro! PTSD is a bitch!"

"What?"

"Shell shock. Like the soldiers who come home from war. Vietnam, for example."

"Korea too?"

"Doesn't matter which. Korea, Iraq, Afghanistan —"

"Maybe I inherited it from my American grandfather."

"Hardly. Something like that isn't hereditary. The soldiers get damaged. Nightmares and stuff. And then they fire a bullet through their heads. Bang!"

I pictured Róbert McKenzie before me and started to sweat. "Yeah, it's kind of like that with me too," I murmured, struggling for air.

"Chin up, lad! No reason to worry! You're a hero! I saw the interview on TV and read a couple of the newspaper articles. The ladies must've gone nuts over you, huh?"

"Well…" I thought about Perla. "There was already one —"

"Respect. And? Did you guys —" Nói made the international hand signal for screwing. I couldn't help but laugh even though I didn't want to.

"No comment!"

"Oh man, what I wouldn't give for just one…"

I decided not to tell Nói that Perla and I had never had sex. I had always been good and kept my trousers on, even when we were lying in bed together.

"But why are you talking about it in the past?"

"Oh, you know, women," I sighed, and Nói understood at once, because friends can tell each other an entire love story from beginning to end in only a few words. This was followed by a brief minute's silence for all the disappointed men in this world.

"Listen, Bear Killer. My mother saw the obituary in the newspaper. And that's why I said to myself, c'mon, Nói, it's high time you got back in touch with the Sheriff!"

"That's how life is. We're all just dirt."

"Word. Only the best die young."

"Grandfather was pretty old."

"What did he actually die of?"

I thought for a moment. "He was just old, he couldn't remember anything, not me nor my mother."

"Alzheimer's."

"He was eighty-five."

"You don't die from that. Did he have Covid?"

"No. I visited him the day before."

"What? You were allowed to visit him? Do you guys not have the pandemic up there?"

"I was allowed to because I wasn't working in the shopping mall any more and just stayed home."

"Weird, but okay. Was he coughing?"

"No."

"Did he have a fever?"

"I don't think so."

"Did he fall over or anything?"

"Yes, but he landed on me, and it didn't hurt him. It hurt me though."

"Have you even read his autopsy report?"

"His what?"

Nói leaned forward and began to type away on his keyboard. I watched him for a while, then I wanted to get a snack from the kitchen, but he called out for me not to leave. So I sat back down again.

"Was your grandfather popular? Did he have enemies?"

"Enemies?" I thought back to the funeral in Sauðanes. "For sure. He sometimes used to fight with the people in Þórshöfn. But only in a suit. And he wanted to start a communist party."

"A Raufarhöfn gulag?"

"And sometimes he bit people."

"Rabies. I'm familiar. Did people cry at his funeral?"

"Do you mean, apart from my mother and my aunt and so on?"

"Correctamundo."

"Nah."

"Bro. Highly interesting. So we can't rule out the possibility he was murdered."

"Murdered?"

"The fact you haven't clapped eyes on the autopsy report makes the matter extremely suspicious, you see?"

"But why would anyone have wanted to murder him? Grandfather would have died soon anyway."

"What about the Pressure Cooker?"

Before I could say anything about Óttar, there was a beeping sound on Nói's side, someone was calling him.

"Later, dude," he said, then ended the call, leaving me sitting there bewildered in front of the laptop.

He was gone. My head felt like a pot of fish soup that someone had stirred rigorously. Had Grandfather been murdered?

I jumped when my old Nokia began to buzz rhythmically in my trouser pocket.

"Kalli, are you still in the village?" It was Hafdís from the town council office. She always got straight to the point. "You speak English pretty well, don't you? English, *por favor*?"

"I think so, yes."

"Good. Because there's a gentleman from America here who wants to take a look at the Arctic Henge, and I don't have the time right now —"

"A *gentleman*?"

"Correcto!" Hafdís suddenly began to whisper: "An American tourist. Kind of old. I'm sure there'll be a good tip in it. Do you have time?"

9

TOURIST

Life is like a boat on the waves. Sometimes it goes up, sometimes it goes down.

While I was waving after my mother until she had driven behind the fish oil tanks, I had assumed I would spend a relaxing day in Raufarhöfn, acting as though everything was perfectly okay. Forget it! Almost as soon as I was back inside the cottage, a freak wave broke over the boat, almost washing me off the sofa. Nói was alive, Grandfather had been murdered, and despite the pandemic a tourist had somehow ended up in Raufarhöfn.

I groaned loudly at the ceiling, pulled myself together, took my cowboy hat down from the hook and pinned the sheriff star to my chest.

Outside, the swathes of fog had dispersed, but the sky was covered with grey clouds. They looked like soft cushions. The air was mild and carried the scent of damp moss and wet stones.

"Hi there, Sheriff. You must be Kalmann!" The tourist threw the words at me in a loud and friendly way, speaking in English, so I slowed my pace a little and studied him discreetly. He was old and looked kind of stiff, but he was standing tall, chin held high. His gaze was assertive. "Thank you so much for showing me everything!" he said, even though I hadn't shown him anything at all yet. But that's how Americans are, super friendly and grateful, even though they're constantly waging wars.

"No problem," I said, giving a military salute. That's how you show your respect in America. And the tourist reciprocated the military salute, swift and professional. His smile disappeared in that moment, like it had been blown away, but his gaze lingered on me, his dim, black eyes as serious and bleak as a Greenland shark's. Yes, suddenly the man in his entirety reminded me of a Greenland shark. It was very strange, I couldn't shake the image. The American's skin was coarse and blotchy too, thick and bumpy, especially around the chin and neck, as though he really was a creature from the deep sea. I quickly looked away. After all, I didn't want to stare at him like the village idiot.

"Kalmann?" The American gave me a friendly smile again and in general looked pretty content. For sure he was a nice guy, a good grandfather who took his grandkids on outings and loved them more than anything. But there was something severe, almost stony, beneath his smile. Deeply sad. Like with the Greenland sharks. Perhaps his wife had died, and that's why he was now here alone.

"Did your wife die?" I asked, because if you don't know something, you have to ask.

The American gave me a solemn look. He was wearing a baseball cap and a thick down jacket with the inscription ARCTIC EXPEDITION 1997 on it. "Yes," he confirmed. "She died recently."

"And that's why you're here?"

He thought for a few seconds. "Yes, that's probably why I'm here. We wanted to do the trip together, but —"

"She probably died of Covid," I presumed, and correctly, because the American nodded.

On the way to the Arctic Henge, he became more talk-ative with every step, and soon he was talking without pause. Probably he was happy to finally be able to speak to someone in his own language. Even though I didn't understand every-thing, I discovered that he used to spend a lot of time in Iceland, that he'd worked for an American agency and visited Keflavík many times. "Good old times!" he said, then went silent, as though all the air had gone out of him. "Good old times," he repeated, almost in a whisper. His steps became smaller, his movements slower, and soon I was a good fifty metres ahead. When I looked around for him, he was leaning forwards and lifted his hand to signal for me to wait for him.

At this point I had almost reached the new parking lot, which was completely empty, even though there would have been space for multiple tourist coaches. Because of the pandemic there were barely any tourists now. Elínborg was pleased about that. She said tourists were a plague, hordes that trampled Iceland's delicate natural landscape. During the Easter holidays, Elínborg had stayed home and not flown to Tenerife as usual. She had used the time to have the meadow in front of the house flattened with a digger, to extend her veranda.

I waved to the American, because I had already got to the wooden path that led up to the Arctic Henge. Here he would have been able to sit on the edge and take a break. But he didn't move from where he was. He rummaged around in a small bag, strapped around his waist, that had been concealed beneath his down jacket. Then he opened the belt of his trousers, pulled them down a little and rammed something into his thigh. Jab! It was a syringe. Quickly, I looked away. I don't like syringes. Then I looked back again. The American had lifted his face towards the sky, his mouth and trousers open, his eyes closed, as though Adam Sandler had pressed the pause button on his magic remote control.

Sitting down on the edge of the wooden path, I waited until the American had caught up with me. He nodded but didn't say a word; he looked pale and sweaty, and his eyes seemed even blacker than before.

Once we arrived at the Arctic Henge, he asked me to explain everything, so I told him about the four dwarves from the old saga. Or tried to, at least. Grandfather would have done it better. He always used to tell me the stories while we were hiking over the Slétta or when we were out at sea, about Grettir the Strong, who was so powerful he carried an ox on his shoulders and defeated a revenant but unfortunately died of blood poisoning when he accidentally hacked an axe into his leg. And Gunnar, who had been banished from Iceland but didn't want to leave because he got homesick, which ultimately cost him his life. About Bárðar, a half-troll, who went into a volcanic mountain covered with glaciers and hasn't come out to this day. Because he was embarrassed and sad. And Grandfather also told me about the four dwarves from the Poetic Edda, who are called North, South, East and West and carry the sky on their shoulders, like the giant stone blocks of the Arctic Henge, although they don't actually look like dwarves. I told the American that in the Poetic Edda there are even more dwarves, who stand for different days of the year, and that's why the stone installation is a kind of Arctic calendar, but unfortunately it's unfinished because Róbert McKenzie ran out of money and the government didn't want to help us.

"Róbert McKenzie?" asked the American, and then I made the mistake of looking at the spot where —

I suddenly felt dizzy, and there was a disco in my chest. An image of the bleeding wound flashed before me, because with this backdrop the memories had an easy job of it. They jostled me from all sides and breathed down the back of my neck. I couldn't get any air into my lungs, and that's why I turned and ran away, wanting to get away from the Arctic Henge, away from the American, who called after me in confusion, asking whether everything was okay.

No, it wasn't.

Nothing was okay!

I climbed over the barbed wire fence and marched towards the horizon, the vastness of the Melrakkaslétta before me, striding over grass mounds and basaltic rocks embellished with colourful flecks, counting backwards from ten like the nice nurse from the psychiatric unit had advised me. And then again. I felt the wanderlust surging inside me, and was relieved I'd left the ghosts behind. All but one. Because even though he was dead, Grandfather was with me, like before, when we'd stridden all across this tundra. Even though its name means "Arctic fox flatland", towards the west it's anything but flat. This becomes particularly evident during the gathering of the sheep, when the ewes hide with their lambs in the furrows and troughs, where they're easily over-looked. For hunting Arctic fox or ptarmigan, however, these uneven surfaces are ideal. It makes it easier to lie in wait for the animals. What I wouldn't have given to go hunting with Grandfather just one last time!

To stop myself from bursting into tears, I ran and howled like an Arctic fox, running and howling until there was no air left inside me. Until I almost had to throw up. Until the cowboy hat fell off my head. And when I turned around, I could see neither the Arctic Henge nor the American. Relieved, I sank down into the moss next to my hat and lis-tened to the sigh of the wind and the silence of the tundra.

10
CARDIAC ARREST

I spent the evening in front of the TV – finally! And I wouldn't move from the sofa for a good while, even if Hafdís called again. I swore it to myself.

Dr Phil is a proper shrink, a genius. He always has a solution at the ready, and it's sometimes so obvious that people are flabbergasted. If you're as smart as Dr Phil, everyone else is stupid. Across from him sat a man who was so overweight he might die of heart failure at any moment; after all, he was lugging two hundred and fifty pounds around with him twenty-four hours a day. He was as spherical as a ball of hay wrapped in plastic.

The shrink concluded that the man urgently needed to lose weight, and the studio audience agreed. Many nodded vigorously.

During the commercial break, I called Nói on Messenger and listened as he eliminated his opponents in *Call of Duty*. "You're getting nervous!" he exclaimed in English, addressing his opponent, who was sitting at a computer somewhere in America or Japan, fighting desperately for their third life. "Take this, you lousy muppet! Bam!" Nói could get pretty worked up at times, and I wondered whether it was healthy for him, I mean, because of his surgery and all. "Bullseye!" he yelled at the top of his voice, and I ducked.

I wasn't in the least bit surprised when the door behind Nói opened and his mother stormed into the room. She threatened to turn off the power if he didn't calm down at once, and while she was waiting for Nói to calm down, she bent down, waved into the camera and said: "Hello, Kalmann, long time no see, how are you doing?"

"Oh, I'm really good, thanks," I replied.

"I'm very sorry your grandfather died."

"I know," I said, and clapped my laptop shut, then instantly regretted it because I'd wanted to talk to Nói about Grandfather's murder.

The next day, Hafdís drove me to Akureyri, even though I had been planning to stay in Raufarhöfn for a while. But because she offered me a ride – after all, I had taken care of the American tourist for her – I accepted. I didn't mention that I had run away and simply left the American standing at the Arctic Henge, though.

At home, my mother showed me the things she had found in my grandfather's old crate. There were carvings, strange stones, a military flask and knife, pressed flowers, some weird military insignia. And above all, photos. "I never knew my father had taken so many photos," said my mother. "It must have been his hobby."

We had a whole pile of photos between us on the living room carpet. My mother told me the stories behind the photos, and all I had to do was look and listen.

There I was, Kalmann, with my first and only bicycle, which I would never use. It had gone rusty behind the house, that I could remember. Kalmann at Christmas, happy because I liked presents, and still do. Kalmann on the first day of school with school bag, left eye taped shut like a pirate's, not happy. Kalmann dressed as a teddy bear, pulling a face, squinting. Kalmann in snow a metre high, wrapped up warmly, rosy-cheeked, runny nose.

I'm sometimes standing a little lopsided in the photos, like a fence post after a fierce winter storm, but my mother made sure I didn't fall over, holding my hand tightly, her smile strained. How young she was back then!

Then I was no longer standing. My first steps at the age of three, Kalmann, a chubby child, a chubby baby, squinting, always drooling. The more we worked our way through the photos, the further we travelled back in time. Before long, I wasn't yet born and my grandmother was alive again, but most of the photos were of my mother and Aunt Guðrún when they were little. Grandfather himself was rarely in the photos, because he had to be behind the camera. Sometimes you saw his shadow. He must have loved his daughters a lot, because he really did take a lot of photos of them, and almost only them, and only very few at home and of my grandmother, who was always busy with something and looked like she didn't have time to be photographed. She looked like unhappiness personified.

"He was always taking us on these long hikes, even though we didn't want to go," said my mother.

I thought back on all the days I'd spent hiking the Melrakkaslétta with Grandfather – without a camera. "But that's not on the Slétta," I said, offended.

My mother turned the photo over and read the letters and numbers scribbled on the back in pencil:

#16-3-5-68 H-2ssw

"Hmm." She turned the photo back over again. "It looks like Langanes. We used to go there a lot!"

"Langanes? How come?"

My mother presumed it was because of Grandmother.

Grandfather had met her in Þórshöfn, after all, where she had grown up, she and Aunt Telma.

"But Grandma isn't in the photos, so she didn't even go."

"Perhaps he just liked it at Langanes. He built the road for the Americans when he was young, after all, and it's really beautiful there. We usually went there by car, sometimes with the boat."

"Petra?"

My mother nodded. "The crossing took forever! But there's an old jetty there, where Telma lives now. Such a recluse. We should go there sometime, you and I. Next summer, maybe, what do you think?"

"With Petra?"

My mother laughed. "God, no! By car, of course! Aunt Telma would be delighted to receive visitors, I'm sure, wouldn't it be great? There's so much nature on Langanes, gannets and puffins and blueberries, Arctic foxes, seals —"

I took the photo from my mother's hand and turned it over again. "What do these numbers and letters mean?"

"No idea. Coordinates perhaps?"

"SSW could mean south-south-west," I conjectured.

"You see? You've got it in the blood!"

"But the numbers?"

"They might be calendar days. Third of May, '68."

"You've got it in the blood too!" I cried. "But what do 16 and H-2 stand for?"

"Pagination, perhaps?"

We looked at the backs of the other photos. There were similar abbreviations on many of them, but it was always the date and sometimes even the time, as well as the compass points. NW or SE, meaning north-west or south-east. On some of the photos, a low mountain stood in the background, and my mother and Aunt Guðrún were mostly in the foreground, with expressions that showed how little enthusiasm they had for these expeditions.

"What mountain is that?"

"No idea," said my mother. "*You're* the map-reading expert, after all."

I hurried straight to my room and studied my map, which I had brought with me from Raufarhöfn and hung over my bed. I immediately found the peninsula of Langanes. I'd often seen it from the boat when I was still sailing out to the lines. " Heiðarfjall!" I called from my room.

"That could be it!" my mother called back.

I sat back down with her. The mountain wasn't so present on all the photos. Grandfather had hiked out further back then, and as I could decipher from the dates of the photos, he had travelled around the peninsula with his daughters repeatedly over the course of three summers. Nói's suspicion came to my mind. "Why did Grandfather die?" I asked my mother straight out.

She sighed and put the photos back on the floor, stacking them carefully. "He was old and had severe dementia."

"But you don't die of that, do you?"

"Hmm. Yes and no. Usually it's organ failure, and that leads to death. And in his case, it was the heart."

"Heart attack!"

"In the end, yes. Cardiac arrest. One of the cleaning staff found him."

"A cleaner?"

"Yes, but it was too late, because he'd already been dead for a while. She fetched help at once, but they weren't able to resuscitate him. Perhaps they could have tried to hook him up to an HLM, but that would have been a step too far in his case. There comes a time when you have to let people go."

I thought about that, which wasn't so easy, because I was angry and sad and confused and proud all at once, because my mother was talking to me as though I were completely normal. Admittedly I had no idea what an HLM was, but I could imagine it was some secret abbreviation that only hospital staff are allowed to understand. Like FBI or H-2.

"Is there an autopsy report?"

"A what?" My mother pulled her head back in such a way that it gave her a double chin. "What makes you ask that?"

"How can we be sure Grandfather wasn't killed?"

"Killed? What kind of nonsense is that?"

I fell silent and went to my room, slamming the door behind me. My mother wouldn't believe me anyway. Luckily I knew someone who would give the murder suspicion their full attention.

Once my mother had set off for her night shift, I went into the living room and took out the blue KALMANN folder containing the newspaper reports, photos, hospital documents and fan mail which my mother had stored in the top compartment of the cabinet after the incident with the polar bear. I found in it a visiting card with the telephone number I'd been looking for.

"Birna here?" She sounded quite curt, like a proper police officer, very professional. But because her voice sounded like I was interrupting her, I said nothing, in the hope she would hang up. "Hello?" I could always try again later. "Kalmann?"

Some people are in the perfect profession. Birna is one of them. How else would she have known I was at the other end of the line? I still didn't say a word.

"Kalmann, if it's you, then say something, you know you can call me any time."

"I know," I mumbled.

"There you are. Hello, Kalmann! How are you?"

"Bad."

"What's happened?"

"Grandfather died."

"Óðinn? Oh, I'm so sorry. Poor Kalmann."

I sniffed, even though I didn't actually need to. "*Takk fyrir.*"

"When did he die?"

"At 14.40."

"What, today?"

"No. It was a while ago now. I had to go to the psychiatric unit."

"Oh, Kalli, I'm so sorry."

"No reason to worry." I only mumbled it.

"When's the funeral?"

"We've already had it. The day before yesterday. In Sauðanes."

"Oh, I'm really sorry. Thank you for calling to tell me, dear Kalmann."

We fell silent. But not for long.

"Are you at your mother's in Akureyri?"

"Yes."

"And what are your plans for the rest of today?"

"At four o'clock I have to go to work at Glerártorg."

"The shopping mall?"

"Correctamundo. That's when everyone gets off work and goes shopping. Someone has to keep things in order in the parking lot. And that someone is me."

"Oh, wonderful! You're a proper guardian of the law. A sheriff, in fact!"

"Grandfather was probably murdered."

"Excuse me?" Birna was caught completely off guard.

"Because people don't just die of Alzheimer's."

"Whew! No, I think they do. And your grandfather was very old, wasn't he?"

"There are people who live to be much older than him. And they brushed the autopsy report under the —"

"The report? So an autopsy was requested?"

"I've no idea."

"But…" Birna thought for a few seconds. "Kalmann, were you told what your grandfather died of?"

"His heart stopped beating."

"Well, then that makes sense. A heart attack. You know, when the cause of death is obvious, no one does an autopsy, because it isn't necessary."

I didn't respond, feeling offended, but because Birna simply let me be silent, I eventually said: "*Maybe* he was killed."

"Kalmann." Birna sighed. "Give me a moment here. What was your grandfather's full name?" I told her. "Okay, let's see. Ah, here we go. Óðinn Arnarson. Deceased 3 October, time of death, that's right, location, Húsavík Care Home, oh, was he still in Húsavík? Okay, further down, found by the cleaner, here we go, this is where it gets more interesting, cause of death, natural causes, heart attack. It's all correct, Kalmann, I'm sorry, your grandfather definitely wasn't killed, I mean, luckily!"

I didn't say anything, because now I felt even more miserable than before, and I didn't know why.

"Kalmann, is everything okay?"

"No reason to worry!" I said, this time a little louder.

Birna sighed and let a few seconds pass, probably contemplating how she could get me off the phone. "Kalli minn, something completely different. Are you keeping our secret?"

"Yes," I said. "I'm not stupid!" I wondered whether people would still like me if they knew what I had done to Róbert McKenzie.

"Good," said Birna. I heard her exhale with relief.

Before we hung up, she gave me another piece of advice: I shouldn't spend any more time thinking about Óðinn's death or how he died, but instead about his life. I should hold on to the beautiful memories of him. "I already know that," I said, and hung up.

I got dressed, looked at myself in the mirror, sighed like someone who has to go to work, and went to work. The people were stupid today too and left their shopping carts all over the parking lot, so I worked up quite a sweat. Sometimes I shoved the carts so forcefully together that everyone turned around to look at me, startled. After work I went back home, and the next day I went to work again, because the cursed carts were all over the parking lot again already, it was like I was jinxed, and then it was finally the weekend, and I went shopping with my mother and to the cinema, and we watched the quiz show on Channel 2 presented by Villi Þór, who my mother found so sexy, and late in the evening I kept Nói company while he was gaming. Then I went back to work, so it was Monday morning, and actually the mall isn't busy then, so I took a small detour past the harbour first, but there was hardly anyone there, not a single cruise ship, no big trawlers I could have taken a look at. The harbour buildings were giant and spotless. I asked a worker where the harbour master's container was, but the worker just gave me a stupid look and shrugged. Completely retarded.

11

LETTER

The day my father's letter arrived was bad from the start. I should have taken it as an omen, stuffed my IKEA bag with clothes and headed off to Raufarhöfn. For good!

Around midday I went to the shopping mall. I was ravenous, and that's why I wanted to eat something at the kebab place, because they serve the best hamburgers in all of Akureyri. But the kiosk was shut. A note taped to the shutter announced that they'd closed down permanently.

I stood in front of the note for a long while, reading the words over and over. It thanked the customers and wished them good health. Eventually my stomach was grumbling so loudly that I had no choice – for the first time in my life, I had to go into the Subway next door.

Cautiously, I put one foot in front of the other and looked around. I asked the masked teenager behind the counter of green stuff if I could get a hamburger. But hamburgers unfortunately weren't on the menu, as he informed me.

"Definitely not?"

"Definitely not."

"Are you sure?"

"Dude!"

I bought a cookie and a cola, so that at least I wouldn't starve.

When I turned around, they almost fell out of my hands, because there was a celebrity sitting at one of the tables and I hadn't even noticed when I walked in! It was Villi Þór from Station 2, from the quiz show we always watched. Sometimes he interviews people who are even more famous than he is.

Villi Þór paid no attention to me; he was taking hurried bites of his sandwich and chewing. His head was large and his dark hair was thick. You could recognize him instantly by his prominent jawline, which my mother found so sexy. There was a man chewing opposite him who wasn't famous and also didn't look like he was. He had a beard and was wearing a wide-brimmed hat – not a proper cowboy hat.

"Good morning!" I exclaimed, then immediately regretted it.

The celebrity glanced up at me. "Hello," he said.

"Are you Villi Þór?"

"Bingo." The celebrity tried to smile with his mouth full. The other man continued chewing, unfazed.

"Could I get a signature?"

"You mean an autograph."

"It's for my mother."

"Can't you see I'm eating?"

"Yes, I can see that."

Now they both looked at me, no longer chewing. I waited until Villi Þór sighed and asked if I had an autograph card and a pen with me.

"I don't," I said.

"Would you perhaps like to take a selfie?"

"I don't have a smartphone," I informed him. "Just an old Nokia phone I use to make calls and send text messages, but it doesn't take photos."

"Understood. Then let us eat in peace, okay? Thanks."

I hesitated. Did he want me to wait until he was done? "I haven't eaten yet either," I said, and now the other man let out a muffled cough, as though something was stuck in his throat.

Villi Þór breathed audibly through his nose, probably because his mouth was full again. "But *I'm* eating now, and when I eat, I don't like to be disturbed."

"All I want is a signature," I said.

"Autograph," Villi Þór growled.

"Does this happen to you a lot?" asked the bearded man, chewing.

"I prefer hamburgers," I said. I have no idea why I said that.

"That doesn't surprise me," said the bearded man.

"Excuse me!" called the Subway guy from behind the counter. "Can you let my customers eat in peace?"

"I'm a customer too," I retorted, lifting my cookie and cola into the air.

Villi Þór leaned back in his chair and groaned: "Oh, come on!"

Suddenly I had an idea. "I have a quiz question that you can use next Saturday on your show. What's the name of the mountain on Langanes?"

Villi Þór glanced over at the Subway employee and spread out his arms.

"Don't you know?" I was surprised now, because Villi Þór always knew the right answer to all the questions. It was his job, after all.

"Seriously?" Villi Þór called to the Subway employee, who had turned towards the sandwich oven and was waiting for the beep.

"Heiðarfjall," I enlightened Villi Þór, and so he wouldn't forget, I repeated the name of the mountain, but this time more slowly: "Hei-ðar-fjall."

"Do us a favour and leave us in peace, okay?"

I would actually have liked to leave, I would really have liked to let the famous talk show host eat in peace, but sometimes that's how I am, I stand there like I'm nailed to the spot and can't move, especially when someone wants to get rid of me.

"Toddle off now!" said the bearded man, as if he were Villi Þór's bodyguard. Maybe he was.

Everyone in Subway was staring at me now, and I clenched my fists. Luckily, I remembered what the nurse from the psychiatric unit had advised me to do. "Ten," I said quietly.

"What?"

"Nine." A little louder.

The bodyguard roared with laughter, and Villi Þór pushed his sandwich away.

"Eight."

"Calm down, okay?"

"Seven."

"Can you please stop counting backwards?"

I raised my voice even louder. "No. Six."

All at once Villi Þór stood up, and his chair almost tipped over.

"Five!"

"What's with the goddamn countdown?"

"Four."

"Kalmann, what are you doing?" I heard a woman say from somewhere behind me. "Are you scaring people again?"

I turned around, startled. Elínborg was standing at the entrance, giving me a reproachful look. Or maybe she looked like that because she was carrying heavy shopping bags in both hands. "Hello, Elínborg," I said, because I couldn't think of anything better to say.

"Does he belong to you?" asked Villi Þór. He, too, had turned around to look at Elínborg.

"Kalmann is harmless," she said. "No need to worry, is there, Kalmann?"

I nodded. "Villi Þór doesn't know the name of the mountain in Langanes," I told her. "I just wanted to help him."

"Heiðarfjall?"

"Correctamundo."

Elínborg shook her head. "That doesn't surprise me these days, Kalmann." She turned around and, as she was walking away, said: "Without GPS, these city folk would be completely screwed. Come on, help me with these bags. Or fetch me a shopping cart, that's your job, isn't it?"

She grumbled for a while longer about reporters, who reported far too little about the rural areas, so it was hardly a surprise people didn't know their way around their own country any more, and then she complained that there were no carts by the entrance, and that I should always make sure there were some available.

"And say hello to your mother from me!"

This day really was turning out to be nothing but stress.

That evening, I waited impatiently for my mother. I wanted to pass on Elínborg's greetings and tell her about Villi Þór, but instead she held a printed-out email in front of my nose and said she needed to talk to me, but that I wasn't to freak out. I even had to promise her I wouldn't.

The paper trembled in her hands as though it were trying to break free, so we didn't have time to put any tea on, we had to immediately see to this email before it fluttered away. And yet my mother must have read it already, because it was from her sperm donor, Quentin Boatwright, my father.

That's how the letter began. That's how every letter usually begins, so initially there was no reason to worry.

He had heard, he wrote, that my grandfather, who had been a kind of father figure to me, had died. *I am so sorry for your loss*, he added. The underlining showed he really meant it. My mother was going to translate the words for me, but I understood them well. Quentin Boatwright wrote that I should never forget I have a father, in other words him, and that he hadn't forgotten me and wished he could be there for me. He had reached a point in his life, *a cross-roads*, he wrote, and *a new beginning*, and this was when my mother explained to me that he was probably deep in a midlife crisis.

I would always be welcome in Mill Creek, he continued, and I should come visit him, and not worry at all about the *China virus*, because he could assure me that all Boatwrights have excellent immune systems.

Boatwright. I hadn't thought about my American surname in ages. I was a Boatwright, too, technically speaking. But when I saw the name there on paper, I felt uneasy. Some years had passed since the last sign of life from my father. It had been a short letter for my eighteenth birthday, but it arrived so late I'd almost begun to look forward to Christmas. Since then: radio silence. I hadn't expected to ever hear from him again. After all, I was a grown-up now and didn't need a father any more. I'd only seen him in person once, and it was so many years ago that I couldn't remember his face.

I stared at the words, lost in thought, as if I could see all the way to America if I only tried hard enough to look between the lines. He wrote *We'd be delighted if you visited us*, but only his name was on the letter. *We* might mean my half-sisters. Did they want to get to know me too?

My mother didn't interrupt my thinking. She gave me all the time in the world, and just looked at me and laid her hand on the table, waiting for me to put mine in hers. Perhaps she was as worried as I was. Was she trying to picture his face too? Or was it burned into her memory because it was the kind of slip-up you never forget?

She usually got angry whenever my father came up. That's why I was expecting her to start cursing. But she looked at me patiently, all peaceful, almost a little dreamy, as if we were watching one of those romantic movies she liked so much. "Kalli minn," she said. "Do you know what I think? I think it's a good idea."

Now I was astounded. "But —" I wanted to say something, but unfortunately couldn't think of a thing, I was completely floored. A bubbling sensation started inside my head.

"It's time you got to know your father, Kalmann Quentinsson," she continued.

"But the pandemic!" I exclaimed. Did my mother really want to send me to America, even though we were strongly advised against foreign travel? Did she want to get rid of me?

She'd already spoken to him on the phone, she told me. And my father thought the trip was definitely feasible, given that there was Covid on both sides anyway, so he would try to register me and take care of all the necessary paperwork. After all, my mother told me, I was even entitled to American citizenship. And she had also contacted the embassy in Reykjavík.

"Don't worry, Kalmann. Your father will take good care of you."

"So am I going to America forever?" I asked, even though it wasn't the question swimming at the top of my fish soup.

"Of course not!" My mother laughed. "Just for a little while. Christmas and New Year. Six weeks max! What do you say?"

I was relieved. So my mother didn't want to get rid of me after all. And I'd seen the Hollywood Christmas movies, so I knew what awaited me: in other words, a Hollywoodesque Christmas! It sounded appealing.

"New Year? But then I'll miss the fireworks in Raufarhöfn!"

My mother had an answer for that too: "The Amis super-size everything. I'm sure that applies to New Year's fireworks as well."

I doubted it, but had to admit her argument was reasonable, and that's why I advised her to buy a plane ticket, and preferably right away, because maybe the planes would soon be booked up, but she only laughed louder and said there was no hurry. First we had a lot to discuss and organize.

"Stop!" I called, jumping to my feet. "I don't even know what he looks like! How am I supposed to recognize him when —"

"Kalmann!" My mother laughed, snorting. As though she had been waiting for this, she conjured up a printed-out photo and handed it to me.

I held it in my hands for a long while. The photo showed my father, Quentin Boatwright, and not only him but also two grown-up women, huddled close to him, smiling broadly. My father was round. That wasn't how I remembered him. He wore a red baseball cap, its rim arched into a semicircle, and his neck was round too, his shoulders broad, his checked shirt straining across his belly. He was a bit chubby perhaps, but sure to be as strong as a bear. A rounded, well-tended goatee with silvery hairs encircled his mouth. My father smiled proudly into the camera and actually looked nice. Did we look alike? I was sure of one thing: I didn't look at all like the women in the picture. "Are those my half-sisters?" They were the same height as my father, but had much wider hips, frizzy hair and beaming faces. Immaculate teeth.

"They're called Allison and Piper – or vice versa, I'm not quite sure any more which one's Piper and which one's Allison. They're not much older than you, they were really little when they lived out in Ásbrú. I'm sure they'll be delighted to meet you."

As my mother prepared dinner, I crept into my room with the photo and quietly shut the door behind me.

Good friends aren't just there to comfort you when you're feeling low, but also to be happy with you when there's something to celebrate. So I called Nói.

12

GORA LETIT

"Biaaatch!" Nói greeted me like a proper American, as though he knew why I was calling him. "You really bring me bad luck!" Nói was immersed in a multiplayer game. "Eat shit, you bitch!" He threw the console on the desk in front of him, carried on swearing for a while, then said: "Kalli, my man. What's up?" He was fully back to his old self again.

"I'm going to the United States."

Nói laughed. He laughed long and hard, holding his belly, even pointing his index finger at the camera, so he was clearly making fun of me. Only friends are allowed to do that. "The States. In the middle of a pandemic. Yeah, right! You can forget that, boy! Do you genuinely think the planes are still flying?"

"Yes, I think so. My father wants me to —"

Nói leaned over and typed on the keyboard. "Hmm," he murmured. "Sheriff, you're right! They're still flying, twice a day. Probably transporting goods. But I don't think it's as easy as just catching a ride. You need authorization, papers, a reason."

"I think I'm an American. My father is —"

Nói interrupted me with a sigh. "You're so shittin' lucky, do you realize that? What I wouldn't give for a green card, or even better, American citizenship! Then I could leave this shitty island forever." Nói made a sound as though he were crying.

91

I tried to comfort him. "Perhaps you can come with me. I mean, you're healthy again now."

"Healthy? Are you retarded? I'm in the highest-risk group. At the moment, in any case. If I catch the big C, I'm done for. That's why I'm in isolation."

"Oh, sorry."

"Yes, I'm sorry too. But when are you going?"

"In December."

"Good, then we still have time."

"For what?"

"To solve the case!"

"Oh, that."

"Have you managed to track down the autopsy report?"

"No. There wasn't one. Birna said they only do that when the cause of death isn't known. If there's suspicion that someone —"

"There *is* suspicion!" cried Nói. "That's exactly the point! When somebody is killed so skilfully that people believe they just keeled over, then it's suspected murder!"

"Oh."

"Sheriff! What's going on with you? Where are your sheriff instincts? Don't you think there's something fishy about this?"

"I do. It's just —"

"What was the official cause of death?"

"Cardiac arrest."

"Yeah, right. Do you know what someone dies of when they're cut in half?"

I didn't know off the top of my head, because I had never thought about it.

"Cardiac arrest!" cried Nói. "Do you know what someone dies of when they get shot in the head?"

I started to feel dizzy.

"Cardiac arrest. Do you know —"

"Nói!" I interrupted. "Do you really think —"

"Damn right I do! What else did you find out?"

"About Grandfather?"

"Yes sir!"

I thought hard, because I didn't want to disappoint my best friend. I almost started to sweat. "He spoke Russian just before he died."

"Say what now?"

"*Suka amerikanets. Gora letit* and so on." The words had burned themselves into my brain.

"*Suka?* Really? I know that! That's what the Russian gamers are always yelling. It probably means bitch or something. *Suka,* they yell, and *idi na khuy!* They're completely nuts. *Amerikanets* must mean Americans. Did he mean your father?"

"No idea. Perhaps he meant all Americans. Do you also know what *gora letit* might mean?"

"*Gora letit.* Give me a second." Nói tapped away on his keyboard again. "There we go. Google Translate, baby! Mountain flying. What the actual fuck?"

"Mountain flying?"

"Perhaps it's 'the mountain flies' or 'flying mountain'. Strange. Doesn't make any sense. What else did he say?"

As it turned out, I could only remember one word: *Opasno.* It means dangerous. I was sure Grandfather had said some other Russian words too, but as hard as I tried, I couldn't remember any of them. And that's why, in the end, we only knew that he didn't like Americans and had wanted to warn me about a flying mountain. So actually I knew nothing at all. When we ended the conversation, I felt a little disappointed, because we hadn't talked about my upcoming America trip, and that had been the real reason for my call.

After dinner, my mother fell asleep on the sofa during a boring cookery show, and I switched over to *Dr. Phil*, but it was an episode I'd already seen. I watched it regardless, because I wanted to practise English, so I repeated the words out loud.

"How about getting a real job," Dr Phil suggested to the skinny guest who still lived with his parents and spent the whole day sitting around. His dream was to make movies, but his depression, the monster that lived inside him, didn't allow it.

Dr Phil usually thinks people should work more. He said that again now, and the skinny man nodded and hung his head.

The funniest wacko I ever saw on there was a man who didn't have a job because he wanted to be a dog, and he would put on a dog costume and chomp dog food out of a bowl on the floor. It made him happy, he explained apologetically. "Better than working!" Dr Phil had mocked him, and the audience laughed and clapped.

Would the audience laugh at me if I was a guest on the show? Would Dr Phil reprimand me too?

My mother had started to snore, so I turned off the television and listened to her for a while. I studied her. Her mouth was slightly open and the back of her hand rested kind of elegantly against her cheek, like in an old painting.

Hopefully I wouldn't run into Dr Phil in America, because it might happen. For sure he'd want to invite me onto his show, given I also still live with my mother.

"*Mamma*," I said softly, stroking her hair. "You've fallen asleep."

13
SNOW

There were two months and sixteen days to go until my trip to the USA, but the wait felt like an entire year.

I had lots of time. It was elastic, like chewing gum that you stretch out lengthways but which doesn't get any bigger for that very reason. I found it hard to fall asleep at night and couldn't concentrate during the day. Sometimes I slouched around in the parking lot in front of the mall, standing around lost in thought for a while and completely forgetting to collect the shopping carts. Nanouk summoned me to his office and said I had to concentrate and couldn't get in the way of the cars, because that was strictly forbidden.

To prepare for America, I spoke to Nói frequently, because he was *the* USA expert, but mostly he wanted to talk about Grandfather's mysterious murder instead, even though by now I had my doubts about the whole thing. But of course I didn't tell him that.

In early December, when the Christmas decorations and lights went up and nothing but Christmas songs trilled from the radio, Akureyri was heavily snowed under. It looked beautiful, admittedly – even our rusty corrugated iron house suddenly looked much more peaceful – but I almost couldn't get to the mall any more. My route to work became a proper expedition, I sweated and my feet got cold all at once, and every time someone got stuck in their car I had to help, pushing and shovelling. And sometimes I found a shopping cart that had been buried in snow in the parking lot, and I had to push and shovel yet again. We never had this much snow in Raufarhöfn, where the wind mostly blew the white powder away, plus Halldór was an expert in snow ploughing, so the roads were never blocked for long. In Akureyri, it's different. Here there are so many streets and houses that the snowploughs don't even know where to push the snow to. In Akureyri they have to transport it away in a truck and tip it into the sea.

So I stayed home, because my muscles were aching from all the shovelling and car pushing. Out of sheer boredom I opened the box my mother had brought with her from Raufarhöfn. In it I found a shoebox taped shut with brown tape. But the tape was already brittle, so I could rip it open like a Christmas present. There were even more photos in the box, of landscapes, snapshots from summer and winter. Grandfather had taken lots of photos from his boat, photographing the coast again and again, and sometimes had taken them of boats he had spotted in the distance. Strange. Back when I was still going out to sea with him, he had never taken photos, nor shown any interest in passing ships. Perhaps he had simply given up his hobby.

Here too were photos of my mother and aunt as little girls. Sometimes there was a woman there too, most likely my grandmother. Among the photos I found small notebooks and loose, yellowed pages, on which Grandfather had scribbled numbers and letters in pencil.

Reading isn't my strong point. When there are lots of words gathered on a piece of paper, they start to dance and rearrange themselves before my eyes. But I could still tell something wasn't right about the letters on these yellowed pages. They were the wrong way round, and sometimes they weren't even proper letters. Was it some kind of secret code? I immediately thought of Nói, but because he wasn't online, I took a few photos with my laptop and sent them to him on Messenger.

Then I ran out of ideas. I went over to the window and watched the snowflakes. They were swirling in all directions, from left to right, from right to left, from down below to up above. Like the letters of the alphabet.

When there's lots of snow outside, it's quieter inside a house too. You can hear yourself think. The blood in my head rushed like a distant river. The thoughts tore me along with them.

I took my grandparents' framed wedding photo down from the dresser and compared my grandmother with the woman in the photos. They looked similar, but weren't the same person. The mysterious woman was sometimes stood leaning against a fence post, sometimes she was sitting on a rusty tractor, laughing. In one, she was relaxing with the children on a picnic blanket.

My laptop began to beep. "Russian," Nói greeted me.

"Russian?"

"The pencil scribblings!"

"Oh, right." I'd already forgotten I'd sent him the snap-shots of the yellowed pages.

"Practice writing, like kids do. Someone was trying to learn Russian."

"Probably my grandfather."

"Where is the car? The car is on the street. How many people are sitting in the car? Three people are sitting in the car. Yawn. I didn't translate all of it, just a few sentences here and there. Seven houses are on the mountain. On the mountain are seven houses. There are also some numerical exercises, but they don't make any sense at all. First the numbers are from one to ten, and then it's complete chaos."

"Oh."

"Is this your grandfather's stuff?"

"Yup."

"That explains everything. He learned Russian back then, for whatever reason. And when he got dementia, these things came back up. That's why the flying mountain doesn't make any sense either. Do you get it?"

"Yes, I think so."

Nói was probably the smartest person I knew.

When my mother came home that evening, I held one of the photos in front of her nose. "Who is this woman?" I asked, instead of greeting her.

"Hello, Kalli," said my mother, and she hugged me even though she was covered with snow.

"*Mamma!*" Ever since I had decided to travel to the United States, she didn't miss a single opportunity to hug me, even though I don't like that. Totally embarrassing.

"Is that a photo from the box?" She pulled off her coat and boots and cursed the snow that fell from her clothing onto the floorboards. I pushed the photo into her hand and bent down, pressed the snow into a ball and threw it in the toilet. Meanwhile my mother went into the living room, where the light was better. "Kalmann!" she cried accusingly. I presumed she had discovered the mess I'd made on the rug with the photos. Private detectives do it like that too, when they want to get an overview of something and see the connections.

"Who is this woman?" I asked again, because I thought the whole thing would make sense if only I knew who she was. I had collected all the photos of her and put them to the side.

"Fancy that!" My mother looked astonished. "It's Aunt Telma, your grandmother's sister."

"Telma?" I said in surprise. "The woman with the funny hat?" What an idiot I was. How had I not thought of that?!

My mother nodded, lost in thought, and looked more closely at the photos. "Yes, my strange Aunt Telma. Wow, she looks so happy! I was surprised she even came to the funeral. She's not come to anything for so long." My mother looked at me, frowning. "Didn't you go to work today?"

"I stayed home, because of the snow."

"The whole day?"

"Muscle ache. But why is Aunt Telma in the photos and not my grandmother?"

"Well," my mother said meaningfully and went into the kitchen, leaving me standing there amid the chaos. But she continued talking loudly enough that I could hear her. "She was good friends with Father. They were both in the Communist Party, as far as I know. She and this Lúlli guy. It was through Telma that he met Mother. Your grandfather and grandmother would never have crossed paths without Telma."

"And why did she break off contact with Grandfather if they were such good friends?"

My mother came back into the lounge with a glass of water in her hand. "Well, that's how it is sometimes. People grow apart, go their own way. Aunt Telma just stopped getting in touch, and Father didn't make an effort either. There was enough going on. You were born, I moved to Raufarhöfn with you and was working a lot. And Telma lived in quite an isolated way, she was a recluse. She's a strange person, orientates herself by the moon and the stars and so on. The last time we invited her to a family gathering, over at Aunt Guðrún's, she said she wouldn't meet with people during that particular constellation." She shook her head thoughtfully. "And now she wants us to go visit her. Any time."

The questions were piling up in my head: why hadn't she come to visit us when the stars *were* positioned correctly? Why had Grandfather never mentioned her?

I took a closer look at her on one of the photos. She was of course much younger than in real life, with long red hair and freckles. She was slim and not at all like you'd imagine the sister of a grandmother to be. On some of the photos she was looking past the lens, as though she hadn't even noticed someone was taking a photo of her, gazing dreamily at the horizon or the children, who were in some of the photos with her. Sometimes she was laughing. I thought she was very beautiful when she laughed. Mostly she was serious, tense. But even then she looked pretty.

Even though Grandfather had taken so many photos, he wasn't a good photographer. Telma, my mother and my aunt were mostly right at the edge of the picture or blurry. But my mother found one that had everyone on it and was nicely in focus too. The girls were laughing, Telma looked content, and the Heiðarfjall mountain was in the background. And if you looked closely, you could even make out the American radar station. On the road that led up to the mountain, a convoy of trucks was whirling up dust.

"Is that the road Grandfather built?"

"I think so. Do you know what, Kalmann, let's get the photo enlarged and frame it!" My mother held the photo away from her as though she were searching for the perfect spot on the wall. She didn't find it, and laid the photo on the dresser.

*

The days fell from the calendar like fish from a conveyor belt, filleted and sorted, packed and away! We had actually planned to visit Aunt Telma on the second day of Advent, the stars were in a good position, but a winter storm got in our way. The road near Tjörnes was shut, so we would only have made it to Húsavík and no further. So instead we went to the mall, ate an ice cream and bought a pale-blue suitcase.

My mother was spending hour after hour on the telephone so that my America trip would run like clockwork and there was no reason for me to worry.

On the day before my departure, it occurred to me that I couldn't leave my mother completely alone in Akureyri. Christmas and New Year were right around the corner, after all, and we had always spent the holidays together, always. Those kind of family traditions are important and are sure to have a reason, every child knows that. So I unpacked my things again, scattering everything on my bedroom floor, and my mother almost flipped out, stuffed things back into the suitcase, quite messily this time, then she sat down on my bed and buried her face in her hands. I stood dumbly next to her and bit my hand, wishing that my father had never got in touch with me, that he had never written the email, and my mother said in a toneless voice, "Kalli, please don't."

It wasn't nice to see her sitting there so tired on my bed. So I let my arms hang by my sides and counted backwards. There was nothing else I could do.

Later we sat down at the kitchen table and drank tea. Obviously. My mother took both my hands in hers, studied the blue flecks my teeth had left on the back of my hand and asked me whether I was scared about the journey, which unfortunately I couldn't deny. She wanted to know where the fear was and took it away, holding in her hands, then she stood up from the chair, went over to the bin, lid open, fear in, lid shut, bang.

"Kalli minn," she said. "You're my everything, do you understand that?"

I may have fish soup in my head, like the kids used to say, but this much I can understand. I'm not stupid. My mother loved me, fish soup here nor there.

"It will do you good to get to know your father. A child should know his father. And you're no longer a child" – she hesitated – "and I think it will do me good too. You know, mothers and sons don't usually spend as much time together as you and I."

So that I didn't need to worry, we went through the entire journey yet again step by step, and one day and 429 kilometres later, when we said goodbye at the airport in Keflavík, everything really was as we had discussed and practised. We put on our masks, checked in at the empty departure hall, bought a few chocolate bars, which I would be allowed to eat whenever I wanted, and slowly went up the steps, where a young woman met us, wearing a badge that showed her name in large letters: Heiðrún Sól. She was dressed nicely and smelled like some sweet I had never tried before. I got a badge too. On it was my name and everything important, telephone numbers and addresses and so on. I said goodbye to my mother, who now didn't say another word, even when I turned around one last time. She was still standing there, with both hands pressed against her mask as though she were trying to keep a scream beneath it, and her eyes swum with tears, which didn't surprise me, because mothers are always so dramatic, that's just how it is.

"*Mamma!*" I cried. "I'll be back soon, no reason to worry!" And she laughed so heartily that her mask almost fell off.

Totally embarrassing! She searched desperately for a tissue, and I went around the corner. I couldn't turn around now, and Heiðrún Sól wouldn't have allowed it anyway.

The security check reminded me of my Mauser, and now I was glad I'd thrown it in the sea, otherwise the machine would have beeped. Everything went smoothly, and Heiðrún Sól, who I had already fallen a little in love with before passport control, but it was just a holiday crush, was happy with me. Nói would burst with envy if he saw me with a woman like this by my side!

Then the waiting began. Heiðrún Sól kept looking at the clock and asking me if I was hungry, and because my mother had told me that when you're travelling by plane you never feel hungry but snack constantly regardless, I said yes. Eventually I was allowed to get on the plane, and Heiðrún Sól was suddenly in a hurry, she said goodbye, wished me luck and a safe journey, and immediately vanished, and I had to sit down and buckle up.

Apart from a load of boxes that were piled on the plastic-covered rows of seats, the plane was practically empty. I had three seats all to myself and each backrest had a screen where you could watch movies. I almost missed the take-off because of it, and jumped when things got very loud, when the lights of the runway outside whooshed past me and I was pushed back into my seat like a Formula One driver. I closed my eyes for a few seconds and counted backwards, from ten to zero, and when I looked out of the window again, I saw the lights of Keflavík beneath me. I was flying for the first time in my life.

Flying is bumpier than you might think. There must be as many potholes in the sky as there are in the streets of Raufarhöfn.

Before long, the lights disappeared and we were over the sea. The water below me looked so black and abandoned that I didn't even want to look out of the window. I chose to watch an Adam Sandler movie instead. Three times back to back. And when I next looked outside, it had become light, even though it was still evening. Despite the fact we had covered 4,700 kilometres and flown across the entire North Atlantic, it was still the same time of day. It felt to me like time travel gone wrong.

14

FATHER

The uniformed border guard's mask covered almost his entire face. I could only see his eyes and the dark bags beneath them. The official studied my passport, then stared at me as though he were trying to figure out whether I posed a danger to the United States. If he had known what would happen, for sure he wouldn't have let me in. "Welcome to the United States, Mr Óðinsson," he said, handing back my documents.

For the first time on this journey, I was alone, with no one looking after me. I took a few cautious steps towards the exit, then stood still.

When you're alone and don't know which direction you're supposed to go in, you have to come to a standstill. My grandfather had often drummed that into me, and once, when we were out hunting Arctic foxes, it actually happened. Grandfather said he needed to take a leak, and for me to go ahead a little. But when I turned around again, it was as though he had been swallowed up by the earth, and I was completely alone on the Slétta. Yep. Definitely reason to worry. So I stood still, and after a while I sat down and waited. For a long time. Hours. It even started to rain. Then I did some firing practice, shooting the rifle at a big rock about fifty metres away from me, bang, upon which Grandfather peered out in shock from behind that very rock, looked around in confusion and wiped the sleep and rain off his face. He cursed.

He must've lost his balance while he was peeing, fallen over, then decided to have a little nap right there. Grandfather was irritable, wet and stiff, and didn't seem well rested. On the contrary. His hip flask was empty, and the fox hunt was over. We went home and then there was trouble, my mother had a go at both of us, but Grandfather defended me, said I'd done exactly the right thing, that I'd stopped right where I was. But my mother pointed out to him that if I'd gone any further, I could have been lost forever. I wouldn't have been the first person to freeze to death out hiking on the Melrakkaslétta, to be lured away by the elves or get eaten by a polar bear.

That's why I stood still now.

Waited.

After a while, a plump woman in a police uniform walked past and said in a really friendly voice: "Straight ahead, young man!"

So I went straight ahead. If a woman in a police uniform tells you to go somewhere, you go. That's the case in every country. But I took tiny steps. Even more people overtook me and cast glances my way, while I looked down at the floor.

Further ahead was an automatic sliding door, like on dating shows when the couple see one another for the first time. My heart was pounding, even though I knew who was behind it.

"Kalmann!"

I saw him immediately, but I paused, and that's why the sliding door closed right in front of my nose – then opened again, because someone overtook me.

"Kalmann! C'mon, don't be shy!" called my father, and I gathered my courage.

How small he was, smaller than me, in any case. I had always thought fathers were bigger than their sons. Perhaps he was shrinking already, because he was significantly older than the photos, but that's normal. The older the photos, the younger the people. My father had silver, closely shorn hair on his temples and the back of his head, and his face had the same goatee as in the photo but whiter. He was wearing jeans, and a black jacket with U.S. ARMY printed on it. His shirt strained beneath, one or even two sizes too small for him.

He gave me a fatherly smile but kept looking around in embarrassment, which made me wonder whether he really was pleased to see me. Eventually he stretched out his short arms towards me, as though he wanted to give me a hug, but he actually wanted to take my suitcase. I was relieved, and even let out a "Phew!"

"Let's go, buddy!" he said, setting off with me behind him like a duckling. Anyone watching us would have immediately seen we were father and son.

Outside, I breathed in the American air, which was nearly as cold as back home. The parking lot was gigantic, and now it was slowly dawning on me that everything in America was gigantic, for example my father's black pickup truck: a RAM 1500. A monster! The truck was almost as long as my boat, Petra, and when I clambered onto the passenger seat and my father began to drive, it felt as though we were sitting in a rocking boat. Suddenly the entire car began to ring, because the RAM was also a travelling phone box. Then my mother's voice came from all directions, from behind and in front and up above and below, and far too loudly.

My mother was wide awake, even though it was night already where she was. With her voice and my father in the car it almost felt like the little whistle-stop tour of the Reykjanes peninsula we did that time years ago. I still remember the hamburger and ice cream, the presents, the cowboy hat, the sheriff's star and the Mauser. It was as though we were all sitting in the car again like a proper family, and my feelings were all knocking together in my belly. I was so worked up I felt like I might explode.

"Kalli minn, are you still there?" My mother noticed I was struggling to follow the conversation, and that's why we broke it off after a brief goodbye.

My father steered the RAM 1500 onto a wide street lined on both sides with American and Mexican, Chinese and Italian restaurants. Cooks from all over the world were gathered here. "You must be hungry," he guessed. He must have heard my stomach rumbling.

I nodded eagerly and picked American cuisine, a McDonald's takeaway, because there was still a way to go before Mill Creek. I liked sitting in the car with my father, even though he was silent most of the time. He concentrated on the driving, devoured his Big Mac and drank small sips of coffee from his gigantic thermos. I stole glances at him, but mostly, because I didn't want to stare at him, I looked out of the window. Just before my eyes began to close after the food, I noticed my father glance at me, he was even smiling, and that's why I fell asleep on the seat of the RAM 1500, feeling relieved because I didn't need to be afraid of anything. My father would look after me. It was a lovely feeling, soft, humming all through my body, a feeling I hadn't known before.

Even though American car seats are very comfortable, you can't sleep in them for long. After all, they're not beds. When I opened my eyes again, we were still driving, so I couldn't have been asleep for longer than an hour, but outside a new landscape was rushing past. The streets had become narrower, the horizon hillier, the trees closer together. There were trees, trees and even more trees in this country. And so many cars!

In between were gas stations, houses and crossings; sometimes gigantic fields and long fences lined the route. It was almost dark now, only the occasional pile of snow beneath the street lamps gleaming brightly. From time to time you could see stars too; it was sure to be a cold night.

"Welcome to West Virginia."

My father was pleased I was awake, and became talkative, but I couldn't possibly pay attention to everything and wasn't always listening because I was also interested in what was flying past the car window. Luckily, I knew a few things already, because my mother had prepared me well. I knew the names of my older half-sisters, Piper and Allison, and I knew I had two younger half-brothers who my father had conceived with his second wife. But they lived over in Salt Lake, so I wouldn't meet them. His third wife, Sharon, who he now lived with, had children too, but they weren't children any more. Piper and Allison would come by; after all, they had also lived in Iceland when my father was stationed there. Their mother, his first wife, lived close by, he admitted to me, but I probably wouldn't meet her. My father also mentioned a few cousins, uncles and aunts, but he must have realized I was no longer listening, because he laughed and patted me on the shoulder, which felt strange.

"It's gonna be all right," he said, and somehow that re-assured me.

Before we reached Mill Creek, it officially became night in the United States too. But my father didn't let this dissuade him from pointing out of the window again and again in order to tell me about his hunting grounds.

"You love hunting too, right?" he asked.

I nodded, but had to confess that I didn't have a gun with me. My father found that funny. A short while later he

109

slowed down the car and pointed at a store at the side of the street where the sign glowed red, blue and white into the night: GUNS.

"I'm sure we'll find something in there."

The houses of Mill Creek lined both sides of the street, and my father drove even slower, pointing at every empty house that could be bought for a ridiculously low price, something he wasn't too happy about. But I almost felt like I was in Raufarhöfn. And yet everything looked completely different. Because in Raufarhöfn there aren't any masts at the sides of the street that are connected to cables. It was kind of chaotic really, the cables being so higgledy-piggledy like that, as though the night sky were divided into geometric areas, a land map for the sky.

We drove past two restaurants and three churches, a gas station and a motel, until the houses were further apart again and the hills stretched up into the night sky on both sides like black, sleeping giants. My father brought the truck to a halt in the middle of the street and looked at me. "Are you ready, son?"

The small, two-storey wooden house looked a little decrepit, admittedly, but it had a pretty, covered veranda, something we don't have anywhere in Iceland, because the Arctic winds would tear them away. Next to the house stood a trailer and a stable, which in America is called a *barn*. So it was a kind of farm without animals.

I should have known what was awaiting me, because five cars were parked in front of the house. Each one of the cars was more expensive than the house itself, and that's why I wasn't sure whether my American family was rich or poor.

My father went ahead, with me behind him. He grinned at me over his shoulder, opened the door and pulled me inside.

The noise was deafening.

"Surprise!" They made a racket like fifty people, and it rained confetti. There were colourful decorations hung up everywhere like at a child's birthday party, everyone was laughing and beaming, clapping their hands and stretching out their arms towards me. A woman, who was surely one of my sisters, lunged at me, and I don't like that, but when an American woman hugs you, you can't get away, they won't let you. If Americans want something, they take it, that's how they're brought up. When the woman let me go so I could catch my breath, I was hugged again, albeit not so tightly, just briefly actually, by my other sister.

I can clearly remember the party in Raufarhöfn when I was made an honorary citizen, but this party in Mill Creek overshadowed everything. Because Americans are world champions at parties. Raufarhöfn wasn't even in the second league.

My father must have noticed I could barely breathe, because he pushed the people away from me and said: "Cut him some slack!"

I didn't know what "slack" was, but I hoped it was cake, because I had spotted a small table with the biggest cake in the world. So I asked my father whether he meant "cake" and pointed at the cake. The whole house shook with the laughter of my American family, and one of my sisters – it was Allison, who had hugged me first – even had tears in her eyes. She was properly crying and not even embarrassed, bawling and laughing as though it were the most normal thing in the whole world.

To my relief I was immediately led to the cake. My tear-drenched sister, Allison, took me by the hand and explained that first I had to blow out the candles, that was the tradition here, people always did it. I got even more embarrassed, because there had to be around fifty candles, more than thirty-five certainly, and it wasn't even my birthday.

More laughter and howling. Damn, it was all getting too much! But even my offended expression prompted delight. So we caught up on all the birthdays that my American family hadn't celebrated with me, at least that's how they explained it. I don't even know whether you are allowed to do that. Because birthdays have a pretty short expiration date.

After I had unwrapped all the presents, my favourite being the brand spanking new snow-white cowboy hat, I locked myself in the bathroom and only came out again when my father assured me he would send the crazy mob home. Admittedly he didn't succeed, but at least they left me in peace after that, talking among themselves.

My sister Allison flopped down onto the sofa next to me with a sigh and an empty paper cup in her hand, and she promised to protect me, like a big sister should. "Piper is totally nuts," she said, pointing discreetly in her sister's direction. "And the guy next to her with the hairy legs is her husband Dan. You'll never see him wearing long pants."

"We can hear you!" cried Piper drily, raising her wine glass to her lips. Dan gave me a wink, then averted his gaze in embarrassment.

I decided Allison was my favourite sister. Piper didn't talk much and now seemed bored; she just drank wine and probably would have left ages ago if Dan wasn't having such a heated discussion with my father about politics.

"The one with the amazing hair and glasses is Sharon, our father's wife, his third. My God! All good things come in threes, don't they?" Allison laughed and Piper shook her head. "And the man chewing gum, with the camouflage baseball cap and ZZ Top beard, is Uncle Bucky. He was in the army with Dad a long time ago, but they're still inseparable, like blood brothers."

It was getting louder and louder inside my father's house. They were talking about the president, saying how he'd given America the best four years, which was really sad, a *goddamn shame*, because now everything would be ruined again. Because the new president wouldn't give a shit about places like Mill Creek, so they might as well pack up.

It was almost like in Raufarhöfn, and all I had to do was close my eyes to feel like I'd been transported home, so I did, but I promptly dozed off on the sofa. Father helped me to my feet and led me outside to the trailer that was to be my home for the coming weeks. Now I felt like I was in a movie, because the trailer was properly luxurious, it even had a TV and a soft bed bigger than mine at home, and I flopped onto the bed and was out within moments. Like I was dead. Bang.

15

MILL CREEK

Apart from being arrested by the FBI, I really liked it in the United States. I liked the food, I liked that the TV was on all the time and I could sit in front of it whenever I wanted. Sharon switched on the TV in the kitchen early in the morning, even before my father had finished his first coffee. But he and Sharon only glanced at it occasionally, mostly listening with one ear while they breakfasted standing up or made a sandwich or planned the day or gave one another a kiss. Sharon only watched TV when the president was on it. Then she would say: "I'll marry this guy one day!" – but just to needle my father. He waved his hand in the air, grumbling, and said she could marry him if she liked, that all she did was cause trouble anyway!

The two of them liked one another a lot, and called each other Baby and Honey. And I liked them too: my father, who greeted me each morning with a handshake and asked whether I had slept well and whether he could do anything for me, and Sharon, who was often in a bad mood, but actually only pretending, because in reality she was fine. She liked complaining, it seemed to make her happy. She took care of everything, was never tired, was the last one to go to bed and the first to get up in the morning. And I never had to help her, even though my mother had told me to. But Sharon wouldn't allow it. I was her "guest of honour", she said. Sometimes she sent me out of the house, because she ran a YouTube channel on which she said only good things about the president. For that she needed absolute peace, because she always talked for a long time, and afterwards she answered all the many comments.

Unfortunately, my sisters were hardly ever there, because they lived quite far away and only visited on weekends. But they never stayed the night, because I was in the trailer. I saw Allison three times, Piper twice. That wasn't so bad, though, no reason to worry, there was enough to do in Mill Creek. My father spent most of the time working in the lumber mill, where he drove large machines, forklifts, trucks, cranes, and sometimes I was allowed to sit in the driver's cabin with him. I learned how to work an old machine saw, after which I was promptly employed, albeit not officially. This is how it works: you stand by the machine saw wearing a helmet, ear protectors and a visor, you have to press the green button from time to time and watch closely as a tree trunk is sawed into planks, press the button, wait, another tree trunk, planks, and yet another trunk, and if something gets stuck you have to press another button, a bright red one, and call Bill. When the saw blades were being sharpened, sparks flew into the air like on New Year's. I liked the smell of the sawed wood and the sparking saw blades a lot.

Sometimes I put on the white cowboy hat and strolled through the village, which was decorated for Christmas. Like in Raufarhöfn, there were lots of older people who watched me from behind their windows or drove past me slowly in their cars and studied me. Occasionally I walked to the gas station to buy myself a chocolate bar. I'd received pocket money from my father; that had been arranged by my mother. Usually a man was sitting on a white plastic chair in front of

115

the gas station, and I wasn't even sure if he worked there or just sat there. The man was a proper American Indian, you could see that right away, and he was the first and only American Indian I saw during my time in the United States. Admittedly he didn't have war paint or feathers on his head, but he had long black hair and a scarred Indian face. He never said hello and only ever nodded at me. So I had to summon all my courage to ask him whether he was perhaps the last Mohican, because I remembered Sæmundur once saying that the fishermen in Raufarhöfn were the last Mohicans, threatened by extinction. He stared at me for a long while, so long that I gave up on getting an answer and was about to leave, because I'd already bought the chocolate bar. But then he grinned and said: "You won't find him here. Sorry."

"Where is he then?" I asked.

"In Hollywood," the American Indian informed me.

"Oh," I said in disappointment.

"I'm a Shawnee. But I know someone who was in the movie. A distant cousin of mine. What's your name?"

"Kalmann."

"Nice to meet you, Kalmann. I'm Bob."

From then on, Bob was really nice, he always said "Hello, Kalmann" and "Goodbye, Kalmann", but when I told Sharon, she acted as though she hadn't heard me.

On Sundays we went to Mass in the truck. We could actually have walked there, because the church was only a few hundred metres away from our house. There were even two churches, directly next to one another, but that's probably the case in every American town.

In Mill Creek you're allowed to talk along during Mass, you can even get loud, you have to call out *hallelujah* and *amen*, and if you're not loud enough, the pastor isn't satisfied and wants to hear it again! It kept making me laugh, and that was allowed too.

The pastor could also get serious, though, and then the people quietened down, because there was so much evil in this world. Often we prayed for the president, who was threatened by dark forces. America's very future was at stake.

"Amen!"

After Mass I was allowed to go with my father and Uncle Bucky to the shooting range, and that's where I fired an M16 for the first time in my life. The kickback from this gun isn't anywhere near as strong as you might think. Because I shot on target, my father suggested taking me along on a hunt. But Uncle Bucky frowned and muttered: "Are you sure?"

"Kalmann's a proper hunter," my father reassured him, giving me a clap on the shoulder. "Isn't that right, son?"

I nodded. "Grandfather taught me everything," I said and looked at the floor, but I noticed that Uncle Bucky's eyes were on me. He always did that, he watched people and the goings-on around him as he chewed gum, his beard waggling. He only rarely joined in the conversation, and when he said something, his lips barely moved. You only saw his teeth if he was opening a beer bottle with them or popping some chewing gum into his mouth. If he brought a bottle to his lips, he stretched out the tip of his tongue.

"Rabbits and squirrels aren't deer," Uncle Bucky said, staring at me.

"There aren't any rabbits or squirrels in Iceland," I informed him. "But sometimes the polar bears come across from Greenland."

Uncle Bucky turned his gaze away from me and looked at my father, as though he wanted to make sure he had heard it too. My father defended me unflinchingly, like a proper father: "Bucky, have you ever brought down a polar bear with a Nazi Mauser?"

"I'd have loved to see that!" Uncle Bucky grinned.

"It was a female," I murmured.

"And the fish I caught was thiiiiiis big!" Uncle Bucky spread his arms out wide.

I thought about the sharks I had caught. They were bigger than Uncle Bucky himself.

That very afternoon, I went hunting with the two of them. The conditions were perfect, there was snow on the hills, and that makes it easier to look for prints. In Uncle Bucky's rusty truck, we drove along a small river, past an old, disused mill, and ever deeper into the leafless forest until we couldn't go any further. End of the road. We climbed out, pulled on fur caps, shouldered our guns and set off upriver through the thicket, tramping through the snow and searching the ground for prints. "Tracking", they call it in America. And we found a lot of tracks, rabbits, badgers, beavers, birds, even deer, but Uncle Bucky said: "Too much noise."

And yet it was really quiet. But my father explained that too many tracks in the snow are confusing, like noise.

"It's not so bad," I said. "You don't always go home with a kill."

"You see?" said my father to Uncle Bucky. "The boy knows what he's talking about!"

Uncle Bucky twitched his shoulders and spat into the snow. "Sure."

My father came to stand next to me. "Bucky, do you see how he holds the gun? Barrel pointing downwards, his fingers not on the trigger. Kalmann is a professional. It's in his blood."

"But can he defend himself?"

"Calm down, Bucky! We're not in Burgan."

"No? Are you sure?" Bucky pointed at the sky. "Don't you see those clouds on the horizon? The storm's coming, mark my words."

I looked at the sky. It was grey and covered with clouds. No storm for far and wide.

"Fine." My father sighed.

"We have to be prepared for anything," Uncle Bucky continued. And, addressing me: "Can you even defend yourself?" He made a quick movement, pulled a pistol out of nowhere, and stared at me. "This is a Walther P99." He held the pistol at a slant in front of his face and pulled the slide back a little, until the cartridge in the chamber came into view. "Nine millimetres, German quality. James Bond's a fan too." He aimed at a tree, then another. "This baby has no safety catch, it's always ready to rock 'n' roll." He took out the magazine and pulled the slide back so hard that the cartridge was ejected from the chamber and spun through the air. My father caught it skilfully, and Uncle Bucky rotated the gun in his hand and held it out to me. "Shoot me!" he ordered.

I don't like it when guns are pointed at people. Nobody does. But because my father was giving me an encouraging look, like there was nothing funnier in the world, I took the pistol and aimed it at Uncle Bucky, and I had to push down the nausea rising inside because Róbert flashed into my mind and so did the polar bear, but the pistol wasn't loaded after all, so no reason to worry. I wouldn't have pulled the trigger anyway, I would just have said bang – but suddenly Uncle Bucky had knocked the gun out of my hand. I'd never seen him move so quickly! Now it was me who was staring down the barrel of the gun, and feeling a bit dazed too.

Uncle Bucky grinned contentedly. "Again!" he said. "But slower this time."

This time he snatched the pistol from me as though in slow motion. He knocked the side of the barrel with his left hand, then grabbed the grip with his right, and it slipped from my hand even though I was holding on tightly, because he rotated the barrel further towards me, a bit like you twist the thigh of a roast chicken before it separates from the rump. So I had no choice but to let go, otherwise Uncle Bucky would have dislocated my hand, and it already hurt. Once again I found myself staring down the barrel of the Walther.

"Now you," Uncle Bucky commanded, aiming the gun at my chest. "Hands up!"

I grabbed the barrel of the gun.

"No, the other hand," my father interjected. "You're right-handed. Don't try to hold the gun, hit it away. You don't want to be on the receiving end of the bullet, that's the most important thing."

So I did it again, smacking the gun barrel with the palm of my hand, and as quickly as I could. Jab!

"Good!" said Uncle Bucky. "Again."

We did that about fifty times. Then I had to try and grab the grip with my other hand after I had knocked the barrel away, or, better still, simultaneously; two flying hands in one single explosive movement. Like trying to swat a mosquito in mid-air. But Uncle Bucky still wasn't satisfied and said I had to exert more force, that I couldn't hesitate under any circumstances.

"Again!" Eventually I got really good at it, and Uncle Bucky said, "Close enough," but we must have wasted an entire hour, our feet were cold, so we decided to let the deer live and head back to the truck. Clocking-off time.

After Christmas we went hunting again, and I even killed a roebuck, which of course made me incredibly proud, because

I managed a clean shot. The buck was about a hundred yards away, on the other side of a swathe that the river had carved into the landscape over many centuries. We didn't even need to wait long at our hideout, because it was a waterside spot well known to hunters, where the animals sometimes went to drink. We had watched the roebuck carefully approach through the thicket, and I exhaled and squeezed the trigger. Bang. His legs gave way beneath him and he slid lifelessly down the slope, almost to the riverbank. I stumbled as we crossed the river and got my feet wet, but didn't let on, because my father was so happy about my clean shot and was praising me the whole time.

Uncle Bucky knelt beside the animal, stroked its head and said a prayer, thanking God the Almighty and the roebuck itself, speaking to it as though the animal could understand us. And as he spoke the words quietly but forcefully, tears rolled down his face, and my father put his hand on his shoulder and mumbled: "It's gonna be all right, buddy. Everything's gonna be all right."

16

Q

Americans are also world champions at celebrating Christmas. They decorate their houses with so many colourful lights, glowing reindeer and Santa Clauses fastened to the chimneys that it can sometimes give you quite a shock. Beneath the massive Christmas trees in the lavishly decorated lounges are so many presents it makes your jaw drop. But the people in Mill Creek don't like it when you peer in through their windows. I was also given so many gifts I wondered how I would ever get them back home. Sharon said I wasn't to worry or think about the journey home yet. But I was thinking about home now, more and more, and after I had opened my many Christmas presents, I missed my mother very much. We spoke on the phone for a long while, and she told me that she had been alone on Christmas Eve for the first time in her life, and – to her surprise – had really enjoyed it. But she had missed me too, of course.

I thought about Grandfather, about our final Christmas celebration a year before, when we'd visited him in the home and I'd had to help him unwrap the present I'd wrapped for him. It was a wooden Arctic fox I'd made in a special carpentry workshop. Grandfather held the fox clasped in his hands the entire evening and didn't even want to let it go when it was time for bed. A nurse told me that on my next visit.

I missed my chats with Nói and was annoyed I hadn't brought my laptop with me. I even missed my ex-girlfriend

Perla. No one got as happy about presents as she did. If something was being unwrapped, she always got so excited that she clapped her hands and jumped around on the sofa in spite of her weight, making everyone laugh and run for safety. I would have liked to send her a Christmas present, but it was too late for that now, it wouldn't have arrived in Akureyri until Easter.

On New Year's Eve morning, I had to help my father and Uncle Bucky prepare the fireworks over in the barn; to mix the different powders and tape the containers shut and so on. I'd never done anything like that before. Sometimes people knocked on the wooden door to buy our fireworks, bangers and rockets, which weren't proper rockets, just flying bangers that exploded loudly and caused proper shock waves. My father and Uncle Bucky drank beer and talked about guns and how they would kit out a small militia. A nine-millimetre Glock would be standard gear, Uncle Bucky and my father immediately agreed on that. But their opinions diverged on rifles, which is why I eventually had to decide whether we would choose a Ruger rifle for our troop, my father's favourite, or a Mossberg pump-action shotgun, which Uncle Bucky thought more appropriate. You could bring down bears with it too, proper bears, he said, staring at me. What's more, the shotgun, with its optional pistol grip and short barrel, was ideal for rioting. Nonetheless I chose my father's hunting rifle, and in reward he pulled the cowboy hat down over my face. Things went dark and I snorted with laughter, even though I thought about running away.

That evening, as we fired our home-made fireworks into the night sky, I held my hands over my ears, and it made me sad not to be in Raufarhöfn, where the spluttering light of the rockets reflected so beautifully on the water. In days gone by, the cartridges of the distress signal rockets were used up at New Year's, because they had an expiry date. Like everything does. I was always allowed to shoot the cartridges into the air from Petra's little deckhouse, because it would have been a shame to simply throw them away.

My father's home-made bombs were one thing above all: loud. Everyone drank a lot of beer that evening and got really overexcited. The conversation revolved around an expedition to Washington DC that we were apparently all going to make. Sharon thought the Communists and Corona-Nazis had stolen office from the rightful president.

"We'll make history!" declared my father happily, and Uncle Bucky, who was holding a beer bottle in one hand and a banger in the other, said that there was no reason for me to be scared, that there weren't any polar bears in Washington, just pigs and roaches and lizard people. Then he threw his banger in a wide arc over his shoulder into the fire, roared: "Fire in the hole!" and spread out his arms like a rock star onstage. Boom. As we fell screaming from the garden chairs, trying to dodge the glowing pieces of wood, Uncle Bucky stood there calmly as though he were enjoying the shower of sparks, as though he had emerged from this very fire. And yet he was unharmed, apart from a few singed beard hairs. He had a thick skin. My father poured a bottle of beer over his head, laughing, and Uncle Bucky's eyes sparked devilishly in the red glow of the blaze.

It was actually that evening that I got a feeling I wasn't at all familiar with. It sat between my lower ribs and pressed on my belly, where joy would have been. But the fact we were going to Washington DC was a done deal, there were no buts, and that was the beginning of the end of my US stay, a last family expedition, a crazy high point of my America trip.

After everyone had slept off their hangovers and we had cleared away the debris from the New Year's party, the preparations began. We washed and polished the truck until it gleamed like it was brand spanking new, and we decorated it with magnetic signs and flags we had bought in the gun store along with extra ammo. We tried on different outfits and painted quotes and letters of the alphabet onto homemade signs which we would wave over our heads to make the president happy. I was given the task of painting one single, big letter on a sign: Q – the first letter of my father's name, Quentin. I suggested painting the first letters of all our names on signs, so K for Kalmann, S for Sharon and B for Bucky, but my father said we didn't have enough hands to hold up all the signs, so I should just leave it at Q.

We went to church and prayed for the president.

We practised at the shooting range.

We cleaned and tended to all our guns.

Once we were finally ready, Sharon prepared a generous picnic early in the morning, Uncle Bucky loaded a crate of beer into the truck, then we drove off towards Washington. It was a cold morning, the sixth of January, so the thirteenth and officially final day of Christmas, and that's why I asked my father whether there would be fireworks in Washington DC like in Iceland. Uncle Bucky replied, as though he were my father's spokesperson: "You can count on it!"

When we drove past the gas station, I saw Bob standing in the middle of the parking lot, leaning on a broom. He stared after us, frowning, but when I waved at him, he turned away.

We weren't the only ones who had come to Washington DC. There were so many people, so many little flags, banners and signs.

My father and Uncle Bucky wore identical baseball caps in camouflage tones, Sharon a pink cowboy hat, and I had my white one on. I also had a small backpack with me, with an Icelandic flag poked into it. This had been Sharon's idea. That way she would always know exactly where I was. I also had my passport, chocolate and a bottle of cola stashed in my bag. But I'd already scoffed the chocolate before I even caught sight of the president. I held my Q sign and got a lot of praise for it, especially from the people who had the same letters on their pullovers and leather jackets.

People were in a good mood and happy about meeting one another. Americans are even in a good mood when they're angry; they're talkative and always ready to have fun, eager to help and generous. Snacks and drinks were handed out, music played from little loudspeakers that were scattered around, and there were garden chairs everywhere. Sharon danced with total strangers, a proper country dance where everyone took small steps to the front, to the back and the side, then turned and clapped their hands. It looked very complicated; I almost got dizzy from watching it.

Later Sharon made a live video with her phone for her fans on YouTube, and she filmed me too. "Our guest of honour all the way from Iceland!" I waved into the camera, embarrassed.

Then the president arrived.

The stage was far away, but luckily someone had set up a huge screen on which you could see the president really well. Sharon clapped both hands to her face, screamed and cried out: "He's so handsome!"

My father furtively wiped a tear from his right eye, and Uncle Bucky smiled, stopped the gum-chewing and even showed his teeth. They were brown. Here no one felt ashamed, neither about brown teeth nor strange cowboy dances. I think the president was emotional too, because he looked around him for a long time. But then he got angry, really angry, because he'd had the presidency stolen from him, and America was going to the dogs, and that's why he was asking everyone to march on the Capitol with him and demand what was rightfully theirs. And lots of people set off at once, leaving their garden chairs behind, they didn't even wait for the president. Uncle Bucky and my father got fidgety and argued with Sharon, who wanted to wait for the president's convoy, but Uncle Bucky said he wouldn't be coming anyway, that he was still the fucking president after all.

The noise around us had increased, and that's why Uncle Bucky was shouting so loudly that I could see a vein throbbing behind his beard. So we set off on the long walk, two kilometres along Pennsylvania Avenue. I got a stitch in my side, and my stupid Q sign got heavier and heavier, even though I wasn't holding it high any more. When it eventually slipped out of my hands, I left it lying there. We were overtaken by beeping trucks, cyclists and in-line skaters. A crowd of people marched with us, some of them disguised or masked, silent military veterans, probably all from American wars, there were even uniformed Confederates. Some were wearing protective armour, military helmets, bike helmets, gas masks, pirate hats, crazy sunglasses, and there was a wheelchair user who looked a bit like Grandfather. But it wasn't him.

As we got closer to the big building whose domed roof I could see even from afar, the people got angrier. Someone even set up gallows like in the Wild West. Now Sharon got nervous and kept calling out for her baby, in other words, my father, but he wouldn't slow down. "Baby, wait for me!" she called, trying not to lose him in the fray.

I clung to Sharon but banged into a broad back, a muscleman in a leather jacket. There was no way I could get past him. My father looked up and turned around to us. "Honey, this house belongs to us!"

The muscleman nodded.

"But what about Kalmann?" Sharon's voice tripped over itself while Uncle Bucky cheered.

"They're really going in! Fuck yeah!" Uncle Bucky dashed forwards. I had never seen him so happy, not even at New Year's when he had thrown the home-made fireworks into the flames and spread out his arms. His long beard swung back and forth, he hopped and whooped, then he disappeared into the mob, who were running up a large staircase, beating down security guards, clambering over barricades and walls. He could no longer be seen among the masses, he had disappeared, and that was the last time I would lay eyes on Uncle Bucky.

Someone knocked the cowboy hat off my head, probably by accident, because lots of people were still waving their little flags and banners over their heads. My beautiful white cowboy hat! It landed on the dirty grass, and I dived after it with outstretched arms, but was shoved so heavily from the side that I fell face forwards.

Legs. Legs everywhere. Like a dark forest in a fairy tale. And my hat got entangled in it, carried away as though by some magical force, vanishing into the thicket. I concentrated on getting back on my feet, because I didn't want to get trampled flat like my hat and be left lying somewhere.

Luckily, a nice Viking pulled me upright. He was wearing a plastic helmet with horns and laughed, patted earth and grass from my little backpack and asked me whether everything was okay.

"I've lost my hat!" I cried in despair.

"Forget the hat!" said the Viking, but he still looked all around him. "What does it look like?"

"It's white! A cowboy hat."

"Forget the hat!" he repeated.

Only then did I realize that I'd not only lost my hat but Sharon too. And my father. So I asked the guy with the horns if he had perhaps seen them, my people, to which he unfortunately said no.

"They're probably going in!" he guessed, pointing at the building. "Everyone's going in now, see? Everyone's invited! This house belongs to us."

He was probably right. Probably I'd be able to find my people inside, along with all the corrupt dirt, the murderous, elite scum, as the guy with the horns explained to me.

"Are you actually okay?"

I nodded, even though I felt the complete opposite of okay, because I had lost my family and my hat. The nice Viking turned away and, bellowing a war cry, disappeared into the crowd.

So there I was. Alone in the midst of thousands of people. I should have stopped where I was, I know. My mistake. Because if you get lost, you have to stop right where you are, until you're found. But I was carried along by the masses like driftwood, so I couldn't do anything else but stumble further and further towards the building, until the crowd came to an abrupt halt. Further forward, acrid smoke rose up, and the people's yelling became deafening. I heard a dull explosion, felt the blast wave in my chest. Boom. I was torn to and fro; some people pushed their way back, while others pressed further forwards. The good mood had completely evaporated with the explosion. I managed to force my way out of the crowd, to the side. I made fists and rowed with my arms, pushing people aside until I was able to move freely again. Only then did I come to a halt, gasping for air, and look around, calling for Sharon, my father and Uncle Bucky, I even called for my mother, dammit, because it seemed to me that she would be the first to find me here. I searched the ground too, and I actually did find a cowboy hat, but it was brown and flat and not mine, so I left it there. I saw a police officer and gathered my courage, wanting to ask him to find my people for me, but then I noticed he was crying. He was sobbing uncontrollably, making his way through the crowd in a seemingly aimless way with his head hanging low, and crying fat tears. I think he was the saddest person I've seen in my entire life, sadder than Róbert McKenzie, sadder than Róbert's daughter Dagbjört after I found his hand. The police officer sniffed and cried, placing one foot in front of the other and paying no attention either to me or what was happening around him. I watched as he was barged and shoved, which didn't seem to bother him. Soon I lost sight of him too, and with that I lost all hope of being found by Sharon or my father, so I turned around and slouched away, heading to where the least people were.

On a street corner, curious bystanders were watching the chaos from a distance. "Happy?" a young woman called to me, pointing her smartphone in my direction. She was probably recording me. Her friends roared: "Racist! Coward! Are you retarded? Oh shit, he really is retarded! Which institution did you break out of?"

I wanted to get across the street but couldn't make it, I got slower and slower, my legs, the blood in them, it got thicker, the noise duller.

"Oops!" crowed someone, but by then I could barely hear a thing. "You're in trouble! Run, Forrest, run!"

I didn't run. I simply came to a halt in the middle of the road, because my legs were now made of concrete and my head was rushing like a cement mixer. I only saw the black Cherokee Jeep which had approached me at a walking pace with flashing lights as though from a great distance, not even realizing its beeping was directed at me. I watched myself as I began to bang my fists against the front of the car, so strongly that my entire body began to buzz like a Nokia phone. The car doors were flung open, FBI agents climbed out, the letters on their vests gleamed yellow; one of the men was Mr García, he twisted my arms across my back and slammed my head down on the warm bonnet of the Cherokee Jeep, and then came the blackout, it finally got dark, lights out.

17
INTERROGATION

I fell silent, suddenly feeling exhausted, my mouth as dry as stockfish. The FBI agent, Dakota Leen, laid the pen down on her notebook and massaged the back of her neck, staring at me, staring right through me, seemingly far away, and that's why I asked if she officially had to arrest me now, after everything I had told her. She shook her head and said that if it were up to her, I wouldn't have been brought to the FBI headquarters in the first place. She sat up a little straighter but still seemed undecided, until Mr García popped his head into the interrogation room. "Leen. Outside!"

Her lips tightened and she threw me a meaningful glance, then got up in a leisurely way and walked out into the corridor, leaving the door open.

"I need you out there, right away!" I heard Mr García say.

"Okay, but…" Dakota Leen cleared her throat. "There are still a few things I need to clear up."

"Are you done with the downser yet?"

"He's not a downser, sir."

"Does he have intel?"

"Lots. I've already passed it on."

"Good. Book him and get kitted up! Full gear. We'll take care of him later."

As Dakota Leen sat back down in her chair, she made a face as though a thousand thoughts were racing around in her head. Eventually she took a deep breath and said: "Let's get on with it. Names and addresses. It won't take much longer." She turned to the laptop and began typing before I had even said anything. "Can you spell your father's name?"

"Q," I said.

"Q?" She looked up.

"Q for Quentin," I said, and Dakota Leen sighed. I couldn't properly spell these American names for her. My mother's name and my grandfather's name I wrote on a piece of paper the FBI agent had torn from her notebook.

She typed the names, letter by letter, into the system. Then she froze and looked at me, dumbfounded, then back at the screen and back at me. "Óðinn Arnarson? This man here?" She turned the laptop around and showed me a picture of Grandfather.

"Yes, that's him!" I cried happily. "But much, much younger."

"Born in 1935?"

"And died last autumn," I added, now no longer happy.

Dakota Leen turned the laptop back towards herself and typed in the year. She seemed amused and confused all at once. "Kalmann, your grandfather!" She held a hand over her mouth as she looked back at the screen. "Your grandfather is quite the individual. We have him in the system!"

"What kind of system?" I wanted to know.

"Well, actually it's a list. A blacklist," she explained, her mouth contorting.

"What's a blacklist?" I asked the question softly, because I had a feeling I might not like the answer.

She hesitated, tilting her head from side to side until she found the right words. "A blacklist is a list of people who, let's say, have done something stupid and have to be arrested if they ever set foot on American soil."

"Arrested? But what did Grandfather do?"

Dakota Leen's lips tightened again. "Well, you said yourself he was a communist, or that the people where you live thought he tried to start a communist party. Did I understand that correctly?" I didn't say a word, and didn't even nod, so she continued: "Well, he really was a communist, but what's worse…" She hesitated again. "Do you know what a spy is?"

I nodded. "James Bond is a spy."

"He is, yes, but…" She glanced over at the door. "Your grandfather was no James Bond. According to CIA intel, he was working for the Soviets, getting hold of classified information – or at least trying to."

"The Soviets?"

"Russians, communists, for the enemy, do you understand? And that's why he's on this blacklist, even though it was all a very long time ago."

"But he's dead!"

"Exactly. And I've now made a note of that in the system: *presumed dead*. So it doesn't actually matter any more. Although…" Dakota Leen gave me a sad look. "I'm afraid I have to put you on a list too. Fortunately it's not quite as black, but you're in our system now."

"And then you have to book me? Meaning lock me up?"

Once again, she thought for a long while, stroking the back of her hand. I longed to know what it felt like to be stroked by her, and tried to imagine it, but she jolted me out of my thoughts. "Listen, Kalmann. I'm sending you home. Today. So by tomorrow you'll be back with your mother, where you belong."

"But Mr García —"

Dakota Leen waved away my objection and telephoned the Icelandic embassy, at which I buried my face in my hands. Only now did the full extent of the realization crash over me like a freak wave on the high seas. Grandfather had been an enemy of the state, and I would never see my father again. It was officially the worst day of my life.

After Dakota Leen had made sure Mr García wasn't lurking outside the door, she led me out of the room and through the long corridors of the gigantic building, which felt to me like a labyrinth. Everything was kicking off now. Uniformed FBI agents in bulletproof vests overtook us or passed us, calling out to one another, orders, directions, rallying cries. Dakota Leen and I moved through the chaos as though in slow motion, as if we weren't part of it. She put her hand on my back and gently pushed me forwards. I felt the warmth radiating through my clothes all the way to my skin. To this day, all I have to do is think about it and I can immediately feel the FBI agent's hand on my back.

She took me to a break room, where there was a vending machine. As I didn't have any money on me, Dakota Leen gave me some, and while I tried to slide the dollar bills into the cash slot, she turned around to me one last time. She had turned pale and was smiling sadly. Maybe she was afraid of facing the angry mob outside. I certainly wouldn't have wanted to swap places with her. But I didn't have time to wish her luck or to say goodbye. I was battling with the vending machine, which kept spitting out my bills, and when it finally worked, I had to tap in the number within mere seconds. Luckily I didn't mistype. The candy bar fell into the collecting container and I turned towards the door in relief, but Dakota Leen was no longer there.

18

MOTHER

In Keflavík I had a little test stick pushed up my nose into my fish soup. Only then did I properly wake up again. Everyone wakes up when they get a tickly little stick pushed up their nose. That's just how it is.

How had I even got to Iceland? I vaguely remembered the stressed woman from the Icelandic embassy who had driven me to the airport and put me on a plane. I had probably flown back in the middle of the night, with a few other passengers even, masked and keeping their distance, masks and pairs of eyes like overly tiny windows, expressionless, distanced bullseyes; and outside the plane, nothing but the blackness of winter.

My mother was waiting for me in the arrival hall. In spite of her mask, I saw immediately that she was sad, perhaps even angry, because she had red eyes and her hair was messy. She hugged me close to her, briefly and tightly, then pulled me outside. She didn't even want to know how it had been at my father's or whether I'd had a good journey, but just drove me silently, and without stopping even once, to Reykjavík, where we had to bunk up in a hotel for five days. Quarantine. Locked into the smallest of rooms, door shut, bang.

The first days in quarantine were the most wonderful of my life! We watched movies, mostly on the laptop, sometimes together, sometimes separately, and we ate proper hotel food or ordered takeaway, pizza and hamburgers for me, sushi for my mother, who didn't have to go to work; she was always there and never went away. I had all the time in the world to tell her what had happened to me in Mill Creek and Washington DC. The next morning, when we woke up next to one another after a long, wonderful sleep, she wanted to know what had happened over there with my father, and because I told her everything, she quickly got angry at her sperm donor. She would have pounded him if he'd turned up here. That's what she said, anyway. She wasn't just angry at him, but at all Americans. And she was angry at herself. She could smack herself around the head, she said, for not having pushed the email into her spam folder, because my father was nothing more than that: spam.

When my father eventually called to ask whether I had arrived safely back in Iceland, my mother gave him short shrift with five brief words: I had landed safely, bless. Then she argued with him for ages, even though she had long since hung up and thrown her phone on the bed. So he couldn't even hear her. But I could! I hadn't even known my mother knew so many swear words, she even called him an "absolute *drullusokkur*". That's a tool you use to unblock a toilet, so it's a useful thing, but no one wants to get shoved head first into a blocked toilet bowl.

After my mother had run out of swear words, I had to tell her everything again, really everything, down to the smallest detail. She listened, transfixed, letting out strange sighs, groaning, shaking her head, running her hand through her hair or pressing a pillow over her face and screaming. It was hilarious. I kept laughing, and eventually my mother laughed too, because you can never be angry for as long as you'd like to be.

On the evening news, they broadcast pictures from Washington DC, and I stood close to the television and commentated on them like a proper reporter. We tried to make out my father or Sharon in the fray, but didn't succeed. I did see someone who looked familiar, though, all too familiar, and I turned to stone, because when you find yourself unexpectedly staring at yourself on television, it's incredibly eerie.

My mother let out a shrill scream that for sure they would have heard in the next room, totally embarrassing. Luckily the scream ebbed away within moments, as though my mother was shocked by it too, but her mouth remained open.

It was a shaky phone recording. There I was, Kalmann Óðinsson, a little blurry, barely recognizable, but the Icelandic flag in my backpack was the proof it could only be me. I was standing on a street corner, surrounded by a gang of young people who were pelting me with insults.

"It looks very much as though one of our own was involved in storming the Capitol," commented the newsreader drily. "Or at least someone with an Icelandic flag, because the identity of the —"

My mother pulled herself out of her trance and turned off the TV, click.

Then we said nothing for about a minute. My mother stared at the black TV screen and I stared at her. The Nokia began to buzz, and my mother jumped. "No!" she hissed. "The media!"

UNKNOWN CALLER. I let the phone buzz until it stopped, and only then did my mother take a breath. But now my laptop was beeping, and my mother bent over double, sank down onto the carpet and buried her face in her hands.

"It's Nói!" I cried in relief, because Nói was my best friend, so there was no reason to worry.

"Nói?" asked my mother. She looked at me in surprise, her hands on her face like blinkers.

"My BFF!" I put my headphones on and hooked myself up to the laptop so my mother could stay sitting on the floor undisturbed.

"You made the evening news, baby! Top audience numbers!"

I didn't always understand what Nói meant, but I gathered that he was happy with me. "Damn media," I said.

Nói laughed. Then he got serious. "Why are you never online? Tell me! How's it all going over there?"

"I'm back already."

"Say what now?"

"I'm an enemy of the state now, I'm on a list, and that's why Dakota Leen sent me home. She's an FBI agent and quite pretty."

"Kalmann, slow down! One thing at a time. Are you back in the Northland?"

"No. I'm in Reykjavík. Five days in quarantine. With my mom."

"Around the corner? Enemy of the state? Hot FBI agent? Your mom? Kalmann, I'm losing my mind here!"

I groaned. I had no choice but to tell Nói the entire story too. But it wasn't like I had anything better to do, and my mother had laid down flat on the carpet, her arms spread out, and was staring at the ceiling as though she were playing dead. And for the first time ever, Nói listened to me attentively without being immersed in a multiplayer game at the same time. He established that we were only 2.7 kilometres away from one another. I suggested visiting him after the quarantine, but he said no. He never knew when he would be home, he said. He had to keep going back to the quack doctors, to rehab, to physio, and besides, he was drowning in work, had deadlines to meet, and couldn't just receive guests at the drop of a hat.

"Working from home is a bitch," Nói said.

"Oh, okay," I said in disappointment and told him a little bit more about the riot in DC, and the crazy people I had met there. I also told him about the FBI agent Dakota Leen, of course. He wanted to know down to the smallest detail what she looked like, and after I had described her, he estimated her as a solid eight, perhaps a nine in her suit. "And she's intelligent!" I added. After all, she had found Grandfather on a blacklist of Russian spies.

"Double-u-tee-eff, Kalmann! A Russian spy? Your grandfather? Bro!"

"Correctamundo! That's why he was also an enemy of the state."

My mother had stood up and was now towering over me, her hands on her hips, eyeing me questioningly. Her nostrils flared in rhythm with her breath. "Enemy of the state?" she growled.

"Ha!" Nói laughed again. "Your grandfather was a Russian spy. In Raufarhöfn. For real?"

"Yes," I whispered, avoiding my mother's gaze.

"Fucking hell. Now it all makes sense! Your grandfather was spying on the Yanks for the Russians! That's why he could speak Russian, and he probably wanted to give you some secret intel. Top secret!"

My mother gestured curtly with her hand that I was to end the call, and right away, but Nói was practically flipping out.

"*The mountain*, remember?"

"Heiðarfjall," I mumbled.

"*Gora letit*! Oh! Fuck me!" Nói leaned back in his chair and smacked his hand on his forehead. I didn't see it, but it made a slapping sound. "They're listening!"

"Who?"

"The FBI! Do you have Anom?"

"What's that?"

"An encrypted chat room."

"No."

"Telegram?"

"I've only got a Nokia."

"Bro!" Nói said, then he disappeared from the screen, just like that.

I was confused. Was someone listening in? Was I being watched and tailed by the FBI? Had Dakota Leen been listening while we were talking about her?

I slowly closed the laptop. My forehead was burning, my palms were clammy.

"Kalmann!" My mother launched into a question she didn't even need to voice, because I knew immediately what she wanted to know. I had completely forgotten to tell her that Grandfather was on an FBI blacklist for espionage. "Was my father a Russian spy? Or was that some weird joke, Kalmann Óðinsson?"

I shrugged, feeling that I had done something stupid.

My mother's expression changed abruptly. She sat down next to me on the bed and placed the laptop on the nightstand. Suddenly she looked very tired. "It's okay, Kalli minn." She rubbed my back. "You couldn't have told me everything at once, I get it, no problem. But just tell me this: what did you find out about Grandfather? Explain it to me word for word."

I told her everything, of course, it wasn't like it was a secret. And only then did I realize that this information was actually

141

the most important, and that I should have started with it, because now everything made sense.

"All those photos!" my mother whispered. "The trips to Langanes, the Americans' radar station…" She stared at me intently. "The radar station!"

"Heiðarfjall," I added.

"H-2." My mother raised her hands and held them in mid-air. "He used us, my sister and I, to photograph the Yanks on the mountain!" Her eyes widened even more. She reached for the laptop again, opened it and launched Google. "H-2," she murmured again, typing it in. And after it: "Heiðarfjall."

"Why didn't he take *me* there?" I asked, feeling almost a little offended now. Apparently I wasn't cut out for espionage.

"The station has been out of service for ages now," said my mother. She told me that the Cold War had ended when I was still little. "Wait, here it is. Bingo! H-2 is the abbreviation for the radar station on Heiðarfjall." She had opened the first link and was scanning the sentences; she clicked on the next link and the one after that, and suddenly she looked amused. "Ha! A storm blew the radar dome away in January 1961!" But it was the next link that caught her attention and made her turn serious again. First she skim-read the text, then she read it aloud to me: "Hazardous waste and contaminants on Heiðarfjall mountain on Langanes. For over forty years, the remains of the American radar station have polluted the subsoil. There is evidence that environmentally damaging waste has been dumped with ordinary waste on the mountain. Chemical residues have been detected in the groundwater of nearby farms. The water is polluted."

"Doesn't Aunt Telma live there?" I asked.

"Yes!" my mother replied.

"Maybe Grandfather took spy photos because of the waste."

"Hardly. The Russians wouldn't have been interested in waste." My mother stared at the screen for a while longer, then took out her phone and called Aunt Guðrún, and talked to her for two whole hours. To begin with I listened, but I kept thinking about Grandfather taking seemingly casual snap-shots of his children as the Americans' military trucks roared through the landscape in the background. And I thought about him standing on Petra's deck out at sea, smoking his pipe and peering through the binoculars, taking notes. Then I got bored and turned on the TV.

My mother had finished talking on the phone.

"Once we get home, we'll take a closer look at those photos and documents!"

I thought that was a great idea, and told her, which made her laugh and give me a little hug. There was a positive out-come from my US adventure in spite of everything; I had found out that Grandfather was a spy. Looking back, I should have told my mother that Grandfather had talked about a flying mountain. And that we were now under surveillance. I should have told her that Grandfather had been murdered because of his espionage past, even if she wouldn't have believed me. That's just how it is with me: if I tell everyone there's a polar bear, they only believe me once it stands up on its hind legs and roars.

The final two days of our hotel quarantine were pretty boring. The room got smaller, the movies longer, and the food that was put in front of our door staler. There were never any Cocoa Puffs. My mother took long showers, read one book after the next and sighed a lot. She made numerous phone calls and wrote long emails, agonizing over them because she didn't want to make any spelling mistakes. I had never spent so much time in one room with her. I almost felt like a spy myself. I watched her. She had three different facial moisturizers: two for the evening, one for the morning. When she was reading a book, her face was completely expressionless, but sometimes she put the book aside to stretch her toes and reflect on what she'd just read. She could sleep in much later than I could, sometimes until ten, even though I was long awake – as though she hadn't slept properly in years. During the night, she never needed to go to the bathroom.

I think that, now Grandfather had died, she was my favourite person, even if she was my mother and sometimes almost drove me insane. Mothers have to annoy their children, that's just the way it is, it's a law of nature. Otherwise, children would want to stay living with their mothers forever. And she really knew how to annoy me! I kept having to tell her about America, as though I were her entertainer or something. She by contrast barely told me anything, least of all about the past, and when I quizzed her about her time in Keflavík or about my childhood, she got irritated. She didn't know any jokes and couldn't draw very well. The hotel staff had put paper and crayons in front of our door, some Red Cross initiative, but my mother gave up quickly because she felt she had so little talent. So we made paper planes instead and threw them out of the window, but that too ended in disaster, because the planes went into tailspins and plummeted to the ground, and an older man who was out for a stroll complained to the Red Cross, claimed we had thrown rubbish out of the window, and threatened to report us to the police.

My mother had become a news junkie during this dumb pandemic. She listened to the radio news once an hour, even though they mostly said the same thing, and then in the evenings she watched the TV news on the state channel, at seven o'clock and ten o'clock. Almost every day at eleven in the morning she watched the Covid-19 press conference, which informed us about the current state of affairs, which usually stayed the same too. The journalists asked the same questions every day, and every day the Covid-19 experts had the same answers. That's why, eventually, everyone was very laid-back.

On one occasion my mother grabbed the laptop, even though I was watching an episode of *Temptation Island*, one I'd already seen, but my complaints fell on deaf ears, because she wanted to find out more about Heiðarfjall, and I was interested in that too. "Misty Mountain!" she cried, after she had researched for a while. "That's what the Yanks called the mountain. Misty Mountain. How fitting."

"Misty Mountain?"

"They gave it back to us, along with the decommissioned radar station, on 1 September 1970. Nice, don't you think?" My mother was sitting in bed with her legs crossed, the computer on her lap. I made myself comfortable next to her on my stomach and turned on the television, but without sound. "We were allowed to keep everything the Yanks hadn't taken with them, the barracks, antennas, all the useless junk. Stupidly, they also left their rubbish behind." My mother scanned through the text, murmuring, then her voice got louder again: "PCB!"

"What's that?" I asked.

"No idea, some contaminant that's now in the ground-water." She googled. "PCB. Polychlorinated biphenyls are poisonous and carcinogenic chlorine compounds. Oh yes. They've been banned worldwide since 2001. Now detectable in the atmosphere, the seas and the ground everywhere. Originating from batteries and transformers. And mercury.

Fuck!" She clapped the laptop shut. "I can't read this," she cried. "Stuff like this makes me furious!"

"*Mamma!*" I was afraid that our room neighbours, who we'd heard coughing for days, would complain again.

"But it's true! The arrogance of the fucking Yanks!"

"You sound like Grandfather!" I blurted out, and for about two seconds my mother was completely still, staring at me aghast, then she burst out laughing, loud and exaggerated, falling onto her back, kicking her legs in such a way that my laptop almost fell off the bed. She lunged at me and tussled my hair. "This fucking room," she cried. "This fucking bed! It's far too soft! These fucking kitschy pictures on the walls! This fucking wannabe-fancy bathroom!"

"*Mamma!*" I almost couldn't catch my breath.

"This fucking pandemic, this fucking virus, this world, it makes me furious!"

Now I couldn't bear any more. I turned over beneath my mother and accidentally hit her in the face. Quite hard, even. More than once, probably.

My mother instantly became still, staring at me in shock, then she buried her face in her hands. I tried to tickle her under the arms so she would laugh again, but she flinched, jumped off the bed and locked herself in the bathroom.

I stayed sitting on the bed.

Thought about nothing.

Waited for the blackout. But I heard her sobbing. My mother was crying in the bathroom, and it was my fault, and that's why I punched myself in the ear, and because I couldn't feel anything, I did it again and again, and suddenly my mother was standing in front of me. She had a glowing cheek, her nose was bleeding and one of her eyes was completely red. She stared at me as though she had lost her mind. Like in a horror movie. "Kalmann," she said with despairing certainty in her voice. "You can't help it. It was a silly accident." She was about to go back in the bathroom, but turned around again. "I'm sorry I flipped out like that, but human beings can be awful, selfish and greedy, they mess up the world, and when you tell them to wear a mask and wash their hands, they make such a fuss as though some huge injustice is being inflicted on them. But you're not like that. You understand what it's all about, and I'm proud of you, I'm proud of what you've become! You can't help it, do you hear me?"

She didn't need to say any more. She was proud of me, that was just how it was, she loved me, she was my mother after all, and that's why I turned up the volume on the TV, and my mother locked herself in the bathroom again, and when we were tested for a final time the next day, received the negative results and checked ourselves out at reception, my mother still had yellow and violet and red flecks on her face, but thanks to the mask you couldn't really see them, and that's why no one asked whether she had fallen down the stairs.

19
LÁRUS

The first thing you do when you get out of quarantine is lift your face to the sky and drink in the air, even if the sky is grey and the air polluted by exhaust fumes from the cars. You're just happy not to be locked up any more. To be free.

We got into my mother's Renault and drove northwards, leaving the capital behind us and with it Nói, who lived somewhere in one of those boring suburbs, and we rejoiced in the snowy mountains that were highlighted by the dark clouds behind, making it look as though the white rocks were glowing from within. The horizon over the sea gleamed faintly, the light a lingering thought. Iceland had never looked so beautiful to me. My mother agreed, even though it was bitterly cold outside. You could tell by the hard-packed snow on the main road and from the horses in the fields, who seemed frozen to the spot despite their scrubby coats, holding their buttocks against the north wind and not daring to move. And that same wind was blowing towards us, trying to stop us from leaving the city, but my mother's Renault battled bravely on even though there are car makes better suited to Arctic conditions, for example American and Russian ones.

When we arrived in Akureyri that evening, my mother quickly got herself ready for a night shift in the hospital, showering and drinking half a litre of filter coffee. But after that she still had a little time, so we got out Grandfather's photos.

Now it was obvious that he had been a spy. In fact, it was astonishing that we hadn't caught on sooner. But why had Grandfather kept these photos? Shouldn't he have sent them to Russia and informed the communists or at least the Icelandic government about the pollution, about what the Americans were doing up there on the mountain?

"Maybe he didn't actually want to be a spy," my mother pondered. "Or maybe he got scared."

"Maybe he decided to keep the photos because you and Aunt Guðrún are in them," I speculated, and my mother decided my idea was the best and rewarded me with a smile. Then she put aside the photos, went over to the mirror and put on some make-up to hide the bruises.

I watched her for a little while and then said that I missed Raufarhöfn.

"Five days locked up with me were probably enough for you," said my mother drily as she packed away her make-up. She even said it was sure to do me good to feel the Raufarhöfn soil under my feet again, to drop anchor, pull up the hand-brake, as she put it. She pulled out her phone and enquired on Facebook whether anyone was driving from Akureyri to Raufarhöfn, and even before she'd put on her winter coat and boots, Ingimar, who hurtled across the Melrakkaslétta in his little dairy truck at least once a week, sent her a message. My mother sighed and stared at her phone for a while, as if she were hoping someone else would get in touch. But Ingimar's response was the only one.

We made a plan to meet at nine the next morning. My mother waved goodbye to me and said she would still be asleep tomorrow, so for me to be quiet, and have fun in Raufarhöfn, and then she was gone, after five days of quarantine, twenty-four hours a day in the same room – it was completely crazy, this time that no longer had Grandfather in it.

It was dark outside, but I didn't feel in the least bit tired, so I called Nói to see if he'd ever heard the name Misty Mountain. He had, of course, in *Lord of the Rings*! He told me it's a treacherous mountain range with goblins and trolls, who throw boulders at travellers and trigger avalanches. Not to be confused with the Lonely Mountain from *The Hobbit*, with Smaug the fire-breathing dragon, who hoarded all the dwarves' treasure. Nói ranted about the awful *Hobbit* movies, which weren't anywhere near as epic as *Lord of the Rings*, but conceded that there were more important things to discuss than fantasy worlds, namely the H-2 radar station and all the poison, the abbreviations that unfortunately I could no longer remember. Nonetheless, Nói seemed happy. "That's it! The motive!"

"The motive?"

"The reason your grandfather was knocked off! He spied on the Americans while they were poisoning the mountain, and that's why he had to be eliminated. Case closed."

"But why only now?"

"Well." Nói swivelled energetically on his chair. "That's the million-dollar question."

"But…" For once, Nói's ponderings made no sense, at least not to my noggin. "Loads of people know the mountain's polluted. It's no secret. My mother googled it."

"You're right, Sherlock," sighed Nói. "Good point. It's nothing new, after all. Americans always leave destruction in their wake. Vietnam, Iraq, Yemen —"

"I'm back in Akureyri, by the way."

"What, you hightailed it back up north? Why didn't you visit me?"

"I don't know where you live. My mother had to work. And so do you, you said!"

"True. I've got enough on my plate."

"Tomorrow I'm going to Raufarhöfn."

"To the end of the world."

"No, the end of the world is further."

"Kalmann, listen up. If there's more information to be found about your grandfather's murder, then it's in Raufarhöfn."

"Or in Húsavík," I said, without thinking.

Nói twitched and slapped his hand theatrically against his chest as though he was having a heart attack. "The care home? Damn it, why didn't I think of that?"

"I don't know."

"Kalli, the surveillance cameras!" He leaned forward slightly and tapped away on his keyboard while the logic unfurled in my head too; perhaps a surveillance camera had captured my grandfather's killer. "Fucking shit!" Nói banged his fists against the keyboard. "I'll never get in there!"

The bedroom door behind Nói opened and his mother peered in. "Nói!" she said firmly. "You —"

"I know, I know!" he interrupted her. "I'm as chilled as a penguin's balls. You can go now, Mom."

His mother hovered there a little longer, said hello to me, then closed the door again.

"Can you hack into the care home?" I asked Nói.

"No chance. But you could go and talk to the security guards. I mean, they know you!"

"There aren't any guards."

Nói sighed impatiently. "Then go in and ask the nurses!"

"Care professionals," I said, and Nói murmured, "Whatever."

I waited at the harbour, standing beneath a street lamp and ignoring the wet snowflakes that occasionally landed on my face. It was still night, pitch-black. Hopefully the clothes my mother had stuffed into an IKEA bag early in the morning weren't getting wet.

Ingimar soon came roaring along, with the windows still steamed up, but he spotted me regardless and came to a halt next to me, then helped me with my bag.

I like sitting in a truck, because you sit much higher than in a car. It feels as though you're flying along the road, as though you're the king and all the other cars are your subjects. But I was a little scared too and belted myself in as quickly as I could, because Ingimar always drives as though he hates every minute he spends in the truck, especially when the roads are covered in snow and the flurries confuse the senses in the darkness. Ingimar is notorious for his overtaking manoeuvres; he overtakes anyone who's going at a snail's pace, and by swerving confusingly. Luckily traffic had significantly reduced since the pandemic, the road was empty, and so we drove silently through the cold night as though we were the only people in the entire world, as though we had nothing more to say to one another because we had already been driving through this darkness for an eternity.

Only after the new tunnel did we catch up with a car that was driving slowly and almost in the middle of the road. "Damn pandemic tourists," grumbled Ingimar. "Step on it, sleepyheads!"

I got myself into position. I knew the drill. When Ingimar got annoyed about a slow-moving car, he wanted to know who was at the wheel. It was a kind of guessing game.

"Tourists, don't you think? Chinese for sure. A young couple, students or something. Did their practical exam in a driving simulator."

I had to press my face against the window to be able to see from above who was behind the wheel. Because of the darkness, I couldn't miss the moment when the truck's headlamps would illuminate the inside of the car.

"No, they're not Chinese," I called out. "Brown people, a full car."

"Aha, Pakistani!" cried Ingimar. "A whole clan, eh? I should have guessed. Where do they get the dough for a holiday in Iceland?"

I didn't know, but couldn't help but think of Grandfather, who had once said that the richest people lived in the poorest countries.

It was a really fun game. Ingimar would say, for example, "There's some old dude sitting at the wheel, I bet, isn't there, Kalmann? Tell me it's an old-timer!" And I'd cry, "Correctamundo!" and my cry would steam up the window. "A very old man, and next to him an old woman. Probably his wife."

"Bingo!" he would cry. Or he would take a guess: "That must be a fox hunter chugging along, the rusty Subaru's on the brink of falling apart. Can you see anything, Kalmann?"

"He's wearing a hat and looking out of the window. He's got his shotgun in his lap!"

"Bingo!" Or he guessed that it was either someone completely retarded at the wheel, or a woman, because they sped up when the road was straight and almost came to a standstill on the bends. "It's a woman, isn't it? Kalmann? It has to be a woman."

"No," I said. "Tourists. Two young men."

"Really? I should have guessed. Dammit!"

Today there was no one to overtake, apart from the Pakistani family, so the drive was relaxed. First we drove to Grenivík, and while Ingimar was delivering dairy products to the hotel and store, I sat patiently in the truck. After that we made a stop at the Goðafoss tourist centre, even though they had barely needed any dairy products there since the pandemic. Mostly Ingimar just replaced the out-of-date Skyr. Eventually, we arrived in Húsavík. He had lots of customers to deliver to here: the care home, the grocery store, hotels, restaurants and the gas station. So I asked him to drop me off at the care home. He gave me half an hour, and not a minute longer.

I ran.

"Kalmann!" a carer called out to me almost as soon as I stepped inside the home. Had she been expecting me? Did she think I was coming to visit Grandfather?

I stopped as though I had run into a wall – not because of the woman but because of the familiar smell. It overpowered me, took my breath away, making me almost fall backwards. The smell contained the memory of Grandfather. Grandfather himself was in it.

The carer marched towards me and called my name again. She was so pleased to see me. Lots of people are pleased when they see me. I got used to that a long time ago. When she was standing in front of me, she said in a sad voice that she was very sorry about my grandfather, and that I should please put on a mask.

For a fraction of a second, I had wondered whether Grandfather was still sitting in his room and staring out of the window. The familiar smell of the care home and the jubilant greeting had confused me. Perhaps Grandfather's death had been a silly dream or a delusion. But if the carer had said it too, then he really was dead. Of course. We had buried him. And I had been there. Strangely, I was relieved not to be suffering from delusions.

No one would actually want the dead to suddenly no longer be dead and rise from the grave. It would be like when you say goodbye to somebody, for example in front of a store, only to realize that you're going the same way. The first few steps are then really embarrassing, because you only just said goodbye.

"Have you come to visit *us*? How nice of you!" She laid her hand on her chest to express her joy.

"I have to go in half an hour," I warned her, because I'd arranged to meet Ingimar by the gas station. "Not a minute longer!"

"Wonderful. That's plenty of time to have a piece of cake, isn't it? Come on, I'll take you to the break room."

We walked through the corridors I knew so well, the carer in front, me behind. When we went around the corner, Kolbeinn was there, staring at me, yellowish, hollow-cheeked. He was kind of slumped over his rollator, and his mask had slipped far beneath his nose, hanging loosely from his ears. He looked shrivelled. "Hello, Kolbeinn," I said, but he didn't recognize me and just stared at me.

"The poor man isn't getting any younger either," said the carer over her shoulder, which I found strange, because no one gets younger; that's nature, it doesn't make exceptions.

Another two carers were sitting in the break room, and I was given a piece of marble cake. I was allowed to take the mask off again now.

"What brings you to see us?" I was asked by one of the other carers, and that's why I told them about Ingimar and his truck, the dairy products —

"What I meant was," they interrupted me carefully, "*why* are you visiting us?"

"I want to find out who…" I hesitated, bit into the cake and chewed. Only then did I finish the sentence, but with a full mouth. "Who was the last person to see my grandfather alive."

"That's why you came?"

"Correctamundo. I'd like to see the recordings from the surveillance cameras."

The carers exchanged glances. The one who had greeted me eventually shrugged. "I think you'll have to speak with Lárus."

"Is he the guard?" I asked.

"Something like that."

The women giggled.

"He's our janitor. Come on, I'll take you to him. He's probably tucked away in his closet. You can ask him yourself."

Lárus was sitting in a dark, windowless room. There wasn't much space for anything beyond a desk and an office chair. If Lárus were to close the door behind him, he would be able to rest his head against it.

On the desk stood a computer and an old bedside lamp, together with all kinds of junk. The wall to the left was covered with tools, the wall to the right hidden behind a cluttered shelving unit. Photos were pinned to the wall above the computer, predominantly of Lárus, grinning, tanned and tattooed, and the tattoos were easy to see because in most of them he was half-naked. He was the youngest and coolest janitor I had ever met.

The nurse left me alone with him but didn't close the door, which reassured me.

Lárus stayed seated, then turned and looked up at me sleepily. His mask dangled loose from one ear. I had seen him around the care home a few times before. He, on the other hand, didn't seem to know who I was, so I had to explain it to him.

"Oh, the guy who dances with polar bears! We haven't seen you here in ages!" He grinned at me.

Something was wrong with his teeth. I would have liked to know why he was a janitor, because he didn't look like one, not like Halldór in Raufarhöfn, for example. Lárus was roughly my age, or at least that was my guess, although he looked a bit washed-out in that dark room, like he'd been to a raucous wake and now had the worst hangover of his life, dark bags under his eyes, thinning hair and stubble. Because he was only wearing a T-shirt – it was warm in the closet – I could study the tattoos on his arms. They were intertwined lines, sometimes thicker, sometimes thinner, like snakes without heads.

"What can I do for you, my friend?" he asked, and I saw that two of his teeth were gold-plated. Maybe he was a rapper.

I explained that I wanted to find out who had seen my grandfather just before he died, something which was sure to be on the security cameras. I pointed towards his computer.

"And why do you want to know that?" Lárus asked, furrowing his brow.

"Because my grandfather may have been murdered," I replied. "Here, in the care home."

Lárus raised his eyebrows and stared at me. Now he was wide awake. I didn't move. Then, suddenly, almost making me jump, he turned to his computer, clicked his tongue and said, "Well, let's see who bumped him off, then. Which room was he in, your grandfather? And don't say 13!"

"No, room nine," I said. "In the Náttfari Corridor."

Lárus clicked around with the mouse until he had found the camera closest to that room. Only then did I notice he was missing a finger, the little one on his right hand. "I've only got one camera there," he muttered. "So the room door isn't visible. Look." He turned the computer screen slightly towards me. "The door to the room is behind the camera, so you can't see when someone leaves or enters the room. You can only see whoever's walking down the corridor."

"Oh," I said, disappointed.

"When did he die?"

"The third of October."

"At what time?"

I thought hard. "They telephoned our house at 2.40."

Lárus studied me. "Are you on the spectrum or something?"

I shrugged. "I don't think so," I said.

"Doesn't matter, everyone's a bit damaged anyway." He turned back to the computer. "If your family got the call at 2.40, then it might've been noticed around two that he'd checked out. The shift manager gets summoned straight away, she establishes whether the person's dead and calls the doctor, and by the time they've confirmed it, a quarter of an hour's gone. And then the relatives have to be informed as quickly as possible."

Lárus typed in the date and approximate time, then played the surveillance camera recording at an accelerated speed. At two in the afternoon, a cleaner shuffled across the screen with her little cart, and in less than two minutes she came back – without the cart. She was clearly in a hurry. Lárus rewound the recording and hit pause.

"Piotra. She's Polish. That'll be her discovering your grandfather's death. Nine minutes past two. Given how she's scurrying, I guarantee you she's seen a dead man. But you want to know who visited your grandfather before he died, right?"

"Correctamundo," I said.

"Correctamundo!" echoed Lárus, amused. "Isn't that from *Pulp Fiction*?"

"No idea," I said, and was reminded of Nói.

Lárus ran the surveillance video backwards, first at the normal speed, and then, because not much was happening, fast again. It probably wouldn't be so easy to establish who had been the last to go in Grandfather's room. There was Kolbeinn, shaking his way slowly backwards down the corridor in his rollator, which looked funny, and I even laughed, and he kept getting overtaken backwards by care staff and cleaners. Once Lárus stopped the recording and pointed at someone. "Look, that's me! With the new Bosch. Amazing hammer drill. But I didn't kill your grandfather, I didn't even visit him, hand on heart."

"Okay." I believed him.

"I was renovating the community room. Thanks to the pandemic, social events and visitors aren't allowed." He glanced at me. "Well, I guess there's the occasional exception."

There really had been other visitors walking through the Náttfari Corridor that day. A care home wasn't a quarantine hotel, after all. There was a mother with her little daughter and an old man wearing a baseball cap, none of whom were part of the inventory, as Lárus put it. A short while later, an old woman with a strange hat, who like everyone else had a mask on, strolled in a leisurely manner along the corridor.

"Stop!" I cried.

"You gave me a fright!" Lárus pressed the pause button.

"Go back!"

He obeyed. "Do you know the old girl?"

"I think so," I said. "That's my grandmother's sister. She has this strange red felt hat with gull feathers."

We established that she had arrived at 13.02 and left again at 13.24.

"Do you think she killed your grandfather?" Lárus asked me.

"I don't know," I admitted, and now I wished Nói had been here, because he was sure to have thought of a logical motive.

"What's her name, your great-aunt? I've seen her here a few times."

"Telma."

"So didn't you know she had visited your grandfather shortly before he died? I mean, she's family!"

I thought for a moment. "I only met her at the funeral."

"Strange family," Lárus declared, leaning back on his office chair a little and running his nine fingers through his hair. "It's certainly suspicious. But unfortunately we can't get any more information from this. We can't even say whether Telma was visiting your grandfather or someone else. Perhaps he just died because he was old, don't you think?"

I shrugged, because I was still thinking. But the more I thought, the less I knew, and that's why I asked Lárus how he had lost his little finger. He looked at the stump, as though he was still grieving his finger.

"Well," he said. "I had to settle an old bill with it. And the other fingers are probably a kind of insurance policy." He moved them as though he were testing their suppleness.

"Oh right," I said, then remembered Ingimar. The half-hour was up for sure, so I ran out of the closet without saying goodbye, neither to Lárus nor the carers, ran all the way to the gas station, even forgetting to take off my mask, and because Ingimar was already sitting in his truck and revving the engine reproachfully, I unfortunately had to sacrifice having a hamburger in the gas station. So my stomach rumbled from Húsavík via Kópasker and all the way to Raufarhöfn.

It was afternoon by the time we arrived, and because it was almost getting dark again already, it felt as though we had been on the road the entire day. I still hadn't eaten any lunch.

20
KLAKABAR

You quickly forget how short the winter days in northern Iceland actually are. Fleeting, like a good mood. There was barely any light remaining over the Melrakkaslétta, just a final glimmer of the embers. It looked as though there were a massive city somewhere beyond the horizon. But I knew very well there was no city there, just a few isolated farms.

Ingimar drove me to my little house, helped me with my bag and nodded goodbye. I stood there for a while on the compacted snow and stared after the rumbling truck until even the exhaust fumes had vanished. Then I took a deep breath of the salty Raufarhöfn air and instantly felt more awake. My little house stood there, completely dark. Was it annoyed with me for having been away so long? There was a light on next door, and when I looked across I spotted Elínborg standing behind the window and lifting her curtain, but when I waved at her she let it drop.

I went in, switched on the light and turned up all three heaters, put the TV on and, with a bag of cheesy popcorn I'd found in the kitchen cupboard, sank onto the sofa.

Dr Phil had a real nutjob in the studio again. Her name was Bailey. She was a pretty girl who lived in the illusion of having a friend, even though the two of them had never met. She was a stalker, but a female one. Dr Phil explained to the audience why Bailey was so disturbed: childhood trauma. Rape. Multiple times. And now he wanted to hear from Bailey, who in the meantime had made herself even smaller on the chair, that she was just imagining being friends with this woman. But Bailey insisted that the friendship was real, and so Dr Phil paused to think for a long while. Only people who like everyone looking at them expectantly can do that.

I thought about Nói, who was my best friend but whom I had never met in person or even properly seen.

Bailey could no longer handle Dr Phil's thinking pause and turned to the audience. "Laugh all you want!" she cried, even though no one was laughing. "I'm clearly a joke to you!"

Dr Phil promptly ended the conversation and sent Bailey away, because he didn't like how she was portraying herself as a victim, and Bailey stumbled off the stage in confusion, wiping tears from her face. Now the people clapped. Some even laughed and shook their heads.

I felt confused. Muting the television, I opened my laptop to call Nói, because I was suddenly no longer sure whether he really existed.

He did exist. But he didn't want to talk about Dr Phil, beyond commenting that he was one of the richest people in the world, and probably the richest shrink. "Have you been to Húsavík yet?" he asked.

"Yes," I said proudly. "I watched the recordings from the surveillance camera!"

"For real? Good work, detective! I didn't think you'd manage."

"It wasn't so hard." I waved my hand. "Lárus showed me everything."

"Everyone likes you. Did you see anything on the recordings?"

"Not much. The camera wasn't aimed at the door to his room. But I saw Telma."

"Telma?"

"My great-aunt." I wondered whether I should even tell Nói about Telma. For sure he would suspect her of being the murderer. "She visited him shortly before his death."

"Hmm." Nói fell silent, thinking. "Most murders happen within the family," he said. "Family relationships are more complex than an Eminem song."

"Oh right," I said.

"Did she have a reason to kill him? A motive?"

I said no and told him I'd only met her at the funeral and that she was actually really nice, not the kind of person who would kill someone.

"Maybe they were having an affair!"

"What do you mean?"

"She and your grandfather. Maybe they used to do it."

"But why?" I asked. "Grandfather would have done it with my grandmother, otherwise my mother and Aunt Guðrún wouldn't exist."

"Man, Kalli, you spoilsport!" Nói explained to me that there was nothing hornier than fucking two sisters at once, which I hadn't realized. I asked him whether he had ever had the pleasure, but he waved his hand dismissively. "Only online," he said.

Then I thought about my ex-girlfriend Perla and how we would sometimes lie in bed together and cuddle, until my arm fell asleep because her head was resting on it.

Usually I don't like it when someone is lying on me. The idea of having to share the narrow bed not just with Perla but her sister too triggered a small panic attack in me. But I kept it to myself, and counted backwards from ten really quietly, and once I arrived at zero, I flipped Nói shut.

*

Outside, I was met by damp air. The sea was loud, a constant thundering and crashing. Sometimes you only have to close your eyes to see the ocean in all its glory. I had put on my cowboy hat and pinned the sheriff star to my chest, and I strolled over to the hotel.

In the lobby I was struck dumb, and stared around in confusion: had I accidentally wandered into the wrong building? I went back out to take another look from the outside, but everything fit: the peeling plaster, the brown window frames, the hotel name on the white tin sign. So I went back in.

The lobby looked completely different. The fishing decor, the nets, buoy lamps, dried starfish and old herring barrels, all of it was gone, in both the lobby and the restaurant. The furniture was new, the seats were upholstered, but on account of their ramrod-straight backrests looked uncomfortable regardless. The lamps were sawed-off pipes, rusty and long, which cast a warm albeit dim light on the tables. The red carpet had been removed; beneath my feet there was now hard, poured concrete with a mirror-like shine. On the walls hung pictures that seemed to gleam vibrantly, but you couldn't tell what they were of. Modern art. Luckily the bar was still as I remembered it. But it had a new name, which had been chalked in white letters on the black wall: KLAKABAR. My bar stool stood in its place, and it was empty. Phew!

"Hello, Kalmann!"

I looked around. Hafdís from the town council was sitting with an unfamiliar woman at a four-person table in the back of the restaurant and waving at me, with two glasses of white wine and a bowl of peanuts in front of her. "Hello!" I waved back.

"Wouldn't you like to join us?"

"No. I'm hungry."

"Of course! Kalmann has to eat when he's hungry."

Further along at the bar sat Siggi, studying me with a mischievous smile. He always looks like that when he's sitting alone at the bar drinking beer. His eyes get a contented gleam, as though a particularly beautiful thought is showing on his face. He raised his beer as if to toast with me. We were the only people in the restaurant. Óttar came out of the kitchen and thundered: "Kalli Kaliber! Long time no see. Where've you been hiding?"

"In America," I confessed point-blank.

"Visiting your father?"

"Correctamundo."

"Did it go okay, the journey I mean? I thought the Yanks had shut the borders?"

I wondered whether Óttar had started to lift weights in the sports hall again. He looked healthier than usual, and his voice was stronger.

"It wasn't a problem."

Óttar looked at me with a frown and put his arms on his sides. "Well, that's not what I heard. But nice to have you back!" He banged the palm of his hand twice on the bar. "Do you like the name? Klakabar! And the new design?"

"It's okay. Actually, no, I don't like it."

A snort of laughter came from Siggi, who had been listening attentively. "I've told you a thousand times! Modern frills don't fit here!"

"Well, you should've told Hörður that!" Óttar retorted. "It wasn't my idea. But he must know what's in fashion nowadays." And, directed at me: "I'm sure you agree, Kalli, that this place was long due a makeover, don't you? I mean, you're still young."

"I just want something to eat," I informed him.

Siggi snorted into his beer glass.

Óttar sighed. "The usual?"

"Hamburger with fries," I confirmed. "And cocktail sauce."

"If it ain't broke, don't fix it. No changes, I've got you!"

I nodded, and Óttar disappeared into the kitchen. Something fell to the floor and made a loud clatter. We heard Óttar swear.

"Kalli minn!" Hafdís had crept up from behind and rubbed the palm of her hand on my back. "Join us for a moment, won't you? Your food will take a little while." I obeyed and followed Hafdís across the restaurant. She guided me towards an empty chair at the table. "Now you can finally meet our village's very own sheriff," she explained to the stranger. "The honorary citizen of Raufarhöfn, who saved us from the clutches of a polar bear!"

The unfamiliar woman looked at me with a friendly smile. For sure she had already heard about it. She had black, tousled hair, and looked as though she had only just got out of bed. She was probably about fifty, maybe even sixty, so around the same as Hafdís, but you can't possibly say that to women of this age – nor should you, as Nói had once explained to me: "If an old woman asks you to guess her age, don't answer under any circumstances, because your guess will always be wrong!"

"I'm Jórunn," said the unfamiliar woman, laying her right hand on her heart.

Hafdís added: "Jórunn comes from Reykjavík and has been staying in the hotel here for a while. She's a proper artist. Do you like the pictures?" Hafdís made a sweeping hand gesture.

"I don't know." My gaze lingered on the bar. How much longer would it take until my hamburger was ready?

167

"Kalmann, there's something I wanted to tell you." Hafdís leaned forward a little and looked at me conspiratorially. "A reporter called me about the mysterious Icelander who was allegedly at the storming of the Capitol. He wanted your phone number. I asked him why, and he said he'd received a tip-off that the Icelander in question was the sheriff of Raufarhöfn!"

"They can be so brazen," said Jórunn, and her eyes narrowed.

"Do you know what I said to him?" Hafdís sat at an angle in her chair, hung one arm casually over the backrest and looked pleased with herself. "I asked whether he had all his marbles! Whether he'd heard of the virus and the small matter of the Americans having locked down several months ago!"

Jórunn laughed up at the ceiling, one single "Ha!"

Hafdís looked at me, her eyes sparkling.

"You're a smooth customer!" said Jórunn to Hafdís, who responded with a smile.

"I told him I had only just run into Kalmann Óðinsson on the street."

"But that's not true!" I interjected. "I really was in the United States of America!"

"Kalmann, sometimes it's okay to lie, don't you think?"

I conceded, thinking about Birna.

"But now tell me, Kalmann. How are you? Were there problems? Was it a close call? Did the Americans let you go again?"

That was a lot of questions, and I didn't have time to answer them all. So I told the women briefly that everything had gone well, I was back and wouldn't go away again, so there was no reason to worry. Hafdís seemed satisfied with my answers and rubbed my back again, saying that I was a really good egg and very brave. That whenever she saw me here in Raufarhöfn, she immediately felt a little safer. Then she told Jórunn that my grandfather had died recently and I was coping brilliantly, even though he and I had been inseparable. And then both the women looked really sorry for me, and because that was unpleasant for me, I said that Grandfather, by the way, had been a Russian spy.

Hafdís laughed in astonishment. "A spy? For the Russians? Kalmann, you've already convinced me!"

"It's true," I mumbled.

"It wouldn't surprise me in the least."

Jórunn, the artist, hadn't laughed. She asked me what there was to spy on.

"He had to watch the American radar station on Heiðarfjall," I explained to them both.

"Because of the toxic waste, I'm sure," presumed Hafdís.

"Toxic waste?" Jórunn's eyebrows shot up.

Hafdís nodded vehemently. "It's still up there! They've been dealing with it in Þórshöfn for years already."

"Where is this mountain?" asked Jórunn.

"On Langanes," I answered.

"Kalmann is right. The Americans probably dumped the fluid they were using for developing the radar films into a trench. And it's still polluting the groundwater now."

"Do people still live out there?"

"Aunt Telma!" I said.

"And the Brimnes brothers," added Hafdís. "They wanted to set up a salmon farm at the foot of the mountain. It's thanks to them that we found out the water is polluted."

Now a voice thundered across to us from the bar. Siggi joined in the conversation at the top of his voice, as though he could no longer hold back: "It was common knowledge even when the Yanks were still on the mountain!" Hafdís and Jórunn turned their heads. Siggi continued: "My uncle used to drive transports for the navy, after the radar station was handed over to them by the air force. Fuel and goods and so on. You know?"

"No," said Hafdís, winking at me.

"Oh yes! And they told him to stay away from the landfill site. Hands off! That's what they said to him." Siggi grabbed his beer, slipped elegantly down from the bar stool and strolled jauntily across the restaurant. "Is this seat free?" He sat down with us, even though Hafdís, who was now sitting bolt upright, hadn't actually answered his question. But he was already at our table, elbows propped on it, beer glass in front of him, as though he had been here the entire time.

Hafdís didn't object. "I thought the Americans were taken to court over it," she said.

Siggi looked at her with feigned tiredness. "Do you really think you can just take the biggest military power in the world to court? They weren't born yesterday. We idiots signed a contract in the year dot!"

"Who do you mean by *we*?" asked Jórunn. She fixed Siggi with her tiny eyes.

"Well, *we*, the Icelandic people! Our foreign minister. In our name. He signed it, the blithering fool. How someone can be so smart in one field and clueless in everything else is beyond me!"

"So what did it say, this contract?"

Siggi cleared his throat theatrically. "The government of the Republic of Iceland blah blah hereby relinquishes in the name of all Icelandic state idiots blah blah any claims against the United States of America on the grounds of damage to persons or property blah blah, forever and ever, amen!"

Hafdís clicked her tongue. "I'm sure you can appeal that kind of contract nowadays."

"At least we summoned the courage to ask the American government what was actually disposed of up there."

"And?"

"Top secret! No comment," I said in English.

Hafdís shook her head and reached for her wine glass. "Awful."

"And the salmon farm?" Jórunn asked.

"Our own food safety authority closed it down. But hold onto your hats, because here comes the worst part!" Siggi took a long gulp from his beer glass, leaving a tiny amount. "Our environment ministry investigated the waters themselves and came to the glorious conclusion that they're not that badly polluted. On the contrary. The other waste sites in Iceland are even worse. But the stupid thing is that the Yanks' landfill isn't right by the sea, as ours usually are, but on a mountain."

"Ooooh!" Hafdís put down her glass and massaged her temples as though her head had started pounding. "We're not one jot better!"

Siggi waved his hand dismissively. "The ocean swallows everything."

Jórunn was confused. "So is the water polluted or not?"

"Well!" Siggi raised his shoulders and spread out his arms. "That depends on which study you choose to believe. The University of Iceland did one too and definitely established the presence of pollution."

"Kalli Kaliber!"

I jumped to my feet.

Óttar placed my plate with hamburger, fries and cocktail sauce on the bar. "Shall I bring it over to you?"

"No!" I ran away from the table.

"Bon appétit!" Hafdís called after me, laughing.

Óttar fished a few ice cubes out of the container with his bare hands and let them tumble down into a glass with a chinking sound. He asked whether I'd been fed properly by the Yanks. He poured cola into the glass, right to the brim, but because I couldn't immediately answer, having just bitten into the hamburger, I shook my head.

"Óttar!" Siggi waved his empty beer glass in the air. He was still sitting with the women. "Refill please! And the same again for the two women." When it came to money, Siggi was what you would call free-handed. "Misty Mountain!" I heard him boom. "More like *Windy* Mountain. At two hundred and sixty metres, you've got Arctic conditions. It didn't just blow away all the radar junk, it even swept the cars off the mountain!"

The two women now seemed to have lost interest in Siggi's stories; they quickly drank down the wine he had bought them and left the hotel restaurant even before I had cleared my plate. They left Siggi alone at the table. He had eaten the whole bowl of peanuts and was lost in his thoughts, shaking his head from time to time. "Misty Mountain," I heard him mumble. "Misty goddamn Mountain."

21
HALLDÓR

A clinking sound woke me. I was still lying on the sofa, so I must have fallen asleep in front of the TV after having the hamburger in the Klakabar.

Again I heard the clinking. It was coming from outside. The weather had turned and it was warmer; the icicles on the roofs were melting and falling to the floor.

With a sigh, I sank back down onto the sofa. There was a soap opera on TV that I didn't like but I watched it anyway, because these two sisters were in love with the same man, which led to an argument, as I had suspected it would. It was afternoon before I got properly dressed and went outside. The roads were hazardous. I had to walk through the village with small steps, placing one foot carefully in front of the other so as not to land on my behind, and because I had put on the cowboy hat and pinned the star to my chest, I had to be extra careful, because a sheriff can't make a fool of himself.

The thermometer at the disused gas station was showing six degrees, which explained why the icy roads were so slippery. This was when the cars' studded tyres came into their own. The sun had just set, so I had missed it once again. I hadn't set eyes on it in days.

On my way to the store, I didn't run into a single pedestrian, which didn't surprise me, because no one wants to break a leg, wrist or skull. Walking is dangerous. Kata raced past me in her old Mitsubishi and gave me a nod. She had her little dog Al Capone on her lap, and he spotted me too and barked in greeting, but I couldn't hear him because the car window was shut.

Bragi was standing by his house in a long dressing gown, holding a steaming cup of coffee in his hand. He had combed back his damp hair. When he noticed me, he raised his cup, toasting me. "You're back!" he established, and stared after me for a long while.

Kata passed me again in her old Mitsubishi, but this time she didn't pay any attention to me, and Al Capone simply looked at me with his dog eyes.

There were three cars in front of the village store: Elínborg's Nissan Pixo, Halldór's red pickup truck and the rusty Toyota Tercel from the Hólmaendar farm. So I immediately knew who was inside. The Pixo was humming contentedly, because Elínborg never turns off the engine when she goes shopping.

Inside, Yrsa was standing at the counter like always, keying in prices. Three young tourists, whose car I hadn't seen outside – so they must have come on foot – had put some groceries on the short conveyor belt and were waiting patiently until Yrsa finished. The conveyor belt didn't move a centimetre; it had never worked, which wasn't a problem, because it was so short Yrsa only needed to stretch out her arm to reach things. But she was scrunching up her nose, which meant she was stressed. No one likes it when everyone goes shopping at the same time. That's why I can't understand why people want to live in Reykjavík, where you do nothing all day long but queue or get stuck in traffic.

Elínborg was chatting with Þóra by the canned goods. I really liked the Hólmaendar sheep farmer, even though we rarely saw her. I liked her husband, Magnús Magnússon, even more. I used to get the horsemeat for the shark bait from him. Þóra greeted me happily, and Elínborg turned towards me and made a face as though she had caught me shoplifting. Halldór pulled his red head out of the freezer cabinet and looked at me questioningly, as though I had said something important. And yet I hadn't even opened my mouth.

"There he is, our American TV star!" cried Elínborg.

Now the three tourists at the checkout looked at me too, not least because Yrsa had stopped keying in the prices and was holding up a packet of spaghetti as though frozen to the spot. Most women can do two things at once. But not Yrsa.

The tourists were three young men, all of them tanned and black-haired. Spaniards, perhaps. I was surprised to see tourists back in Raufarhöfn already despite the stupid pandemic, but Óttar had once said there would always be tourists, regardless of what was happening in this world. Even if a volcano erupts, they still come running. Right now, he said, trendy locations were the ones without any Covid restrictions or where the population density was low and you could move around freely, in other words places like Raufarhöfn.

"Wasn't it dangerous over there in Washington?" Þóra wanted to know.

"It was," I said. "Very dangerous."

"Were you also inside the —"

"No, I waited outside until the FBI sent me home."

"That's how it is when the fascists are in power," grunted Elínborg. "Did you see him, at least?"

"My father?"

"No, the president, of course!"

"Oh, him, yes, I did."

175

Yrsa's jaw dropped. "Impressive!" she said, holding the pack of spaghetti higher up in the air.

"Our Kalmann is probably the first person from Raufarhöfn to see an American president in real life!" presumed Þóra.

"Agent Orange!" cried Halldór. Nothing more.

"The Americans will miss him soon enough," Elínborg replied.

"Bandits, the lot of them, regardless which party they belong to," said Halldór. He stared at me across the shelves. "Why don't you go out to sea any more?"

"Let him tell us about his trip!" called Elínborg, but I didn't want to talk about my US adventure yet again, and Halldór had asked me a question, after all, so I said I didn't have time to go out to sea, because I had to solve a murder.

"That's our Kalmann!" cried Þóra delightedly.

"Was it the polar bear again?" asked Elínborg, with a quick, dry laugh.

"No chance."

"So who was murdered this time?"

"Grandfather," I said, adding a "probably" to be on the safe side.

"Murdered?"

"He was a commie and spy," I explained.

"Of course," said Elínborg. "A proper James Bond, our Óðinn."

"No, not a James Bond," I murmured.

Halldór came over to join us. In his shopping basket were blueberry Skyr, SS sausages and frozen cauliflower. "A person doesn't get murdered just for being a communist," he said. "Though it does happen the other way round. Then it's a one-way ticket to a labour camp."

"In the end, these criminals all kill themselves," Elínborg interjected.

"Hitler, yes," commented Halldór. "He shot himself. Lenin and Stalin died of natural causes, heart attacks."

"Sorry, but can we pay?" asked one of the tourists, and Yrsa looked at him, wrinkling her nose, pondered the question and eventually tapped in the price for the spaghetti. The tourist spoke up again. "You already did the spaghetti." He said it in English, but it sounded like Italian.

"What?"

"The packet in your hand!" I said, coming to the tourists' aid. "You've already keyed in the *spaghetti*!"

Yrsa started over. With everything. The tourists sneaked glances at me.

"But what makes you think old Óðinn was murdered?" enquired Elínborg, as always asking the questions nobody wants to answer.

"I don't know," I mumbled, and fell silent, because the thing about the autopsy that hadn't been done was somehow difficult to explain.

"Well, sure," Elínborg said thoughtfully. "Your grandfather certainly wouldn't have won a popularity contest back in the day."

"Do we have one here?" I asked, astonished.

"It's just an expression," Þóra explained, but I still pondered over who would win a popularity contest in Raufarhöfn if there was one. Probably Hafdís. Or me.

Halldór said, "If anyone had wanted to kill old Óðinn, then I'd guess Róbert, but he's not around any more."

"Don't forget Stebbi Senior!" said Þóra, laughing and then waving her hand dismissively as if she hadn't intended to mention him.

177

"No one's seen him in ages," said Elínborg, although everyone already knew that – everyone, that is, except the tourists. They were now pulling coins out of their wallets and inspecting each one as if they wanted one last look at the treasures before handing them over. Yrsa cupped her hands, resting her elbows on the conveyor belt.

"Why would Róbert have wanted to kill my grandfather?" I asked. I knew they had never liked one another, but that wasn't a reason to kill someone. Was it?

Halldór looked at me with a frown. "The thing with the golf course got pretty serious. Óðinn used to have his drying hut over there, but you were still a baby back then, so you didn't even know about it."

"Was the drying shed on the golf course then?"

"No, next to it. Róbert had it moved."

Now Þóra joined in: "Wasn't that about the access road, though? I thought it had to be widened so Róbert's friends could drive there in their fancy cars."

"Bullshit!" You could see by looking at Halldór that he was getting bored of the discussion. "It had to be widened so the snow plough could get through."

"But who plays golf in winter?"

Halldór said that he didn't make the laws. That every street has a minimum width, that's just how it is. In any case, Róbert and Grandfather had had a bit of a rumpus, that was the key point.

"That's putting it mildly," Elínborg called out. "Róbert came away with a bite wound. He had to go straight to the doctor to get a rabies shot, just imagine!"

"You don't have to remind me." Halldór gnashed his teeth. "I drove him there."

"The whole village should get a rabies shot," said Þóra,

only in jest, but Elínborg didn't find it funny in the slightest and suddenly started talking about Covid, I've no idea why, but she thought getting everyone vaccinated was a terrible idea, the consequences would be catastrophic, and she also said something about communism, but no one reacted.

"Not enough," said Yrsa loudly and clearly once she had counted out the Italians' coins. She handed the coins back.

The tourists pulled out a banknote in despair and grimaced when Yrsa gave them a handful of coins as change. *Now* they had enough coins to pay for their groceries. But they had already done that.

Elínborg and Þóra were still standing by the canned goods when I left the store empty-handed. I didn't need anything; after all, I had enough Cocoa Puffs and butter cookies at home. The three tourists headed off towards the Hotel Arctica, holding their shopping bags outstretched at their sides to help keep their balance on the icy street. It was almost dark by now.

"Kalli!" Halldór opened the door of his red pickup truck and waved me over. "Come on, I'll drive you home!"

I clambered into the passenger seat next to him, Halldór's shopping bags between my feet, and I wanted to say something, but nothing occurred to me.

"Make sure you don't tread on my eggs!"

Halldór turned the truck on the slippery parking lot, and the spikes left behind scratch marks on the ice. I don't think anyone can drive as well as he can. After all, it is his job. Sometimes he has to drive the ambulance to Húsavík or Þórshöfn, even when the road is shut.

"That was quite the interrogation!" he said.

"It's just how Elínborg is," I said. "She always wants to know everything, but when you tell her something, she already knew it."

Halldór shook his head and didn't respond. He was a man of few words, but unfortunately also one who wasn't good at listening. Back when I was a child, I used to be afraid of him.

I asked anyway. "Do you know anybody who would have wanted to kill Grandfather? I mean, someone who's still alive?"

Halldór studied me thoughtfully. "Well, your grandfather didn't have many friends around here. And this Stebbi Senior was quite the character. He divorced Linda in the nineties and sold his entire quota to Dalvík. Two dozen jobs gone, just like that. He moved to Selfoss to live with his girlfriend, who was twenty-five years younger than him. He kept his villa as a summer home. But he never dared set foot in Raufarhöfn again."

"Does the villa still belong to him?" I interrupted Halldór.

"Yes, that's why it's empty. He's letting it fall to ruin, and we have to live with the rubble. Nothing but ghosts in this village."

"Perhaps *he* killed Grandfather, so he can finally come back to Raufarhöfn," I mused.

Halldór laughed tiredly. "It would be the first time someone had killed in order to live in Raufarhöfn!"

"But Grandfather was spying for the Russians! Perhaps he was killed because of that."

"Espionage?" Halldór thought for a moment. "Nonsense. That communism stuff wasn't anything serious. A long time ago, there were still proper communists in Iceland. And hard-core Nazis. But the communists became socialists, and the socialists became sofa communists, spoiled hippies, nothing more. Unbearably naive, but completely harmless." Halldór waved his hand and told me about Neskaupstaður, which apparently used to be a socialist nest and had therefore been nicknamed Little Moscow. "There, people made sure that the cooperative society and the fishing trade stayed in the village, in line with the motto 'Work for All!' Even for people like me. They built a hospital and a school, but when the speculations with the fishing quotas were allowed and heavy industry promised jobs…"

Halldór broke off mid-sentence. He must have noticed I was no longer listening, and I only understood half of what he was saying anyway. He had never talked to me this much, and that confused me. Probably he was so chatty because he felt at home inside a car, like Sæmundur inside his container. He brought the pickup to a halt in the middle of the road. You're not allowed to do that, that's the law, but because there was no traffic, it wasn't bothering anyone.

Halldór looked at me. "Why don't you talk to Lúlli Lenin?"

"Who?"

"He hasn't left his house for years now. You've probably never met him."

Even though we had almost arrived at my little house, Halldór turned the pickup around and drove back down the main road, back past the store, the gas station, the school, then steered right into a driveway and parked between two houses. Before us, in the evening shadow of the slope, a small, run-down house with peeling red paint was huddled between snow-covered rocks.

"But no one lives there!" I said in astonishment.

Halldór grinned. "I can assure you someone does!"

"But there's no light on! No one's home."

"There is a light on. Look more closely, the window to the right."

181

And there actually was a weak glimmer, probably from a bedside lamp, barely noticeable in fact, because the street lamp and the remaining daylight over the horizon were reflected in the panes, making all the windows in the house look old and dull. Suddenly I noticed a shadow moving behind the window. Slowly, admittedly but it was clearly a movement. "Something moved!" I said under my breath.

Halldór ducked. "Dammit!" he exclaimed. "The old boy spotted us."

"Who?"

"Lúlli Lenin, of course. The last commie in the village! He and your grandfather were dyed-in-the-wool comrades, pretty much until Lúlli's wife Ásrún died. Shortly after that, he had a stroke, and he never fully recovered."

We sat there motionless and continued to stare at the window, but there was no more movement.

"But how can he survive if he never leaves the house?"

"Yrsa brings him something to eat every few days. I mean, he doesn't need much. Liver pâté. Oats and coffee."

I thought of Grandfather, who also hadn't wanted to eat much in his final days.

Halldór looked at me. "Go knock on the door, Kalmann! If there's anyone who can tell you about your grandfather, it's Lúlli Lenin."

"Okay," I said, and put the plan off to another day.

"Well, go on then!"

"What, now?"

"Of course!" Halldór looked back at the window and squinted. "He's watching us, he's waiting for you. Ask him when he's got time to talk. I'll wait here in the car."

*

The wet snow in front of the dark house squelched beneath the soles of my shoes. No one had shovelled it away, which is why the house looked uninhabited. I knocked on the door and let a few seconds pass, but nothing happened. Halldór signalled to me to knock harder. So I pounded on the door. My heart pounded too, and I really wanted to get back in the pickup, but at that moment the door opened a crack, and the crack was even blacker than the evening sky above me. And yet I was sure someone was there. I could hear him breathing.

"What do you want?" A high voice, a croaky voice. It belonged to an old man who didn't like opening his mouth.

"Good morning," I said. "I'm —"

"Kalmann, it's about time!" the old man interrupted me and opened the door a little wider so that we were standing opposite one another, though I could only see half of him. Because the distant street lamp was the only source of light, the old man's face shimmered as grey as the old ice on the street. He had a grey, bushy beard concealing his mouth. There were no hairs left on his head, though, just dark flecks, like craters on the moon.

"You know me?" I asked, stunned.

"Of course I know Óðinn's retarded grandson. I mean, you've been roaming all over the village for years in your silly hat, always on your way somewhere but never arriving, and once you clambered up the slope behind my house and trampled my potatoes!" The old man croaked out the words without his mouth moving behind his beard. He should have been on TV with a talking puppet, like one of those old-time entertainers.

"Oh."

"Yes, that's what I said too: Oh. Now he's even traipsing over my potatoes!"

"I'm sorry."

The old man waved his hand sullenly. "It was a while ago now. Nothing grows here anyway. Why did it take you so long to come?"

I didn't know. So I said that.

"Well, you're here now. And who's that waiting in the car?"

"Halldór," I said.

"Halldór." The old man wasn't happy about that either. "Too lazy to clear the snow up to my house!"

Now I understood why Halldór hadn't wanted to get out of the car.

"I'm sure you want to know what your grandfather and I got up to back in the day, don't you?"

I nodded and was about to say something, but then I noticed a black rivulet dripping out of Lúlli Lenin's nose onto his beard. It looked like blood, but stickier, blacker, as though darkness was flowing out of his nose. "Your nose!" I said, pointing my finger at his face.

"Hmm," muttered the old man, pulling out a handkerchief covered in black stains and wiping his beard with it.

I ventured a question: "Why didn't you come to Grandfather's funeral?"

Lúlli Lenin put away the handkerchief. Something metallic banged against the door. Tock. "I'll see the old mule soon enough, don't you worry. He'll be coming for me."

"Who's coming for you?"

"And if you're not careful, he'll fetch you too!"

I suddenly felt cold. "Do you mean Grandfather?"

"Of course not. Do you really think Óðinn just happened to die?"

"Actually I don't. Nói thinks he was murdered."

"He's right, this Nói fellow." The old man gave a tired

sigh. "Listen here, boy. I'll tell you everything, but not now. I'm missing the radio news because of you. Come tomorrow morning at twenty past ten, after the weather forecast. Bring a snow shovel. You can shovel my walk when the obituaries are read at eleven."

When Lúlli Lenin took a step backwards, I saw the barrel of his shotgun. The door slammed shut in front of my nose and was illuminated once again by the street lamp, as though a crevice in the earth had closed right before my eyes.

"Well?"

I had never known Halldór to be in such a good mood, and that's why I didn't feel so afraid any more. He put the truck in reverse and backed speedily towards the main road as though we were in a getaway car!

"So what did the old guy say?"

"That you're too lazy to clear the snow right up to his house," I told him, and that I had therefore been assigned the task of shovelling the snow tomorrow.

"Ha!" Halldór laughed. "The old guy doesn't even leave his house any more! So why should I shovel —"

Suddenly everything became blindingly bright and a car came to a halt centimetres from us. It had come along the main road and would have crashed into the side of us had the driver not slammed on the brakes. The spikes scratched loudly on the icy street. Halldór quickly put the truck into first gear, stepped on the gas and took his foot off the clutch so quickly that the wheels hissed on the ice, accompanied by the scream of the engine. We slid back into the driveway.

"Goddammit!" cursed Halldór, slamming on the brakes so we didn't crash into Lúlli Lenin's house. "You distracted me!" He stared intently into the rear-view mirror and waited.

The other car just stood there on the road. It didn't even beep. It was a white jeep, a rental, as I could tell from my experience with Ingimar, but because it was night-time already, I couldn't make out whether it perhaps belonged to the three Italian tourists I'd seen in the store.

"Come on then, drive on!" shouted Halldór, as though the Italians in the rental car could hear him. "No harm done!"

After a few more uncomfortable seconds, the white jeep finally set into motion, rumbling slowly past behind us and disappearing into the bottomless darkness of the winter's night, its red rear lights like the glowing eyes of a monster.

I shuddered. An oppressive feeling overcame me, as though I had come face to face with something dangerous, like back when the polar bear had let out its throaty cry on the Melrakkaslétta.

"Damn tourists. You can't escape them, even during a pandemic!"

Muttering away, Halldór drove back onto the main road, but this time more carefully. Probably he was feeling a little shocked too. I wondered whether he perhaps wasn't the best driver in the world after all – but for sure he was the best driver in Raufarhöfn.

As we slowly put some distance between us and the scene of the almost-accident, I remembered the old man. "Lúlli Lenin also thinks Grandfather was killed."

"That nincompoop," said Halldór, probably glad to be distracted from thinking about the white rental car.

"His nose was bleeding, but it wasn't blood."

"Snuff tobacco! It was always like that with him. It drips out of his nose. Disgusting."

"Snuff tobacco," I echoed, and was relieved and exhausted when Halldór dropped me off in front of my little house.

"Don't do anything silly now!" he said before he drove away.

"No reason to worry," I murmured, concentrating on getting myself inside. For the first time in my entire life, I wondered if I should lock the door.

22

LÚLLI LENIN

I slept badly. I felt like a white ptarmigan in the spring once the snow has melted away. During the night I had to pee several times; I had probably drunk too much Coca-Cola. I'd also gone to bed far too late, because I'd spent ages chatting with Nói. He had scoured the internet for the old communist, but had only found out that Lúlli Lenin's real name was Lúðvík Birgisson, that he'd been widowed for over thirty years, and that he was a few years younger than my grandfather. Nói was convinced they were all spies, including my great-aunt Telma, and that they had perhaps even killed people for the Russians. He called them the Melrakkaslétta KGB, and suspected that Róbert McKenzie had also been involved in some way. I was to remember to ask Lúlli Lenin about Róbert's disappearance, he said. My only response was to nod; I didn't tell Nói that Róbert McKenzie's disappearance had absolutely nothing to do with it.

Then he had turned his attention back to the abbreviation H-2, the American radar station on Heiðarfjall mountain, and he'd even found the University of Reykjavík's report on all the pollution, but he might as well have been speaking in Chinese, because I didn't understand a word.

Over a bowl of Cocoa Puffs, I ran through the previous day in my mind, almost forgetting to eat in the process. A strange feeling plagued me, as though I were close to solving the puzzle even though I didn't know exactly what the puzzle was.

Around ten o'clock, when it was almost light, I shouldered a snow shovel and marched off, and because I arrived at Lúlli Lenin's house, previously believed abandoned, five minutes early, I began to shovel the walk, but I quickly got tired, because the snow was wet and heavy and collapsed in on itself, and that's why I waited in front of the door until it was precisely twenty past ten, down to the second.

I pressed my ear against the door, held my breath and listened. The radio presenter's voice was muffled but audible. I could even understand what was being said, but because it wasn't a weather report or an obituary, which Lúlli Lenin seemed to really like listening to, I pounded on the door. No one answered, and by now it was already twenty-two minutes past ten, so I carefully tried the handle and was surprised to find that the door simply opened.

Yesterday's blackness inside the house had slunk away into the drawers and cupboards, but it was still gloomy. The radio presenter's voice droned through the hallway, talking about a composer who had died on this day one hundred years ago.

"Hello!" I cried. "Are you home, Lúlli Lenin? Hello!"

No answer.

The composer had died unexpectedly, because he might have been poisoned, but this wasn't something that could have been confirmed back then.

I found a light switch and flicked it on, looked around the hallway, my gaze sweeping over the black-flecked brown carpet, the dark sideboard, the yellowed newspapers, the old telephone on the wall, the closet, the dusty clothes hangers, the fur coat, the faded photographs. The reddish glass shade on the ceiling light bathed everything in a matt, warm glow. The house interior was old and dusty, time-worn and stuffy. Someone had stayed between these walls for decades, and it smelled like it too; liver pâté and cold coffee, stale air and burned hair. At some point, possibly thirty years ago, time had come to a standstill.

"Lúlli Lenin?" Still no answer.

The composer had been in love with a man but had married a woman, because back then two men weren't allowed to love one another. Maybe the composer hadn't been poisoned after all but instead had died of heartache. Because the radio presenter's voice was so loud, though, I couldn't think about that, there simply wasn't enough space in my head. What's more, the voice was coming from two sides: from the lounge and the kitchen. So there must have been two radios on.

First I turned the radio in the kitchen off, and when I turned around and looked through the kitchen door into the lounge, I saw the second radio, on a little table whose only purpose was to hold it. Then I noticed the old man's slippers. And inside the slippers were feet.

I made my way over, taking tiny steps, and put my hand instinctively towards my hip, where my Mauser used to be, but touched only emptiness. My heart was pounding, and I took one last step.

Well. And then I saw him. He was sitting there slackly in the armchair, Lúlli Lenin, staring at me with an empty gaze. The shotgun lay in his lap, his finger still on the trigger, and this black mass clung to his beard, a mixture of snuff tobacco and snot, and in the middle of his forehead gaped a small hole just about big enough to poke a finger into. The blood that had seeped alongside his nose into the thicket of his beard was no longer glistening, it was almost dry. His pullover was saturated too, I noticed now, right where I presumed Lúlli Lenin's heart was. Heart shot.

Sometimes I have a mental blackout. That's why I don't know how long I stood there staring into the hole, into Lúlli Lenin's skull, as though I was searching for answers in it.

A new radio presenter tore me out of my rigid state, announcing that she was about to read the death notices, which is why I wondered whether the presenter would already mention his demise, but that was nonsense of course, it doesn't happen that quickly, somebody would have had to inform the radio station that Lúlli Lenin was dead. Somebody like me. Probably no one else knew besides me – me and the person who had made the small holes in the old man's head and heart. It was, of course, completely impossible that Lúlli had killed himself; he was still holding his shotgun in his hands, after all, and if he had shot himself in the head there wouldn't have been much left of it.

So who had made the two holes? Was I perhaps not even alone in the house?

I decided I'd seen enough, said "bless", turned around and ran outside without turning off the lounge radio, which was now announcing the names of the recently deceased and their surviving family.

The snow was higher in the shelter of the slope, as is usually the case. The sunbeams played with the parched lupins at the upper edge of the rise and petered out towards the sea. There wasn't a soul to be seen. The children were surely at school, the store didn't open until the afternoon today, and the harbour was quite a distance from Lúlli Lenin's house.

For a long while I stood there in the snow, because it wouldn't have been right to go home and act as though it were a completely normal day.

Sometimes I get annoyed about my head. It doesn't always function properly. I was seriously asking myself whether it would be simplest to feed Lúlli Lenin to the sharks. Because then I wouldn't need to tell anyone that I had found him dead. And if Halldór had asked me about him, I could have said Lúlli Lenin wasn't there, which in a way would have been true; not completely there *in spirit*. But just the thought of all the work involved, the preparation of the bait pieces and the secret boat journeys, was very tiring.

Should I ring 112? Should I inform Yrsa that she didn't need to bring Lúlli Lenin any more food supplies?

I stared indecisively at the front door and asked myself what Grandfather would have done. Maybe he would have left the old man sitting there in his armchair and gone home, fished some singed sheepshead out of the cooking pot, peeled off the thin layer of flesh with a knife and put it in his mouth. Maybe, while he was chewing, it would have occurred to him what he had to do. But for sure he wouldn't have called 112, because Lúlli Lenin was as dead as a door-nail, so even Halldór with his ambulance wouldn't have been able to help.

Sometimes, when you don't know what to do, you simply have to do something that has nothing at all to do with the thing. I spotted my snow shovel next to the entrance and decided to clear the small path to the front door. After all, I'd already started to do it. And while I shovelled, a thought shot into my head: Telma! I paused. She belonged to the Melrakkaslétta KGB too! Was she in danger? So maybe 112 after all? Should I have called Birna? But what would I have said? That there was an old woman on Langanes called Telma who had spied for the Russians along with Grandfather and Lúlli Lenin and that she was going to be murdered because of it, that she was in mortal danger, perhaps even dead already? Birna wouldn't believe me.

Was Telma even still alive?

I propped the snow shovel against the wall of the house, pulled out my phone and tried to call her. But her phone was turned off or the battery was dead. I kept reaching the same automatic voice, so I couldn't warn her. I repeated the process about five times, all in vain.

Never in my entire life had I had so many thoughts all at the same time. It felt like a firework. When your head explodes and the fish soup spills over, it's unpleasant. So I closed my eyes, counted backwards from ten to zero and thought about Grandfather. I thought about the past, the wide skies over the Slétta, the clouds that sometimes looked like sheep, sometimes like broad paint stripes or like a giant soup lid, I thought about the sea, about us together on the boat, crowded into the small deckhouse. Grandfather looking contentedly out over the water, lost in thought and steering straight for the endless horizon, which never came closer, regardless of how far out we went, because that's how horizons are. Unreachable. Always.

Suddenly I missed Grandfather so much it hurt. I stood there with my head hanging and shoulders drooping, missing the smell of petrol and wet wood, the warmth and noise of the engine. I used to like looking at Grandfather's hands, because they were so completely different, bigger than mine or my mother's. Hard, calloused, indestructible. These hands didn't need gloves.

"Grandfather," I murmured, "what should I do?"

He would probably have pondered the question until he found an answer, which sometimes took a long time. But then he would have looked at me – and now I knew what I had to do.

23

PETRA

I left Lúlli Lenin where he was, dead in his armchair, and headed off, goose-stepping through the village –

"Kalmann!"

– because I wanted to go down to the harbour –

"Hello! Kalmann?"

– knowing exactly what I had to do.

"Kalmann, stop right there, for the love of Heimdall!"

I gave a start and turned around. The village poet Bragi had tried to stop me, he was even running after me and therefore out of breath. After all, he wasn't young any more, and hadn't been for years. He was wearing an anorak and a white captain's cap with a black visor and a shimmering golden anchor. Perhaps the hat was real. His hands were tucked inside leather gloves, so I couldn't see what colour his fingernails were today.

"I'm busy," I said.

"Wait! Hell, whenever Kalmann walks past without noticing me, there's reason to worry."

"There really is!"

"Where are you going?"

"To the harbour. Bless." I turned around and walked on.

"Could I at least accompany you?"

I groaned up at the sky, but stood still and waited until he had caught up. Then I quickened my steps so that Bragi would struggle to keep pace.

"Are you. Going. To your hall?" He almost didn't have enough breath for the question. He also had to be damn careful not to slip on the wet but still icy road.

"No comment."

"Arc you. Going. Out to sea?"

"Perhaps."

"What, today? Now? Alone? Have you. Seen. The sea yet?"

I didn't answer, having already revealed too much. "I'm not saying another word!" I informed Bragi, because then he could save himself all the questions and concentrate better on breathing.

Harbour master Sæmundur must have spotted us, because he had stepped out of his container and was squinting sleepily in the low-lying winter sun. His clothes were anything but wintry; he was in jogging bottoms and a T-shirt, so he wouldn't last long out here.

"Sæmundur!" cried Bragi with relief. "I think Kalmann wants to go out to sea. That can't be a good idea, can it?"

Sæmundur looked up at the sky, inhaled deeply and let his gaze sweep across the estuary. "Well," he said. "Why not? The wind is gentle and steady, blowing from the north-east, that's why it's got colder again, and it'll probably stay like this for the next few hours. But why do you want to go out, Kalli minn? You haven't laid any lines."

I came to a halt. I hadn't thought about that. Sæmundur wouldn't let me go. He wasn't allowed to. He was the harbour master, after all. I needed an escort.

"I just want to go out. Bragi can accompany me," I said. "Is that forbidden?"

"No, not technically speaking." Sæmundur rubbed his hairy forearms. It seemed he was getting cold now. He glanced at Bragi and shrugged. "What do you think?"

"No winter storm on the cards?" Bragi asked.

"Just wind and sun, and temperatures around freezing. Siggi and Jújú are out too, up in Sléttugrunn."

"I'll only go out a little," I lied. "We'll be back in an hour or two." Lying is allowed if you do it to protect someone.

"Well, have fun then!" Sæmundur said. "But don't stay out too long, okay? Dusk sets in around three."

I jumped onto Petra to warm up her engine, and called to Bragi to untie the ropes. Now I was happy to have him with me, because I had never gone out alone to where I wanted to go today.

Bragi tossed the lines onto the boat and hopped on behind them. His movements seemed practised and he didn't fall, and that's why I remembered that during the herring boom he had gone out to sea like almost everyone up here. He was grinning broadly.

I knew the feeling. Going out to sea is like leaving the hotel after a long quarantine. You feel relieved and happy. You want to whoop for joy and sing.

Bragi joined me in the little deckhouse, took off my cowboy hat and put his captain's hat on me. "Right then, Captain. Where are we headed?"

"To the south." I ground my teeth, tore the captain's hat off my head, pressed it against Bragi's chest and put the cowboy hat back on.

"Fine," said Bragi, turning his hat over in his hands in embarrassment. "To the south. Like migrating birds. With the north wind on our backs."

We chugged out of the harbour. The village glided past to starboard, the lighthouse port side. I directed Petra towards the south-east, the headland of Melrakkanes with its lighthouse in my sights, planning to steer the boat past it, so staying near the coast initially, in order to then make a small change in course and head straight to Heiðarfjall, right across the Þistilfjord.

"Listen, Kalmann. You don't have to tell me why you so urgently want to go out to sea. But I am your ship's poet now, and I'd like to know where we're going and what the aim of the mission is. Or when we're going back."

"Ship's poet? Does that job really exist?" Bragi was probably pulling my leg, but I didn't know all the ranks. After all, I had only ever been out on this little fishing boat, never on a big trawler.

"Cradle me / oh soft embrace / of your white-crested wave / Love me / I lie untraced / in your deep, wet grave."

"Langanes," I murmured, because my ship's poet's poem had depressed me.

"What's on Langanes?"

I hesitated. "Telma."

"Your great-aunt?"

"You know her?"

"Naturally. From way back. I talked to her at the funeral. An unusual woman, you have to admit. And she's never been married, even though there are plenty of old bachelors in Þórshöfn."

Of course he knew her. Everyone knows more than I do. Because I'm such an idiot. That's just how it is. And that's why I would stay quiet from now on, because I had to be careful not to reveal any more details.

"So you want to go to Langanes," Bragi continued. "Okay. Do you know how long it will take us to get there?"

"No idea." It was a good question.

"Do you have a map, Captain?"

"Of course!"

Bragi measured the distance between Raufarhöfn and Langanes. "My boy! Forty kilometres! That's over twenty nautical miles, isn't it? That'll take forever! How quickly does this old box go anyway?"

"Petra does eight knots."

Bragi thought for a while. "Kalmann, it'll take between two and three hours to get there!"

"Correctamundo!"

"Do you even have a full tank?"

I looked at the fuel gauge in shock. "It's full!" I cried in relief.

"We could have taken my car. Then we would've got there much quicker!"

"I don't care," I said, because I didn't want to turn around. I also knew from experience that Bragi wasn't a very good driver. He always drove very slowly and usually far across the line painted in the middle of the road.

Bragi sighed. "Okay then. Does this Petra of yours at least have a comfortable cabin?"

"Yes," I said, even though I actually found it much more comfortable in the little deckhouse, where you could also see something of the surroundings. "Down there it's dark and narrow and you bang your head on the ceiling or the door frame if you're not careful."

"Put autopilot on, then we can make ourselves comfortable downstairs and play cards if you have any with you."

"Grandfather said I'm not allowed to do that."

"Oh really? So he never used autopilot?"

"He did. But there were two of us then."

"There are two of us now!"

I thought about it, but came to the conclusion that it had always served me well to follow Grandfather's advice.

Once, back when I was still a little boy, Grandfather had let Petra chug back to Raufarhöfn with two magnificent grey sharks in tow, and said he'd sit in the cabin, just for a little while, and for me to make sure we stayed on course.

As we came closer to the shore, I went down for a quick look and there he lay, arms outstretched, upper body on the small integrated table. He was snoring. And I couldn't wake him. So I went back up, sat in the deckhouse and watched the cormorants and gulls on the islet in the strait, watched as Petra glided past the black cliffs and, a short while later, ran aground on the stony beach at Bakki, and forcefully too, as though she were one of those old row-boats that used to be pulled up onto the beach, as easily as that, to unload the cargo. I almost crashed through the window, and Grandfather staggered up into the daylight with a cut on his head, cursing and stammering, and then word spread, even though it wasn't so bad, because Petra came away from it with just a few scratches. But people made fun of us, and Grandfather kept his distance from the harbour for a while, taking long hikes across the Melrakkaslétta and talking to himself.

In hindsight, it was a good thing, because after that Grandfather always had to blow into this thing for harbour master Sæmundur. It meant he wasn't allowed to drink Brennivín any more, which back then we used to get from the moonshiners in the valleys, who from then on had to get their hákarl somewhere else.

"No autopilot!" I said. "We might fall asleep and let the boat head straight for the cliffs. It happens more often than you'd think!"

"Kalmann, do you have a good answer to every question?" Bragi asked.

"No," I said, and Bragi said that was a good answer too. After pausing to think, he added: "But I don't understand why we need to visit Telma so urgently. Can you please explain that to me?"

I almost opened my mouth to reply, but then Bragi's phone rang. It was Sæmundur, I could tell straight away, because the phone volume was set very loud. He wanted to know if we were okay, why I hadn't switched on the radio, and where in God's name we were headed.

"No reason to worry!" Bragi said, giving me a wink. "We're heading towards Langanes, you can see that yourself. A family visit. Seems urgent... okay. I'll pass that on to the captain."

Bragi put away the phone and reported that I wasn't to steer too close to the Melrakkanes lighthouse, but a smidgen further east. That because of the crosswind we had driftage.

I loaded the course, and after that we were silent for a long while. The snowy landscape drifted past, white and wide, the sky streaked with cirrus clouds, the sea deep blue, almost black actually. Ahead of us on the horizon, the flat silhouette of Langanes appeared. Soon the winter sun hung so low that, as we went further eastwards, it disappeared behind the Selfjöll rise and remained hidden. Its faint light was cast from below on the ever-increasing blanket of cloud that was making its way like a giant UFO across the Melrakkaslétta and out to sea. The sky's cool colour gave way to a warm, almost otherworldly light that hovered in the air as though you could touch it. The sea now turned completely black, but the waves gave off a warm glow which, although it looked beautiful, signalled clearly that the weather was about to turn.

If you go out to the sea in winter, it's better not to have any weather. At least we had the wind diagonally behind us, and so we made good progress.

"So do you know where Telma lives? She's not in Þórshöfn itself, is she?"

"She lives at the foot of Heiðarfjall. There's a jetty there too."

"Where the trading post used to be?"

"I think so."

"So have we been invited?"

I shrugged. "She's not answering her phone."

"Well, let's just drop by then," Bragi murmured. He seemed a little despondent. "We'll survive, I'm sure."

The Melrakkanes lighthouse drifted past us and the sea widened. The coast retreated into the distance.

"I need some fresh air," Bragi said, going outside, gripping onto the deckhouse with one hand, unbuttoning his trousers with the other and peeing over the railing – or trying to, at least, because the wind complicated things. Once Bragi had relieved himself, he gazed at the lighthouse for a while, then came back inside, damp patches on his trousers. He took off his leather gloves and shoved them into the pockets of his anorak. His fingernails were painted red. "Damn wind," he said. "It's about to turn, I can smell it. Maybe even snow. Listen, Kalmann. Hadn't we better turn back?"

I shook my head. "Telma might be in danger."

"Well I never! Why?"

"Nói thinks Grandfather was murdered, and Lúlli Lenin —"

"Who's Nói?"

"My best friend. He's helping me solve the murder."

"Murder. Of course." Bragi sounded disbelieving, and I regretted having said anything.

"It doesn't matter," I mumbled.

"No, my dear boy. Now you have to tell me what's going on here! Are we heading to see Telma purely because this

Nói fellow thinks your grandfather was murdered? And that Telma's next in line, is that the gist of it?"

"No idea."

"No idea? Kalmann. Shouldn't we call 112?"

"I called Birna, she's a proper police inspector, but she didn't believe me. Nobody believes me. And you don't either."

Bragi took a deep breath, sighed, then said very gently: "Listen, Kalmann. Do you remember the thing with Róbert? I haven't told anyone about it, just like I promised, because I think Róbert is fine where he is. We're accomplices, you and me, do you understand? I'm *also* your friend. So you can tell me anything!"

I looked at him. I hadn't realized we were friends! But he really meant it, so I told him that Grandfather, together with Telma, used to spy on the Heiðarfjall radar station for the Russians. That he had kept numerous photographs of the mountain and the radar station in our house, and that, shortly before he died, he had started to speak Russian.

"I've heard about that," Bragi said, nodding thoughtfully. "It's astonishing what the human brain's capable of."

"There's poison in the mountain," I said. "The whole mountain is polluted."

"That's common knowledge too."

"Telma didn't answer my call, so that's why we're going there."

"And you suspect she's going to be murdered too?"

"Yes. Like Lúlli Lenin."

Bragi whistled through his teeth. "Like Lúlli Lenin, would you listen to that! The things you say!" He glanced at his watch.

I swallowed down a lump in my throat and felt glad we were steadily approaching the curved Langanes peninsula, which looks like a blackbird from above. I could even make out Telma's house already.

The daylight had grown weaker now; the sky gleamed dully. The sea was green, turbulent, the waves low and wild. Petra made little hops, meaning that the sea spray sometimes splashed against the windows. The wind direction had clearly changed, and I realized there was no way we could get back home with Petra. No chance.

Bragi had been trying to call Sæmundur for a while, but he didn't have any phone signal out here, and I lied, telling him the radio wasn't working. He had no choice but to mutter a few expletives. Nonetheless, I was glad he was with me.

24

TELMA

The jetty was pretty dilapidated. I clambered onto the rotten planks, fastened Petra's bow and stern lines to the rusty bollards and wondered when a boat had last been moored here. Bragi climbed onto the jetty too, testing the planks with the tips of his shoes.

It was only about two hundred metres to my great-aunt's house; from the jetty, a dirt track led straight across the meadow, which held the visible remains of building foundations. A small settlement had once stood here, but the houses had been torn down and transported away, and wind and frost were now eating away at the foundations.

Bragi had pulled his leather gloves back on. He tugged the captain's hat lower on his face, buttoned up his anorak and stared worriedly up at the sky. "There's a storm brewing!" he called. "The weather's turning, did you notice the warm air?"

"South-easterly." I'd noticed it a while ago.

Bragi was far from happy. He suggested taking Petra across to Þórshöfn, in order to organize a ride back to Raufarhöfn should Telma not be home.

I didn't have any objections and merely nodded, because I was precisely where I wanted to be.

Telma's house stood completely alone on the hillside. It had just two neighbours: the sleeping mountain and the surging sea. The path that led across the meadow held a light covering of snow, because it was a windswept spot, you could see that at once, with no tree far and wide, and the brown grass stems that poked out of the snow were trembling.

As we got closer to the house, I noticed two cars parked behind it: a yellow Lada and a white tourist jeep, a Mazda. "Wait!" I cried, and leaving Bragi standing there on the meadow, I ran back to the jetty, climbed into the boat and fetched my flare gun, making sure it was loaded and tucking it into my waistband. I was so frustrated that I'd thrown my Mauser into the ocean back then. What an idiot! How I wished I'd brought my American father's entire arsenal of weapons back home with me, and even my father and Uncle Bucky along with them! We would have been a private militia armed to the teeth. But all I had was a simple maritime flare gun – and a ship's poet.

Bragi was waiting for me, shivering. "Telma has visitors!" He seemed relieved. He was probably hoping for a cup of coffee and a four-wheeled ride back home.

"Come on!" I said, and marched forwards.

The mountain loomed up behind the house. You couldn't see the radar station from down here, just a part of the road that led up to it. In the distance, a few kilometres away, I spotted the little church of Sauðanes, where Grandfather lay buried next to Grandmother in the cemetery. Hopefully they weren't cold.

I waited outside the house until Bragi had caught up with me, then, to his great unease, pulled out the flare gun, aimed it at the floor and opened the front door without knocking.

Warmth and silence spilled towards us. Even though I had never been in this house before, I immediately felt at home. Bragi glanced at me uncertainly and moved his lips but didn't make a sound. I signalled to him to stay quiet, because I knew from the TV how to creep into a house. So I stepped cautiously into the hallway, leaned forwards a little so I could peer through the door into the kitchen, and saw my great-aunt sitting stiff and upright at the table. She looked at me sadly and gently shook her head.

"Give me that!" said a voice in English, and right next to me, but because I had the barrel of a gun pressed up against my temple, I couldn't turn around after that. I knew who the voice belonged to, though: the American tourist to whom I'd given the tour of the Arctic Henge, the old man with the eyes of a Greenland shark. I would have liked to take a look at him, but I couldn't move. The old man must have waited for me behind the door until I'd stepped into the hallway, every inch the professional. So he wasn't a tourist at all. He was a contract killer or a secret agent. He grabbed my flare gun, stepped two paces away and waved Bragi and me further into the house with his gun.

Now I could see him properly. He still looked like an American tourist, but far less friendly now; he was bitter and tired like a Greenland shark who'd had enough after 412 years in the blackness of the deep sea.

Bragi was making strange sniffing sounds, and Telma groaned with pain.

"Come in!" said the old man. "Both of you. Sit down with Telma at the kitchen table and make yourselves comfortable." Apart from the fact that he was pointing a gun at us, it sounded very inviting.

Bragi exhaled in a strained way, which sounded like the air coming out of a tractor tyre. He made a face to match, and I almost didn't recognize him. He was shaking, and I felt afraid he was about to keel over. "Kalmann," he gasped. "What in God's name —"

"Sit down and be quiet!" the old man ordered, waving us into the kitchen with his gun.

Telma looked at us sadly. "I'm so sorry," she said, and that surprised me, because she hadn't done anything wrong. After all, we had come to save her! The old American was the one who should have been sorry – or me, because I'd fallen into his trap like the village idiot, even though I'd suspected Telma was in danger.

We sat down at the table to the left and right with Telma sandwiched between us, like at a press conference, as though we were a committee. The American definitely had some explaining to do. He stayed in the doorway and studied us, the gun pointed slackly at us. It was a Glock.

"Is he going to kill us?" breathed Bragi.

"I think so," I said.

"*Andskotans djöfulsins helvítis helvíti,*" cursed Bragi tearfully.

"Why did you dimwits even come?" whispered Telma.

While we were conversing, the American studied us mockingly.

"He killed Grandfather and Lúlli Lenin," I explained to her.

"Don't say that!" hissed Bragi. Finally he believed me.

"It's true!" the American interrupted loudly. "I knocked Lúlli off, the old bastard. One bullet between the eyes, one in the heart."

Had he understood us? Could he speak Icelandic? We exchanged glances. Telma ground out a few English words between her teeth: "You despicable monster!"

I wondered whether it was smart to be impolite to a contract killer who was pointing a Glock at you. But the old American didn't seem in the least insulted.

"I actually didn't intend to kill Lúlli," he said, defending himself. "I just wanted to pay him a visit, have a chat with him about the good old days. He was sitting there in the armchair with his loaded shotgun and seemed to have been waiting for me, said for me to give Óðinn his best. But" – the American raised his Glock apologetically – "I was quicker."

Now I understood that he must have been following me since the walk to the Arctic Henge, or perhaps even before that. How else would he have stumbled across Lúlli Lenin? And Telma! Grandfather! Had I led him directly to his victims?

"Why did you murder Grandfather?" I blurted out.

Telma grabbed my hand beneath the kitchen table, and that distracted me a little, because she was warm and her skin smooth but her grip was hard.

"Murdered?" The old man studied me thoughtfully. "Did I murder him? A good question. A philosophical question, really. Óðinn was as good as gone anyway. He didn't recognize me, he just growled at me. But then I said two words, and that was enough. Suddenly he knew exactly who I was."

"Misty Mountain," breathed Telma, and a cold shiver ran down my back.

"Misty Mountain, precisely!" The American shook his head in amusement. "Your grandfather's eyes got so wide! He stared at me open-mouthed and began to shake, and then he grabbed his chest and slumped. By God, I swear it! Maybe I did him a favour with my visit. I released him, don't you think, Kalmann?"

"Don't answer!" Telma commanded, and that's why I didn't give the American an answer, but I did ask him another question: "So why did you have to visit him?"

"You're not anywhere near as stupid as everyone says, Kalmann Óðinsson," he said, praising me. "I had assumed the old man was long dead and that he'd taken our secret with him to the grave. I was even going into retirement, leaving all of that behind me, and had other worries anyway on account of the diagnosis. But then, one cursed evening, one of those seemingly never-ending evenings so goddamn lonely you start to talk to yourself..." The American's gaze drifted off into the distance, as though he were staring into a bottomless abyss which sucked all the life out of his eyes.

I knew this look. It's the same one Greenland sharks have when they're pulled out of the water. They're not happy to finally see daylight or the sun, the blue sky. They've long since become accustomed to the darkness, and have perhaps even forgotten light exists. But when they're pulled out of the water, they know that they're dying.

"Loneliness is the worst enemy," said the old American, as though he had read my thoughts. He stared at me. "The loneliness" – he paused – "it devoured me. From the inside, do you understand?" He shook the memory away. "So I'm sitting in front of the TV and watching the news, it must be almost two years ago now, and my Glock's in my lap, I'm not even properly listening, because I've made a decision. Today I want to conquer the loneliness, this illness, blow it out of my head. The barrel of the gun between my teeth, my finger on the trigger, one final thought, and in that very moment you appear, Kalmann, my dear Kalmann, as though you were heaven-sent! Your face fills the entire screen. You stare directly into the camera and into my lounge, fearful and sullen but curious too. It's a long time since anyone looked at me like that! It's as though you've caught me in the act. And suddenly I feel ashamed, I start to shake, let the gun drop. Kalmann, you saved my life, do you understand?" The American smiled. Did he have tears in his eyes? "I turn up the volume. They're talking about Iceland, about a remote fishing village, about Raufarhöfn and its retarded village sheriff, who heroically protected the inhabitants from a polar bear attack. And then your name appears on the screen." The American chuckled in amusement. "Kalmann *fucking* Óðinsson. And this Kalmann had apparently learned how to hunt foxes and sharks from his grandfather, but the grandfather was very old and in a home." The American shook his head, grinning, and actually wiped a tear from his eye. His voice sounded broken. "I felt like I'd been hit by lightning. A gift of fate! The old man was still alive? Was he keeping our agreement? Was our secret safe? That's when I realized my time on this earth wasn't yet up! My work wasn't over yet. I'd retired too early. Well. A short while later I travelled to Iceland, after all these years. It's crazy how much has changed here! The roads are surfaced now, there are restaurants and hotels and museums everywhere, even in the small villages, I really like it here. And you, Kalmann, I quickly found you. I mean, you're a proper celebrity! And you led me to your grandfather. But I wasn't planning to confront him. I stayed in the background, went unnoticed, and was about to leave when someone said the old man had begun to speak Russian. So I didn't have any choice but to pay him a visit, you can understand that, right? I had to make sure he wouldn't accidentally blabber everything. He promised me faithfully back then, all those years ago, that he would stop the espionage. Because I had given him a choice. If he continued to spy, and opened his mouth, first his wife would feel the consequences, then his daughters. If he kept quiet, then everyone would live happily ever after. Simple." The American waved the pistol. "A kind of oral contract, you understand, Kalmann? And you, Telma, you remember too! It's not complicated, is it?"

Telma snarled and gave the American an angry look. "I can't believe I was taken in by you back then! You're the biggest mistake of my life, I'll admit that. But I'm telling you one thing. I won't make that mistake again."

"You didn't see me coming!" the American reminded my great-aunt. "Not this time either."

"You're a wolf," she retorted. "There's no place for wolves up here."

I couldn't help but think of the wolf fish, but the American waved his hand tiredly. "Anyway, Lúlli Lenin did see me coming, you have to give him that."

"You idiot! Lúlli has been waiting for you all these years!"

"Was he? Crazy Viking!" The American laughed drily. "All of you are." He took a deep breath, as though he had to make a decision that wouldn't be easy.

Telma broke the oppressive silence. "Neither Kalmann nor the village poet know what all this is about. Let them go! How much longer are you going to keep guarding your cursed mountain? It's ancient history. The Cold War is over!"

The American gave her a wistful smile. "The Cold War is far from over," he murmured. "It's only just begun. Kalmann and his friend here know what I've done. Tell me, Telma, what other choice do I have?"

"Let them go, I'm begging you!" Her voice was suddenly tearful. That shocked me. "They have nothing to do with the mountain."

The American thought for a long time. Perhaps he wasn't anywhere near as intelligent as I'd initially believed.

Bragi swallowed heavily, and the American came to a decision. "We're going for a spin," he said. "We'll drive up to the…"

25
MOUNTAIN

We had to get in the Mazda, which was a stupid idea. A tourist jeep like that is essentially a normal car, just bigger and more luxurious. My great-aunt's old Lada, by contrast, was a small tractor that looked like a car. In that, we could have driven in a straight line up the mountain. But the American was still pointing the Glock at us, so it was better not to start any arguments.

Bragi was given the task of sitting at the wheel and driving up the road towards the radar station. That wasn't a good idea either; the American clearly didn't know Bragi is an appalling driver.

Desperately, Bragi searched for the ignition key, but the Mazda merely had a button you have to press to start the engine. The American sat in the passenger seat, the pistol pointed constantly at Bragi. He laid my flare gun on the dashboard. Telma and I had climbed in the back.

Luckily the road up the mountain was in good condition and drivable, having been well constructed back in its day. Bragi steered the heavy Mazda carefully along the snow-covered road, while the automatic transmission couldn't decide on the correct gear and constantly switched from third to second – and back again. The American stayed silent, but kept his eyes on us.

With every metre of increasing altitude, Bragi became paler. He was sweating and mumbled something incomprehensible.

It would definitely have been better to let Telma drive. She sought out my gaze and smiled at me, but fear lurked behind her eyes.

"Your plan is absurd. The car tracks in the snow, Kalmann's boat, all the bodies you're leaving in your wake… All the clues lead to you! You're a textbook idiot."

The American gave a bored sigh. "Telma, my love, I took an oath back then, I swore on my flag, my nation and God to protect America and sacrifice my life for it. That's something you lot probably aren't familiar with here. Loyalty, integrity, honour. These values still exist for us."

"At least we understand something about geography," mocked Telma. "America is a continent, not a country, you jackass!"

"You won't succeed in provoking me," said the American, his lips tightening.

"How many people did you kill during your CIA years? Do they haunt you in your sleep? Did Claire leave you because it got too cramped in bed for her with all the ghosts?"

The American shook his head almost imperceptibly. His eyes turned black. He murmured: "This mountain is my legacy," as though he were talking to himself. "It's my life's work. I'll protect it until my dying day. And that's the end."

"Too right!" scoffed Telma. "This mountain is your grave!"

Bragi decelerated, because the snowdrifts on the rocks were getting deeper with every metre of altitude. The road got steeper, and the Mazda decided on first gear. We were almost at the top already and had a wonderful view over all of Þistilfjord. The water was dark, but it still had that strange green tone. Cold mist lay over the fjord, veiling the Melrakkaslétta towards the north-western horizon. The lighthouse was gone too. Off in the distance, you could make out the tiny light of a trawler. Siggi and Jújú were sure to be back in the harbour by now.

As we steered around the next bend, my aunt's house appeared far below us momentarily, the red corrugated iron roof, but then immediately disappeared again behind the cliffs. Telma stared sadly out of the window.

Suddenly the Mazda switched back into second gear and almost came to a standstill, so Bragi stepped desperately on the gas. That was a mistake. The engine roared, the wheels spun and lost their grip. The car swerved towards the rocks and Bragi wrenched the wheel around. Now the American tried to intervene, holding the steering wheel with his free hand, but we had already come off the road. The jeep tilted to the side and skidded into the ditch, luckily on the mountain side. Bragi jolted the steering wheel wildly and stepped even harder on the gas, making the wheels spray up snow – which only made the situation worse. The Mazda burrowed itself in deeper, and we sank down and got stuck.

"Stop!" cried the American angrily, and Bragi finally took his foot off the gas pedal. "You idiot! Put it in reverse!"

Telma sniggered. Apart from the wheels of the car, nothing moved.

"Goddamn Japanese piece of shit!" cursed the American. He slumped back in his seat and fell silent, thinking.

Telma interrupted him. "With the Lada, we'd be at the top by now."

"Get out!" The American was furious now. Perhaps he regretted having taken us with him. "We'll continue on foot." He climbed out, stomped around the jeep and aimed the gun at us. "The poet first, then Kalmann, then you, Telma!"

We looked at one another, probably all making the same face because we didn't feel like getting out, but we couldn't drive away either.

"112," whispered Bragi, looking at Telma intensely, but she shook her head a little. "No reception up here," she murmured.

"Get out!" roared the American again. "Right now!"

Bragi made a strange sound, which I would usually have associated with a nervous Arctic fox pup, hung his head and got out.

"Now the village idiot!"

Usually I get angry when someone calls me that. But up there on Heiðarfjall, I felt a little like I was looking at myself sitting in the car, with someone insulting me as I got out.

I positioned myself right next to Bragi, and Telma joined us. We stood like a wall of football players, but we would probably have been the worst football team in the world. Telma was smaller than us men, and now she looked even older. Hopefully the American wouldn't chase us all too far through the snow. Where was he taking us?

A few stones' throws away I saw a large ruin, a brown monstrosity consisting of crumbling concrete blocks. So we had almost reached the old radar station. All the windows in the building were broken, and the wind was whistling through the holes. Right at the top of the levelled mountaintop stood rusty masts and struts; beyond that, there wasn't much left of the station. All the other buildings had been torn down, razed to the ground or transported away. There must have been a good dozen barracks directly beneath the metal framework, and these big satellite bowls had stood somewhere further back. I almost couldn't imagine there had once been bustling activity and hundreds of American soldiers stationed here.

"Let's go, guys! Time's up!"

We had to go in front. The old American followed us at a few metres' distance, the gun aimed at our backs. Telma linked arms with me; I was a great help to her.

"All the way to the top!"

The northern horizon was as black and impenetrable as a wall. The sun had long since set, and the remaining daylight lay over Langanes as though it had been left behind. Perhaps the snow had saved some of it. We battled against the wind, stumbled over concrete foundations where the soldiers' barracks had once stood, passed electricity masts here and there, which, crooked and forgotten, feigned a connection with the rest of the world. We climbed up unsound concrete steps, which seemed haphazardly distributed across the sloping wasteland. Telma leaned more and more heavily on my arm, hanging at an angle and holding onto me with the dregs of her strength; on one occasion she stumbled over a nasty piece of iron that jutted out of the ground. But eventually we made it, arriving exhausted right at the top by the metal framework. One last step led to a concrete platform and, from there, into nothingness. "Stairway to heaven," murmured Bragi sadly.

At our feet lay the rest of the Langanes peninsula. We could see to the outermost tip, but because no one had lived there for years, besides ghosts and the hidden people, there were no lights twinkling; not a single sign of life. This place really did feel like the end of the world, and that's why I swiftly averted my gaze.

The American had fallen far behind and was a good fifty metres away. I spotted him pulling up his trousers and putting away the syringe in his bag. Bragi had noticed too. He shot me a despairing look. "We're such idiots!" he said. "He's sick. We could have overpowered him!"

"It's possible," I said, feeling a little annoyed that I'd forgotten the thing about the syringe.

Telma grabbed my arm and looked at me insistently. "Kalmann," she hissed. "Run, fetch help, go!"

"Run, Kalmann, run!" said Bragi too.

I shook my head. "No chance," I said. "I'm not leaving you two alone."

Where would I have run to? Down to Telma's house, to call help from there, or to drive to Þórshöfn in the Lada? I could easily make out the village from here, there were lights on. But by the time I'd informed someone, Telma and Bragi would have been long dead. Then I would have had to live with that.

The American came slowly towards us. The Glock in his hand seemed to have become heavier.

"Run, Kalmann!" yelled Bragi, trying to push me away, but I didn't move from the spot. I stood like a tree.

"Stop it!" I growled. "I'm staying with you."

Now we heard the American shout. "Don't go getting any stupid ideas!" He aimed the gun at us, so we stayed put until he had caught up. The Glock shook in his hand. "No stupid ideas," he repeated, gasping for breath. There were pearls of sweat on his forehead.

I was getting cold. The plateau of the mountain was almost empty of snow; the concrete foundations lay bare beside a few snowdrifts. The wind had continually blown away the white powder. It whistled around the metal framework and free-standing reinforcing rods that jutted out of the ground like finger bones, as though a giant had been cemented into the mountain. The whistling of the wind sounded like a warning signal, a siren, a creepy orchestra. There was no living thing far and wide. No tracks. No ptarmigan, no Arctic foxes, no ravens. The animals probably didn't like the poisoned mountain. And the mountain didn't like people, that's why its coldness was so tangible. It wanted to be left in peace, it wanted to sleep, because that's the only thing mountains like.

The American tore me out of my thoughts. "Stand over there, all of you, and don't do anything stupid!"

We obeyed, huddling together like penguins at the South Pole who had long since made their peace with living in a cold world. The American looked around him to all sides and seemed to find what he was looking for, namely a rusty barrel which was split in half and filled with rocks the size of fists. Bragi and I were assigned the task of taking the rocks out of the barrel so that we could push it away.

Once again, we obeyed. But why? The thoughts raced in my head. Should I try to smash the American's head in with one of these rocks? Why was I finding it so difficult to work up the courage to defend myself?

Beneath the barrel, a grey manhole cover came into view, embedded in the concrete slab and almost unrecognizable. The American seemed relieved and even praised us. He produced an iron hook from his down jacket and handed it to me. "Open it!" he said.

The piece of iron reminded me of a fish hook for sharks, but it was thicker and rounded, so completely useless for shark hunting. I hooked it into the heavy manhole cover, lifted it a little and pulled it away, let it drop next to the opening and stared into the black hole. Here, outside, wasn't anywhere near as dark as in there. Inside the mountain lurked the kind of blackness that can probably only otherwise be found on the ocean floor. An unpleasant, indescribable smell rose from the hole. I almost threw up. Telma covered her nose with her hand and Bragi began to tremble all over.

"Give it back!" The American wanted his hook back and held out his hand, while the other pointed the Glock at me.

I obeyed.

Yet again.

The old man waved us towards the shaft opening with his gun. "One after the other. In you go!"

"No!" Telma flung her arm around me. "That's enough!"

The American sighed. "Either I shoot you all on the spot and throw you into the shaft, or you can climb into the mountain alive, it's your choice. I don't care either way."

"Then do it!" said Telma coldly.

A whimper escaped Bragi's mouth.

I thought of Grandfather, pictured him before me. He made an angry face.

"Really?" asked the American. "Nobody? You perhaps?" He pointed the gun at Bragi, who ducked and scrunched his eyes shut but didn't move from the spot. "All right, so be it." The American aimed the Glock at me. "I'll start with the retarded sheriff."

Retarded.

I know these words. There are lots of them, and in all languages too. Retard, idiot, moron, downser, spastic, mongo, cripple, simpleton, dolt, blockhead. And I usually can't stand people who call me those names.

I lowered my head, let my arms hang and took a step to the side, away from Telma and Bragi. I suddenly felt a pulling and tugging in my upper arms, an uncomfortable feeling. Like heat. It spread through my entire body, making a loud rushing sound in my head. I watched the American moving his lips and coming towards me, but I couldn't hear what he was saying. I just looked at him. He raised the gun and pointed it at my head, and I stared into the barrel of the Glock – another awful black hole, albeit much smaller than the shaft.

They say your life flashes before your eyes right before you die. That's not entirely true. More than anything you see faces, because life is a collection of encounters. You see them all in front of you, but not just the people you like the most, no, you see all kinds of faces. Because as well as Grandfather and my mother, I also saw Róbert McKenzie and that famous TV presenter, Villi Þór, the one I met in the shopping mall. Strange. Why him of all people? I saw Birna, I saw FBI agent Dakota Leen and my sisters Allison and Piper. I saw Óttar's wife Lin, and Yrsa, and many other faces. I missed them all, regardless of whether I liked them or not. I even saw Sharon and my father, who had abandoned me amid all that commotion. They were all my life.

Then I saw Uncle Bucky, and it was like something clicked into place inside me, like in a gearbox, as though the gears in my head, which had been running backwards for years, had, with one final click, settled into the correct position. Without stopping to think, I yanked my head to the left and simultaneously hit the barrel of the Glock to the right with my left hand, grabbed the grip with my right and pushed it backwards with my left like a chicken bone. It was one single, lightning-fast movement, like Uncle Bucky had taught me. With one difference: his gun had never been loaded, nor was he an experienced CIA hitman. But that's just how it is: you can't always choose your enemies.

A shot rang out, bang, but I had other worries, I had to act. To the American's immense surprise, his gun was now suddenly in my hand, and so he pulled a funny face, one that's hard to describe. One thing was certain: he hadn't reckoned on me taking the gun from him.

"Kalmann!" Bragi shouted from far, far away in the distance, and that's why it took a few seconds for his shout to arrive in my brain. I almost fired a bullet into the old American's chest. Heart shot. Because a shot to the head isn't always deadly. But then I would have killed a human being, and that wouldn't have been good, not in the slightest, because then he would have visited me in my dreams and possibly haunted me.

I took a step backwards, because I could see from the American's expression that he had sniffed an opportunity and might try to overpower me. I lowered the Glock, aimed at his left knee. The American raised his hands and said "No!" and I pulled the trigger.

Bang.

A hole appeared in his trousers, slightly to the side, and because the old man still seemed to be thinking about all kinds of things other than worrying about his injury, I pulled the trigger again.

Bang.

And then again.

Bang.

His trouser leg was in tatters now, and the American tumbled over. I had felled him like a tree. The old machine saw in Mill Creek flashed before my eyes.

"Kalmann, that's enough!"

If it hadn't been for Bragi, I would have fired the entire magazine into the old American, because with every pull of the trigger a little more of the anger ebbed out of my limbs; the anger that my grandfather had died, that my father had left me standing there in the confusion, that the American had wanted to trap me inside the poisoned mountain and leave me to suffocate. That I was the way I was. But I was the sheriff, after all. So I pulled the trigger one last time.

26
BANG

Telma would have let me for sure. Because when I paused, took my finger off the trigger and aimed the Glock at the ground, she said, as though from a great distance, "Kalmann, give me the gun!" Did she want to shoot the American?

Bragi intervened. His voice was muffled too, I almost couldn't understand him. "We're not murderers!"

He was right, of course, and that's why I was genuinely glad of his company. And besides, the danger had passed, because the American was lying on the floor. With his leg injured, he would no longer be able to herd us around like sheep. All we had to do was head back down the mountain to call the police from Telma's landline or Petra's radio. Birna would be amazed!

"Kalmann, give me the gun!" The coldness in Telma's voice was really clear.

Bragi positioned himself between us, his face bright red. "Kalmann clearly knows his way around a gun better." And, addressing me, still so quietly, as though I had cotton wool in my ears: "Don't give it to her! Kalmann, you're the sheriff!"

So I didn't hand over the Glock, and was even a little proud to be called the sheriff. But Telma wouldn't give up. "We can end this here and now!" she cried. "I don't want to spend the rest of my life looking over my shoulder, waiting for him to turn up again —"

"The American's no use to us dead," Bragi interrupted, and I wondered what he meant by that. Because he was no use to us alive either. But I didn't get involved. After all, my job was to keep hold of the Glock, and to make sure order was restored. To keep my eye on the American.

Telma hissed angrily. I'd never seen her like this. And she wasn't anywhere near as exhausted as she'd had us believe. She glared at the American, watching with satisfaction as he pressed his hands against his knee and tried to keep his cries of pain captive behind his tightened lips. He was staring at the floor and had lost interest in us. He was probably trying to come to terms with the new situation.

Throwing her hands up in the air, Telma turned and marched across the concrete foundations and down the steps back to the road, stomping towards the car as though she were suddenly ten years younger. Bragi looked first at the American, then at me, his eyes wide. "Your ear!" he said dully. "We have to go back at once."

Now I felt the warm blood; it was dripping down my neck. Had the bullet the American fired caught me after all? I touched my damaged ear with my fingertips and found loose tatters where my outer ear should have been. "Okay!" I cried.

We walked after Telma in silence, keeping our distance, simply leaving the American there on the ground. I tucked his gun into my waistband and pressed my palm against the damaged ear so it wouldn't fall off completely. I looked back one more time, but the American had disappeared, he was nowhere to be seen, and so I stood still in amazement.

"Where did he go?"

Bragi looked around too. He cursed. "He's probably climbed down into the shaft. Come on!" He grabbed my arm and pulled me onwards, as if there were no reason to worry.

At the rental car, we took a short break, because I was feeling dizzy. We debated whether we could push the Mazda out of the ditch and back onto the road, but I suspected it was too heavy for us. Pushing two tons of car through the snow isn't easy, and we didn't have a shovel with us either. Luckily, Telma had a better idea: Bragi was to get in the car with me. We could fire up the engine to keep warm, but we weren't to take our eyes off the radar station. Meanwhile, she would run down to the house to fetch help, then come to get us in the Lada.

It was an excellent idea, and she could have counted on our unanimous agreement, but at that moment a hole appeared in the Mazda's front window, a really small, round hole. That wasn't good. A short while later we heard a shot being fired. Bang. I turned and stared up at the remains of the metal framework, but the American was still nowhere to be seen. Only when I saw something flash on the ground did I presume he was up on the concrete platform, a few hundred metres from us. The second bullet hit the rocks behind the car, making a horrible whizzing sound.

"Kalmann!"

Incredible. The American must have climbed down into the shaft, despite his gunshot wounds, and found an old rifle there; there was no other explanation for it. The distance was too great for a pistol, and I had his Glock.

"Kalmann, wake up!"

The Mazda's headlamp shattered immediately next to my right leg. The people at the car rental company would scratch their heads in astonishment when they got the car back.

"Kalli!"

Telma and Bragi had dived behind the Mazda and were frantically waving me over. Something hit my left bicep,

225

and scraps of fabric flew through the air. Then I heard the shot, because a bullet is always faster than its sound. I sat down with them in the snow, feeling all fuzzy. My left arm was numb.

"We should have killed the bastard!" Telma swore.

"That's no help now!" Bragi snapped. He turned to me with a look of concern. "Did he get you?"

"Just grazed," I guessed. "It doesn't hurt. I can't feel anything. No reason —"

Another bullet zipped past us.

"At least we're safe behind the car," Telma said.

"But for how long?" Bragi interjected. "We have to get help!"

"Then he'll pick us off like ptarmigan."

"Kalmann, can you shoot him with the pistol?"

"No chance," I said. Bragi wasn't very knowledgeable about firearms. But I'd had a better idea, anyway, and suddenly knew what to do. There was no time to waste, either, because by now I was feeling really floppy, and perhaps I would even faint soon. I would have liked to lie down in the car for a while, on the back seat, and take a nap. Maybe it was the blood loss, or maybe I was tired from all the excitement. I also hadn't eaten anything for hours. So I had to act, now, immediately. I waited until the next bullet made a hole in the Mazda, then I crept around the car, opened the passenger door and climbed in. Bragi and Telma yelled at me, wanting me to come back and huddle with them. It was totally embarrassing. A second hole appeared in the front window, and then in the seat upholstery next to me, but I reached for the flare gun on the dashboard, climbed out of the car, stood wide-legged in the snow and aimed at the sky, my arm outstretched, probably looking like that singer from Queen, except instead of a microphone I had a gun.

I didn't hesitate for a second.

I pulled the trigger.

Bang.

27

FIREWORK

The projectile from the flare gun flew diagonally into the air. Would someone in Þórshöfn or Sauðanes see it, perhaps the trawler I had spotted out at sea? It was our only hope, possibly our last. Because we needed help, and urgently. Someone simply had to spot us up here, because we didn't want to be targets any more, nobody likes that.

Amid the scattered snowflakes in the gloomy evening sky, the flare's glow was red and intense, sparking and hissing. I watched it like you would watch a New Year's firework; filled with wonder and joyful anticipation of the imminent bang.

A gust of wind ruffled my hair as I stared after the glowing dot, which hovered about a hundred metres above the mountain and then began to fall slowly. The gust was followed by a distant bang. The bullet must have flown within millimetres of my head. And there I was standing next to the car like an idiot, staring up at the sky. But that's how I am sometimes. And I only vaguely noticed when the window next to me shattered, unable to tolerate a third hole. Fireworks hypnotize me.

The flare was now heading directly for the metal structure of the radar station – even though I'd intended to fire it towards Þórshöfn so someone would notice it. The Mazda slumped a little; the bullet had hit a tyre. Shortly after, scraps of my jacket flew through the air and mingled with the snowflakes. Bragi and Telma's shouts, pleas for me to take cover, barely registered. I was in a fireworks mood now, not wanting to miss a thing, and stared captivated as the glowing flare fell onto the concrete behind the old American. But instead of remaining there on the ground, it disappeared as though by magic.

"Ha!" I laughed in astonishment. "What a coincidence!" The flare must have fallen into the open shaft, spraying its red light into the inside of the mountain, which would definitely have looked spooky.

The American had noticed it too. He arduously pulled himself up with the help of the rifle, putting his weight on it, and stood there hunched; his wounded leg was surely hurting him. He was probably trying to gather his strength, and seemed to succeed, because he was hobbling on the spot a little, trying to find his balance, and eventually he stood still and upright. Looked in my direction. Shouldered the rifle. I saw it in spite of the darkness. What was he doing? Stiffly and slowly, he raised his right arm and brought the tips of his fingers to his temple, then gave a military salute into the night and became a soldier statue – a small black silhouette on the horizon. Was the salute for me? Was he paying me his respects?

Sometimes I need a long time, longer than other people, to put two and two together. But now, having seen the flare disappear into the shaft as though the mountain had swallowed it, and now the American had paid his respects to me with the military salute, a light was turned on in the darkest depths of my noggin, a switch flipped, and the gears finally began to move again: I suddenly remembered – the pollution, the chemicals! The odd smell, the secrecy surrounding the mountain, the espionage, the threats, the wide road,

the haulage trucks, my grandfather's many photographs…
Grandfather! "The mountain's flying," I murmured. "It's
flying in the air."

Then it came to life.

Booom!

The mountain rose before my eyes, straightening up as
though in slow motion – or was it the giant who had been
concreted into the mountain back in the day, or perhaps a
dragon guarding golden treasure?

Detached from its torso, the entire upper section of the
mountain lifted and flew into the air, a blindingly bright fireball which instantaneously absorbed the American. Smoke
shot upwards, surging on all sides, billowing and expanding,
whirling up stones like medieval missiles. The old American
had been eaten by the dragon, trampled by the giant, tossed
aside, and no longer posed any danger. I rose now too,
gripped by the pressure wave of the explosion. I stared along
my arms and legs and was flung backwards through the air,
flying past the Mazda, which in spite of everything was still
stuck in the ditch. Bragi and Telma watched me pass, and if
it hadn't all happened so quickly, I would have waved.

Even while I was flying through the air, I realized that it
was neither a giant nor a dragon nor the mountain itself that
had risen, but an ammunition dump that was exploding into
the air. Nói would laugh! He would list all the chemicals he
had read about in the university report, and he would say:
"An epic cocktail, baby!"

I was already looking forward to telling him about the
badass explosion, but I still had the landing ahead of me,
though I didn't register any of it, because everything went
black, click, lights out.

*

I woke up seconds later, so it wasn't over yet, even though I felt kind of dead, like a lifeless piece of meat, a fish in a barrel, a soggy teabag in an empty cup.

The noise from the ongoing explosions now sounded like a roaring, a screeching and shrieking, a moaning and groaning. The mountain wailed, raged, rose with one last battle cry and in its despair flung giant rock boulders, which now crashed onto the ground around me. I pulled myself up a little, resting on my elbows, stared along my body – and marvelled. It wasn't me lying here, but someone who had been pushed through a meat grinder. My trousers were tattered and dirty, my feet were in bloody socks, my shoes were gone. The earth beneath me trembled and tremored, as though a giant were stomping around angrily up on the mountain, or as if the dragon were raging, but gradually the intensity subsided. The mountain was getting tired.

It had a crater now, almost like a volcano, and from this crater billowed black smoke, while flames, rock fragments and rockets darted skywards. It was loud, louder than at New Year's in Mill Creek, because the rockets weren't actually fireworks and not home-made ones either but bombs and large-calibre missiles, and when they explode, it makes a mighty boom. The air vibrated and burned.

Bragi waved to me from the shelter of the Mazda rental car, and seemed relieved when I waved back. He began to shovel snow out from beneath the car with his bare hands to create a protective den. Telma kept her head down low and held both hands pressed against her ears, trying to crawl under the car at the same time. That's usually how it is: old people don't know how to appreciate a good firework show. Even Grandfather had lost pleasure in it in his final years and was usually asleep before midnight. In any case, he had left it to me to fire the old projectiles from the flare gun. But now I was getting the show of my life!

We knew we were much too close to the ammunition dump, because the rockets sometimes exploded really close by, meaning that little stones kept hailing down on us. The people at the car rental company would have a heart attack when they saw the Mazda! The white paint had peeled off, the chassis was covered with little holes, and all the windows were shattered.

I watched as the remains of the American radar station, the brown hulk of prefabricated concrete blocks, was hit by multiple rockets and exploded in a mighty fireball. The gloomy sky above us went black, and a boulder came loose from the edge of the crater and rolled down the slope, as though in slow motion. Now it was time to cross our fingers, because Telma's house was somewhere down there.

Suddenly Bragi was leaning over me. He had a graze on his head and a filthy face. "Under the car!" he shouted, but I couldn't move, I was far too exhausted.

Everything went bright, earth rained down, and Bragi fell on his behind, held his arm protectively in front of his face and screamed. He pulled himself up again, grabbed me beneath the armpits and pulled me backwards through the dirty snow. I left a trail of blood behind me, looked down at the legs I could barely feel, and was happy and relieved when they stayed attached. Bragi fell over a few times but eventually managed to drag me to the Mazda, where he pushed me beneath the car while Telma tugged on my clothes. The Mazda rocked and the ground vibrated like one of those massage chairs in the shopping mall in Akureyri. The shuddering of the mountain was so pleasant that my eyes rolled back in my head and I fell into a deep sleep.

*

Grandfather stopped in his tracks. He turned around in shock and swore: "*Andskotans!*"

We were somewhere on the Melrakkaslétta, barely an hour away from Raufarhöfn, on a fox hunt. I was carrying the plastic bag with the bait, lamb leftovers, leg bones, which we would lay on moss somewhere on a suitable baiting spot to watch from a good distance until an Arctic fox set to work on the delicacies. The lamb's hooves poked out of the top of the bag. Grandfather had the rifle on a carrying strap, it was a beautiful sunny day, the warm breeze brushed against our faces. The conditions were perfect.

"What's wrong?" I asked Grandfather. He looked exhausted; over recent months he had become old and slow. This wasn't our first hunt; after all these years we were a practised team, and we sometimes spent many hours together on the Slétta without even exchanging a word – which is advisable, by the way, because Arctic foxes have excellent hearing.

But Grandfather was confused. "The camera. Goddamn it! I forgot it."

"The camera?"

Grandfather looked at me, scowling. "I have to go get it!"

"What do you need a camera for?"

He searched for an explanation but became increasingly impatient, staring at me as though he were regretting bringing me with him on the hunt; yes, that's it, as though he wasn't too sure why I'd come with him. It didn't matter, he said eventually, and his eyes took on this anxious glimmer. He looked around and then at me surreptitiously, his beard quivered in the wind, he chewed his lips. Then he sat down, slumped into the moss and laid the rifle carelessly next to himself.

"Are you tired already?" I asked, and he nodded. I wasn't

tired yet, so I went to take a little look around, leaving Grandfather sitting there. Suddenly, just a few metres away from me, a whimbrel fluttered out of a hollow, flew through the air, whistling loudly, and circled above me. No question: there was a nest up there. And I soon found it. Four green eggs mottled with brown. Wonderful. Every egg looked like it was hand-painted.

"Don't touch it!" cried Grandfather from some distance. He was still grumpy. "Leave the nest alone, otherwise the bird won't come back! How often do I have to tell you!" I sulkily trudged back over to him. "Sit down next to me, Kalmann." We gazed towards the north, the sun on our backs, the wide plain before us. "Listen…" He searched for the words. "I won't always be able to go hunting with you. You know that, don't you?"

"Yes." I took the cowboy hat off my head, turned it over in my hands and murmured: "Nothing in this world is forever." The sun warmed my hair, the wind cooled my brow.

"That's right." Grandfather was content with my answer but stayed silent for a long time, so long that I got a damp bottom. "Kalmann, this is what we're going to do. You go on ahead alone, and I'll go back."

"To get the camera?"

"No, Kalmann. Forget the camera. And by the way, don't mention that to your mother. Understood?"

"Yes sir."

"And don't 'yes sir' me!"

"Yes sir!" I repeated, and Grandfather shook his head, but he wasn't in as bad a mood as before.

"I'll go back and lie down for a bit. I'm so tired."

I nodded.

Grandfather hung the rifle over my shoulder. "You carry on, hunt foxes, keep going straight. But don't stay too long.

And if you don't catch any – it doesn't matter. Not every hunt ends with a kill."

I must have looked at him blankly, because he gave me an encouraging clap on the shoulder, asked me to help him to his feet, then turned eastwards and headed off, leaving me there alone in the middle of the Melrakkaslétta. For the first time in my life.

I stared after him for a long while as he made his way with small, careful steps across the uneven plain, like a person might walk across a frozen lake, unsure of whether the layer of ice will hold. Just before disappearing behind a small hill, he turned and looked back, lifting his hand like in a Western when the lonesome hero says goodbye. I waved back with my cowboy hat in my hand, waved and waved until Grandfather had disappeared behind the hill. Then I put the hat back on my head, turned towards the wind and strode bravely on. It was my first time going fox hunting alone, armed to the teeth, the rifle hanging from my shoulder, the Mauser in my holster, and I had a knife with me too. I felt proud and at the same time scared shitless.

Given that I could walk more quickly now than before, I went a long way, then I put the bait on the soft moss and hid myself about a hundred metres away from it behind a big rock, which was covered with white and yellow and orange flecks, and made sure the wind was always blowing nicely into my face, because even though foxes have tiny nostrils, their sense of smell is better than ours. I kept thinking about Grandfather, who had recently become so old and fearful, grumpy, sullen, and because I was thinking so much, I fell asleep behind the rock and only woke up again once the sun was low in the west.

The bait was gone.

You can sleep really well under a Mazda, even in winter, I know that now. So it seems they're good for something after all. I slept so deeply that apparently there was some concern as to whether I would ever emerge. A few minutes felt to me like weeks. But eventually I did wake up, though not under the Mazda but in an ambulance that was tilted at such an angle I thought I'd been strung up by my feet. So we were still on the mountain. I was on a stretcher, and the booming explosions could still be heard outside. From time to time, little stones hailed down onto the roof.

"Halldór, you can drive off!" I heard Bragi call, and the vehicle began to move, swaying violently from side to side because the road was covered with rubble, which meant I was immediately rocked back to sleep, there was nothing I could do to stop it.

"Kalmann, you carry on, hunt foxes, keep going straight ahead!"

Halldór drove down the mountain at breakneck speed while Bragi leaned over me, trying to fasten me more securely to the stretcher. "Don't worry!" he snapped at me, and told me to stop pulling the thin tube out of my arm.

I looked down and saw I was wearing only my underwear, and I had bandages on my arms and legs that were saturated with red blood. My head was wrapped tightly in bandages too; I must have looked like a mummy. My ribcage felt heavy. Every breath I took sounded like someone rattling a half-full box of nails. "Where's Telma?" I asked Bragi in a whisper.

"Sitting up front!" Bragi shouted, adding that we were still on Langanes, somewhere near Sauðanes.

I couldn't help but think of Grandfather again, because if I had died right then and there they could have just stopped and laid me down with him. But Bragi assured me once again that there was no reason to worry, and if I could please leave the bandages and the IV alone and goddamn relax!

Because I know from the movies that you have to count backwards on the operating table to fall asleep, I counted backwards from ten, but I think I only made it to eight.

"And if you don't get any foxes – it doesn't matter. Understood?"

I woke up again. Bragi was having a loud discussion with Halldór, who in turn was yelling into a radio set, and it was only then I realized that there was indeed reason to worry. I had vomited blood and my pulse was pretty weak. We were driving on a tarmacked road now, so there was no more lurching, and Halldór could step on the gas as hard as he wanted. He was enquiring about the whereabouts of the helicopter, and the voice on the radio said it was still in the Westfjords, busy rescuing a four-man boat crew who had run aground on the rocky coast.

"Autopilot," I murmured.

"What's that?" Bragi asked me, but now I turned the autopilot on too and closed my eyes, and even Grandfather said it was okay, all of it, that it was all perfectly okay.

Suddenly things got very loud. A storm broke out. And then I saw the ambulance far beneath me, although only briefly, with Halldór, Bragi and Telma standing next to it, gazing up at me with their arms raised and eyes narrowed. So now I was dead, and already moving towards heaven. That's what I thought. It was nonsense, of course. The stretcher I was on was being winched up into the coastguard's helicopter. Probably the pilot hadn't been able to find a suitable place to land at short notice. It was snowing heavily; the snowflakes were whirling in all directions. The stretcher began to lurch and so the ambulance rotated beneath me. Everything was spinning and I closed my eyes again.

It's a lot louder inside a helicopter than you think. Particularly when the pilot has to hurry. The helicopter tilted sideways, turned, and so I could still make out the lights of the ambulance below, the three figures standing next to it. Outside the window it was getting dark already, with only the helicopter's flashing lights to illuminate the snow flurries.

A man in a helmet glanced at me and gave me the thumbs up. I would have liked to return the gesture, thumbs up, no reason to worry, but for numerous reasons I couldn't.

28
HOSPITAL

The waking-up process was slow, more like a battling really, a struggling, a desperate resurfacing and coming up for air.

My mother leaned over me and moved her lips. That calmed me for a moment, and I gave up the battle and sank back down into the depths, feeling relieved this time. When I woke up again, a day later, my mother was still there.

It took a long time before I completely came to, before I could separate reality from dreams and grasp what was actually going on. This was because I had sustained some really bad injuries. I had been patched together and sewn up, had about fifty bandages, and was hooked up to tubes. The rifle bullet in my left arm had been removed and a nasty graze wound doctored with fish skin from the Western fjords. I was half-man, half-fish. They had managed to sew up the mangled ear to a certain extent, there was just one piece missing, but the ear was still in thick bandages, which meant I could only listen with the other one when the doctor was talking to my mother about my injuries. A few of my bones were broken, including my ribs, because when you get flung through the air, it usually ends in a crash landing. The ruptured lung, blood loss and other internal injuries caused by the pressure wave of the explosion had almost finished me off. According to the doctor, I had been at a crossroads. One path led back here, and the other, well, to the other side, probably to Valhalla.

Grandfather. He had waved to me from the distance! I had dreamed about him when I was napping under the Mazda. It had been our last hunt together. I had chosen the Melrakkaslétta. I had chosen life. Fox hunting. Grandfather had wanted it that way. He hadn't let me go with him.

I had to stay lying in the hospital bed for a very long time and was even operated on a second time.

Telma and Bragi had come away with minor injuries and scrapes. They had already been discharged from hospital, and had come back to visit me, but I was asleep. The painkillers made me foggy.

Luckily I was awake when the police came: two men in uniform and Birna. How happy I was! Birna was happy too, she even took off her mask so I could see her beaming smile, and she laid her hand on my cheek as though she were in love with me or something. Her colleagues exchanged glances, because of course we weren't allowed to touch due to the stupid pandemic, but if a police officer breaks the rules, people usually turn a blind eye.

I had to tell her everything, because there was this one thing that was really silly, namely the murder of Lúlli Lenin. The old American, who had been a retired CIA secret agent, was nowhere to be found; his true identity, even his existence, couldn't be proven with a hundred per cent certainty. Because when you fly up into the air with an ammunition dump, there's not much left of you. His Glock, which I had taken off him, matched the weapon Lúlli Lenin had been shot with. And that's why I was left there like an idiot, because my fingerprints were the only ones on the weapon. What's more, I had visited Lúlli Lenin shortly before his death, shovelled snow in front of his house and left my shovel there, so I was also officially the last person on earth to visit him, and that's why Birna had to question me, that's the law. I had no choice but to explain to her that my grandfather had been scared to death. I advised her to get in touch with Lárus, the tattooed janitor at the care home in Húsavík, who would be able to help her find the American on the surveillance camera recordings, and for sure there would also be a white Mazda in front of the building.

Birna turned her colleagues and said: "Didn't I tell you? Kalmann is a proper sheriff!" She laughed happily, and her two colleagues grinned, nodding with approval.

We talked for a while longer about my US adventure; it was a relaxed conversation among friends. Birna told me that Sæmundur had had a bad feeling and asked Halldór to drive the ambulance to Langanes, even before the mountain had exploded. And almost as soon as Halldór arrived on Langanes, he spotted the flare in the night sky high above Heiðarfjall – and drove straight up to the mountain, which burst apart before his eyes. He didn't hesitate for even a second, speeding the ambulance along the snow-covered road and through the avalanche of stones up the mountain until he spotted the Mazda in the ditch.

As soon as I got the opportunity, I should thank Halldór and Sæmundur for saving my life, Birna suggested, something I firmly resolved to do.

Then she gave me some well-meaning advice: I was to say "no" more frequently during the coming days and weeks. And I obediently followed this advice. I said no to all the interview requests and didn't answer any phone calls either. A police officer stood in front of the door, making sure no one pushed their way into the room uninvited. So I had my peace and quiet. I could sleep and watch TV as much as I wanted. There were a lot of reports about the old H-2 radar station that had turned out to be an ammunition dump. It became an international affair, because the Americans had constructed radar stations all over the world but were unwilling to disclose more detailed information. Given that, thanks to me, people now knew these stations could also be ammunition dumps, my name was almost always mentioned, with a photo and everything. Even though I'd only blown up the mountain by accident. An expert on TV said he doubted that the projectile from my flare gun could have exploded an entire ammo dump, and that maybe a chemical reaction had caused it, or the American had triggered the explosion himself, but no one would ever be able to say with certainty. Other examples were named in this context, comparisons made with other ammo dumps which had also exploded: in the United States, in Russia, Poland, Germany, Switzerland… Iceland was now part of a long list.

And so the conversations revolved around old war munitions, how and where they were stored and the danger they posed. There was talk about the conservation of nature and water, for the damage was enormous here too, the entire mountain had to be cordoned off because there were unexploded munitions lying around everywhere. And that's why people were pretty mad at the Americans, even though they eventually agreed to pay the damages. But what does a broken mountain cost? And how can you patch it together? These were good questions that still haven't been answered.

Soon the focus shifted to the old American, who until now had remained a mystery, but eventually some things were discovered about him. Birna had managed to prove his existence. He really had been a CIA secret agent, in the espionage department, stationed in Iceland during the Cold War, but he had been retired for years and working on his own missions.

He had lived alone, was divorced, with grown-up children who had broken contact with him ages ago and wanted nothing to do with any of this. Despite the clean-up operation, his remains were never found. My suspicion was therefore the closest: the force of the explosion had carried him out to sea, where the Greenland shark and wolf fish would take care of him.

Because he was nowhere to be found, the journalists had to turn their attention elsewhere, and they got wind of Grandfather's work as a spy. It was simply unending! My mother had to hand over all the photos and files to the police so they could gauge the extent of the ammunition dump. Thanks to these photos, they now knew how much scree the Americans had transported away and how many truckloads of munitions had been driven up the mountain. After all these years, Grandfather's photos were fulfilling their purpose after all.

As I had been his most loyal companion, the journalists' interest led back to me. The demands for an interview became more and more insistent, the phone calls mounted up, and that's why my mother negotiated an exclusive TV interview with Channel 2.

Before the famous talk-show master Villi Þór could ask his first question – we did the interview in the hospital room – I asked him whether he now knew what the mountain on Langanes was called. "Of course!" he said with an embarrassed grin. "Heiðarfjall. Thanks to you, the whole world knows!"

My mother, who was standing behind the camera and following the conversation from there, glowed with pride. Had she put on make-up?

As soon as the interview was broadcast on TV, Nói called me on Messenger: "Sheriff, why didn't you mention me? I helped you solve the case!"

He was right. I smacked my palm against my forehead. "I'm sorry!"

Nói waved his hand forgivingly. "No, I'm happy to pass on all the media frenzy, thank you very much. Someone has to pull the strings in the background, after all."

"Oh right."

"I'm the puppet master!"

"Who?"

Nói opened a can of Red Bull, said he was toasting me, and chugged it down in one go. "Don't pull that face! We did it. We achieved something amazing." He burped. "The world is a better place! Thanks to us, there's one less murderer. And you avenged your grandfather."

"Do you think?" A strange feeling crept into my chest. It constricted, which hurt.

"Bro!" Nói laughed. He leaned back in his chair, meaning that for the first time in my life I could see his mouth. "You pulverized the heavyweight. Sick. I sooo wish I could've seen it!" Nói's mouth was small and narrow, his lips colourless.

"The mountain really lifted up," I confirmed. "The rocks flew around my ears."

"The mountain's flying!" laughed Nói. "*Gora letit*, right?"

"*Gora letit*," I echoed, then I immediately repeated it, because for some reason the words did me good. "*Gora letit, gora letit!*" I saw Grandfather bury his face in my chest and cry "*Gora letit!*" and I felt as though I were about to explode, and I must have waved my arms around, because I accidentally swept the laptop off the hospital bed and it fell to the floor and instantly conked out, bang, dead. The screen was black and cracked, Nói was gone, and now I was happy I'd got lots of money for the interview with Villi Þór, because I could buy myself a new laptop with it.

29
NO REASON TO WORRY

By the time I had completely recovered, physically at least, and dared to venture back anywhere in the vicinity of the mountain I had blown up, it was early summer. Finally I was ready to take a trip with my mother to the Langanes peninsula to lay flowers on my grandparents' graves in Sauðanes, and then visit Aunt Telma in her solitary house, which, fortunately, had survived the explosion of the ammunition dump unscathed.

As we hurtled across the Melrakkaslétta in my mother's Renault, counting wild geese and whooper swans, I felt very happy – up until we drove across Hálsar and the Heiðarfjall mountain appeared in the far distance, its crater clearly visible even from here: a black, gaping wound in the grey ridge. I bit my hand so hard that it hurt.

"Everything okay?" asked my mother, touching my shoulder. "Should we turn around?"

"No," I said, studying the indent in my hand. It was white at first, then it turned green and red. The original skin tone was slow to return. Even then, the indents remained. "No reason to worry."

"Good," said my mother, letting out a contented sigh.

Perhaps it was really true. Perhaps there really was no reason to worry. Sure, I had accidentally dispatched an American into the afterlife and blown a hole in the Heiðarfjall mountain, but it wasn't like it was the most beautiful mountain in the world, it was just a slightly rounded elevation which from a distance looked like a rowing boat lying upturned on the beach, except much bigger. Heiðarfjall wasn't even that high – at least not what you could see of it.

In Hawaii there's a volcanic island which is only a few thousand metres in height, but beneath the water's surface it goes down much deeper into the depths, and that's why this volcanic island in its entirety is bigger than the highest mountain in the world. Just imagine! A volcanic mountain, ten thousand metres high, and most people don't even know its name. At the foot of this volcano, in the blackest depths, live the most unbelievable creatures, spearfish and vampire squid, giant spiders and sad blobfish, possibly wolf fish, but certainly no Greenland sharks, because they prefer the cold.

Perhaps Heiðarfjall was that kind of mountain too, and what we could see of it was just the tip, a tiny fragment of the whole, like with icebergs. And that reminded me of the American, whose remains lay down there on the ocean floor, the tattered limbs and scraps of clothing, his little bag, everything nicely scattered. For sure the sharks had smelled the roasted meat and bit appreciatively into his flesh, and the wolf fish were grinding the American's bones until nothing remained of him but white bone sand, which would be carried away by the tide and washed up on the beach at Langanes and simply belong there, becoming part of nature, and that's why there was no reason to worry.

"It was full of pack ice," said my mother. "The whole bay, and stretching right out!"

"*Mamma!*" I cried. "Don't start up about the pack ice again!"

She smiled at me with a wink and told me about a white, shapeless world that had formed overnight, as though two universes had collided.

In Þórshöfn, at my request, we ate a gas station hot dog. Three quite dirty roadworkers had gone in ahead of us and were queuing up, because it was lunchtime, and because people get bored when they're standing in a queue, they all turned around and stared at me, studied my strange ear, my cowboy hat and my sheriff's star. I had got used to that a long time ago. To being famous, I mean. The woman at the counter even squealed when she recognized me. "Well, if it isn't the Sheriff of Raufarhöfn!"

Then the penny dropped with the workmen too, they grinned and nodded to me, but they still didn't let me go in front of them. "Chief blaster Kalmann!" said one, and they all laughed.

The woman at the counter wanted to know whether we were visiting Telma, because then we could take along a replacement part she had ordered for the Lada.

One roadworker, who had already received his hot dog, said with a full mouth: "Didn't she have to move away because of the clean-up operation?"

"Forget it!" said his colleague. "You won't get the communist aunt away from there."

"She's got the right idea, if you ask me," said the woman at the counter. "I think everyone should live where they feel most comfortable. After all, there are catastrophes everywhere. In the western fjords the avalanches thunder down from the mountains, in the south there are volcanoes, and here in the east, mountains sometimes explode. That's just how it is!"

"And Reykjavík is overrun with tourists!" I said, which prompted laughter, even though I hadn't made a joke.

When we arrived at my grandparents' graves in Sauðanes, we set down the flowers, sat on the grass for a while and said nothing. When you're sitting at a grave, words are unnecessary. The earth connects you, almost like a telephone. You just have to think. Preferably about the time when Grandfather was still alive.

Once, when I was visiting him in the care home like I did every Saturday, he asked me irritably why I was there. I had sat down next to him on a chair and was chomping on a chocolate bar.

"I'm Kalmann," I said, bored and nothing more, because I'd given up explaining to him that I was his grandson and that I came to visit him every week. He didn't believe me anyway.

"Kalmann?" Grandfather scratched his beard. "Hmm." He leaned back and thought for a moment. "Kalmann!" Suddenly his face brightened. "My grandson's called that too! Like you. Kalmann. A strange name. It means Dove. Kalmann Óðinsson is his full name. He's named after me, even though I... oh." Grandfather waved his hand as though none of it had anything to do with me. But he continued to mumble that his grandson was a good boy, a decent young man. His gaze was watery, as though he were looking inside himself and finding me, because I was there, somewhere deep inside.

Now he lay beneath me in the ground, and I plucked grass, and my mother held her face up to the sun. The Arctic terns squawked over the meadows, and the oystercatchers ran around on the beach. Further back, where an old plane wreck lay in the meadow, probably another remnant from the Americans, a few sheep and horses lolled around. My mother stroked her hand over my back and looked at me. Her smile was happy and sad all at once, and that's why I remembered that she had been keeping something for me, and this whole time too! So I reached over, stretched out my hand and touched her pullover, really carefully, right where her heart was.

My mother flinched, looked at me in astonishment and then began to beam all over her face, because I had taken it from her, I had freed her from it and now held it captured in my closed hand, *my* grief, that my mother had kept for me since I'd been released from the psychiatric unit. Because now I was ready for it, ready for my grief, and I put it where it belonged, in my heart, because I wanted to carry it in me, it would remind me of my grandfather. Until the end of my life.

She laughed and pulled me close, but only briefly, because she knew I don't really like that. There are lots of people who can live very happily with not being constantly hugged and embraced and squeezed. We're not cuddly toys, after all. Grandfather was one of these people. He had never hugged anyone, and he had never wanted to be hugged.

I remembered the day when he had fallen out of his wheelchair and ended up lying on top of me, in my arms, even though he possibly hadn't wanted that, but the force of gravity was stronger, he couldn't resist it, because it's a law of nature that keeps us on the ground so we don't fly away like paragliders in the wind.

"Do you want to stay here for a while?" My mother was already standing up and brushing blades of grass from her jeans.

"No," I said, and jumped to my feet. "Aunt Telma must be waiting for us." I cast one last glance at my grandparents' graves, took a deep breath and said: "Bless."

THE END

Acknowledgements

I would like to thank all the people who continually help me make my books better, and to ultimately make them a reality – without mentioning them all by name, because they know how much I treasure their help, our conversations and friendships.

I would like to mention by name my helpers in Þórshöfn: Guðlaug Jónasdóttir, Heiðrún Óladóttir, Líney Sigurðardóttir, Páll Jónasson and his son Jónas Helgi Pálsson. Thank you for opening your doors to me.

The inhabitants of Raufarhöfn must be mentioned too, without a doubt. They are and always will be my stars. Every visit is a celebration; these encounters are heartfelt and uplifting. They swiftly accepted Kalmann into their ranks. That's why they're especially delighted when tourists ask them about Kalmann. My heartfelt thanks also go to Svava, Nanna and Birna, who made my visit to Raufarhöfn possible and filled me up with coffee and stories; to Rögnvaldur and Magga, who chauffeured me; and to harbour master Gunnar and hotel director Hólmsteinn, from whom I was able to coax a few stories while playing pool – but was thrashed in the process: *Takk samt!*

I would like to say goodbye, with deep gratitude, to Jónas Friðrik Guðnason, from whom I once again borrowed a few lines of poetry for the opening of this novel. Thank you for everything, and safe travels, dear Jónas.

I would also like to thank Einar Björn Jóhannesson and Natasha S.

And I thank my wife, Kristín Elva, and my children, Heiðdís and Rögnvald, who are part of this story. Without them, Kalmann wouldn't exist.